New York Times and *USA Today* bestselling author Emily March lives in Texas with her husband and their beloved boxer, Doc, who tolerates a revolving doggie door of rescue foster dogs sharing his kingdom until they find their forever homes. A graduate of Texas A&M University, Emily is an avid fan of Aggie sports, and her recipe for jalapeño relish has made her a tailgating legend. You can find out more about Emily March and her books at www.emilymarch.com and follow her on Twitter @emilymarchbooks

Praise for Emily March:

'With passion, romance, and revealing moments that will touch your heart, [Emily March] takes readers on an unhurried journey where past mistakes are redeemed and a more beautiful future is forged – one miracle at a time' *USA Today*

'Emily March's stories are heart-wrenching and soul-satisfying. For a wonderful read, don't miss a visit to Eternity Springs' Lisa Kleypas

'Characters you adore, a world you want to visit, and stories that tug your heartstrings. Bravo, Emily March. I love Eternity Springs' Christina Dodd

'Readers will be breathless as Eternity Springs works its romantic magic once again' *Publishers Weekly* Starred Review

By Emily March

Eternity Springs Series
Angel's Rest
Hummingbird Lake
Heartache Falls
Mistletoe Mine (e-novella)
Lover's Leap
Nightingale Way

Heartache Falls
EMILY MARCH

ETERNAL
ROMANCE

Published by arrangement with Ballantine Books,
an imprint of The Random House Publishing Group,
a division of Random House, Inc.

First published in Great Britain in 2013
by ETERNAL ROMANCE
An imprint of HEADLINE PUBLISHING GROUP

1

Cataloguing in Publication Data is available from the British Library

ISBN 978 1 4722 0196 6

Offset in Sabon by Avon DataSet Ltd, Bidford-on-Avon, Warwickshire

Printed and bound by CPI Group (UK) Ltd, Croydon, CR0 4YY

Headline's policy is to use papers that are natural, renewable and
recyclable products and made from wood grown in sustainable forests.
The logging and manufacturing processes are expected to conform to the
environmental regulations of the country of origin.

HEADLINE PUBLISHING GROUP
An Hachette UK Company
338 Euston Road
London NW1 3BH

www.eternalromancebooks.co.uk
www.headline.co.uk
www.hachette.co.uk

For Mary Lou

Sisters, sisters . . .

Thanks for going with me to Eternity Springs. Next time, I'll drive over the mountain pass if we hit a thunderstorm, though I still have dibs on being Louise. You're Thelma.

Love seems the swiftest, but it is the slowest of all growths. No mans or woman really knows what perfect love is until they have been married a quarter of a century.

—MARK TWAIN

PROLOGUE

Byron R. White Federal Courthouse
Denver, Colorado

"So help me God."

Lowering his right hand, Mackenzie S. Timberlake shook the hand of the chief justice, who had just sworn him in as the newest member of the United States District Court for the District of Colorado.

"Congratulations, Judge Timberlake," the chief justice said. "We're glad to have you aboard, Mac."

"Thank you, sir. I'm honored. I look forward to working with you."

He turned to his wife, Ali, who held the family Bible against her chest, and they exchanged a quick hug. "I'm so proud of you, Mac," she murmured. "Congratulations."

"Thanks, honey." Then, as he turned to face the witnesses in the courtroom—his colleagues, his friends, and especially his family—his heart swelled with emotion as they broke into applause.

This grand and glorious moment was the culmination of a long-cherished dream. It was almost surreal.

His gaze fell on his longtime secretary, Louise, whose maternal smile beamed with pride and approval, then to his former law partners, then to Charles Cavanaugh, his mentor from the very beginnings of his legal career. Charles was also his father-in-law and the only father figure Mac had ever known. Meeting his gaze, Charles nodded once, a regal bow of his head. Pride rose within Mac. Having this man's approval meant the world to him.

Next Mac met the warm gazes of the young adults who were his children. The pride in Stephen's and Chase's eyes made him feel ten feet tall. The hero worship in Caitlin's reassured him that even though his little girl was almost all grown up, her daddy was still her prince.

Finally he turned back to Ali. In her eyes, he saw . . . everything. Pride, respect, encouragement, admiration, love. Always love. Classically beautiful, outrageously generous, and infinitely supportive, for more than twenty years she'd been his wife, his lover, his biggest cheerleader. She was his heart.

I am blessed.

Tradition required that he give a bit of a speech, but Mac kept his remarks short and limited them primarily to expressions of thanks and appreciation to those who had assisted him along this journey. He accepted handshakes and hugs, verbal jabs and kisses until slowly his guests departed for the reception to be hosted by his father-in-law at the Brown Palace Hotel. As the crowd flowed through the doors and out into the hall, Mac hung back. Once the courtroom had emptied, he paused and turned around.

Mac drew in a deep breath, then slowly exhaled. A courtroom. *My courtroom.*

He thought back to the day he'd had his first look

at a courtroom. Nine years old and scared to death. The public defender smelled of grilled onions. The prosecutor wore gold cuff links with stones that winked in the sunlight beaming through a dusty window. The courtroom was muggy and hot, the air-conditioning system unable to keep up on an August afternoon in southern Oklahoma.

Towering above him, his robe black as midnight and his hair white as snow, was the judge. The judge could make his mother do something. The judge could make sure his mom *didn't* do something. This was a man who would change Mac's world.

A man who held all the power.

To the nine-year-old boy who'd watched the huge, white-haired man bang his gavel and have his mother handcuffed and marched away, the judge was a god. In that moment, Mac's life path had been blazed. He wanted that power, that prestige, that authority. He wanted to be a god.

He wanted to be a judge.

And now, after decades of study and sacrifice, hard work and determination, he'd achieved his goal.

From behind him, Ali spoke. "Mac? The cab is waiting."

Turning to look at her, his heart gave a twist and his conscience whispered, *But at what cost?*

ONE

❦

Two years later

In the bedroom she shared with her husband, Ali Timberlake tucked her makeup case neatly into her suitcase, then zipped it shut just as her husband emerged from his closet, a duffel bag in one hand. "Are you sure about this, honey?" Mac asked, his brow knitted with concern. "We can still change the plan."

"Right," Ali replied, her tone dry. "And for the rest of my life I'll get to listen to Stephen and Chase talk about the one that got away."

"Hey, we can go fishing in Alaska another—"

Ali interrupted. "No, it's okay. I'm glad you're getting to go. It's a minor miracle that your schedule and those of the boys meshed this time. If Caitlin wanted you with her, that would be different, but she's flexing her wings and feeling independent and ready to take on Vanderbilt University."

Her lips twisted as she added, "Frankly, I'm not sure she really wants *me* to go with her to Nashville. We haven't exactly been getting along very well lately."

Her husband tossed his duffel onto their bed, then

gave Ali a rueful look. "She did tell me you packed her toothbrush three days ago. She thinks you can't wait for her to go."

"After the way she's been acting lately, can you blame me?"

"Now, sweetheart."

"Oh, I know." Ali shrugged and waved her hand in a dismissive gesture. "She's emotional. I'm emotional. It's not every day that your youngest child and only daughter goes off to college for the first time."

"Exactly." Mac grimaced and rubbed the back of his neck. "That's why I think I should be there. The boys could go to Alaska without me. No reason why they couldn't."

He truly appeared torn, so Ali swallowed her own misgivings and pasted on a smile. "Actually, there is. This is a father-son trip. You can't very well have a father-son trip if the father is a no-show. You went with me and Cait to orientation, and that was the important trip. This will be fun for me and Caitlin. An August road trip. A mother-daughter adventure. We'll do just fine."

He gave her a long, searching look, then nodded. "Okay. If you're sure."

"I'm sure." She smiled with a brightness she didn't feel. "Now I'd better get downstairs and see to breakfast."

"Leave your suitcase. I'll carry it down when I come."

"Thanks."

Ali tried to shake off her melancholy as she made her way downstairs to prepare a meal for her family. She wanted today's breakfast to be extra special since this was Caitlin's big day, the day she flew out of the nest and off to college. It was also the first time in months that the entire family would sit down to a meal together and likely the last meal they'd all share until Thanksgiving.

Throughout the children's lives, Ali had made the family supper a big deal. It was the Timberlake family together time, and everyone was expected to make a real effort to be there. Since Mac had worked at her father's firm while the kids were growing up, she had invoked the boss's daughter privilege in that respect alone. Mac had rarely missed dinner with the family. That had changed since he took the seat on the bench, but by then the crucial years were behind them, the precedent had been set. Their family was stronger because of it.

After today, family meals would be few and far between.

Ali briefly closed her eyes. *Don't go there.*

She'd have the kids set the table in the dining room and make it a celebration. Maybe even use her mother's china. The kids would complain about having to hand-wash the dishes, but if you didn't go to the trouble to make an occasion an occasion, it became just one more meal in a lifetime of meals.

Mentally she reviewed the contents of her fridge and pantry. Yes, she could do a Hollandaise sauce. She had fresh spinach. If she did eggs Florentine, at least the boys would have one serving of a vegetable today. Fresh berries. She could make pigs in a blanket for Caitlin. They were her favorite.

As she approached her kitchen, the aroma drifting in the air gave her warning. Bacon? Someone was already cooking? Her eyes rounded with surprise. What alternate reality was this?

Ali stepped into the kitchen and halted abruptly. The kitchen table was set with a "Bon Voyage" paper tablecloth. A SpongeBob SquarePants paper center-piece adorned the center of the table. Paper plates proclaimed "Happy St. Patrick's Day," and helium-filled Mylar balloons that read "Over the Hill" had been tied to the back of each of the chairs.

Each of her three grown children turned to look at her, and Ali desperately wished she had a camera. Stephen, looking like a lawyer already with his neatly trimmed hair, freshly shaved face, and button-down shirt. Chase, the outdoorsman, with his three-day beard and longish hair drawn back and tied at the nape of his neck with a leather lace. And Caitlin, blond and beautiful and brimming with life, a typical college coed. Ten minutes ago these young adults had been grade-schoolers riding their bikes on the side-walk. Where had the years gone?

Familiar impish grins spread across their faces, telling Ali that they were tickled pink that they'd sur-prised her. *Some things never change, thank good-ness.* They'd recognized that this was an important family moment. Something she'd tried too hard to teach them had stuck. Happiness bloomed inside Ali like a springtime flower, and she didn't try to keep the smile off her face as she said, "Caitlin, did your brothers actually cook for you to mark your special day?"

"Sort of," Caitlin replied, glancing at the boys. "But not exactly."

"We are cooking breakfast," Stephen clarified as he

removed the last piece of bacon from the frying pan and placed it on a paper towel to drain. He was a younger version of Mac, with his father's dark hair and brown eyes that now sparkled mischievously. "I know it's shocking, and I'm glad we didn't give you a heart attack. At your advanced age, I worried about that."

"Just because you are in law school, young man, doesn't mean I can't still send you to your room," Ali fired back. Her gaze fixed on the table, she asked, "Happy St. Patrick's Day?"

"We shopped the bargain bin at the party store," Chase explained. "G'morning, Mom."

"Good morning, son." She eyed the activity at the stovetop, counter, and kitchen table. Apparently the menu included bacon, scrambled eggs, toast, orange juice, Ali's usual yogurt and fruit, and of course Chase's favorite, Froot Loops. "So, who is going to clue me in? What does Cait mean when she says 'sorta'?"

Chase opened his mouth, but Caitlin stopped him with an elbow to his side, then pushed the lever on the toaster and gave Stephen, their eldest, a look that said, *Go on*.

"We thought it was important to mark the occasion because today is a special day," Stephen said as Mac joined the family in the kitchen. Mac placed his hand on Ali's shoulder while their eldest continued, "The last of your chicks is officially flying from the nest today. It *is* a special day for Caitlin, and that's why we bought her a princess crown to wear during breakfast. But it's also a special day for you and Dad. We thought it was an appropriate time for the three

of us to tell you both how much we love you and ﹍
much we appreciate all you've done for us."

Oh. Ali brought a hand to her chest. *Wow.*

Stephen nodded toward Chase, then cracked another egg into a bowl. Ali's middle child flashed his father's grin, then said, "I'll keep my part short because I know you, Mom. You'll start bawling, and we don't want you dribbling snot into your yogurt."

"Cha-a-ase!" Caitlin protested as the toast popped up.

"Well, it's true."

"Yeah, but you don't have to be gross about it. Are you ever gonna grow up?"

"Probably not."

Probably not, Ali silently agreed. Chase had been such a terror, such a daredevil, when he was little. Such a challenge to parent, yet so much fun.

"You are the greatest mom in the world, Mom," he continued. "You've always been there for us, and we always knew we could count on you. I was always proud that you were my mother."

Ali started blinking. She was moments away from bawling. *My kids know me so well.*

Chase made a sweeping gesture toward Caitlin. Ali's daughter, now a young, idealistic woman, stepped forward. Lacing her fingers, she spoke with solemn sincerity. "You guys gave us a firm, stable foundation on which to build our hopes and dreams. That's something few of my friends had. Actually, none of my friends had the great home and family life we have had. I know that makes me a stronger person, and it makes today easier for me.

"Today is my Independence Day, but it's also your

Freedom Day. Especially for you, Mom." Then, with a loving smile, sweet, tender-hearted Caitlin shot the arrow through the very center of Ali's heart. "You're not a stay-at-home mom anymore."

Mac's hand gave her shoulder a reassuring squeeze while Ali stood there bleeding.

"So," Caitlin continued, "the boys and I thought it'd be nice to mark this special day with a special thank-you—a family meal we prepared."

"Besides," Chase piped up, "we knew if we didn't do something first, then you'd go all out and we'd be stuck washing Grandmother's dishes."

Ali couldn't speak past the lump of emotion in her throat. Mac stepped forward and covered for her. "This is a real nice surprise. How long before it's ready? I'm starved."

Breakfast was delicious, boisterous, and fun. The kids teased one another as usual, and for just a little while Ali could pretend the old days were back. All too soon, however, breakfast was finished, the paper plates relegated to the trash, and the pots and pans washed and stored away. Mac glanced at the clock. "You girls had better hit the road. Kansas City is a long drive."

"Don't remind me," Caitlin groaned. But excitement shone in her eyes as she hurried upstairs, saying, "I'll be ready in five, Mom."

A few minutes later, out beside the car, Mac studied the load and grimaced. "We should have shipped half of this stuff. If you have a flat tire . . ." He exhaled a heavy sigh and shook his head. Then he gave Ali a long look and said, "Last chance."

"We'll be fine."

"I'll worry about you being on the road for the next week."

"I'll worry that you'll be eaten by a grizzly bear."

Caitlin bounded out of the house carrying her purse and a tennis racket that she somehow found space for in the back of Mac's SUV. She exchanged hugs and more good-natured teasing with her brothers, then her father took her hands. Mac's voice was a little gruff as he spoke his traditional farewell: "Be careful, kitten. Wear sunscreen. Drink lots of water."

"*Dad*-dy!"

Mac grinned, then pulled her into his embrace and hugged her hard. "Seriously, though, do be careful. Listen to your instincts. Go to class. Make smart decisions."

"I will, Daddy."

He kissed her forehead, then said, "I'm so proud of you, Caitlin. I'm going to miss you so much."

"I'll miss you, too, Daddy, and I'll be home for Thanksgiving before you know it. Shoot, with the hours you've been working, you won't even notice I'm gone."

"Finally, something good to come out of all of those hours." He gave her one more kiss, one more hug, then opened the door for her. "Buckle your seat belt. If you're driving, don't talk on the cell phone, and especially don't text."

Caitlin rolled her eyes as she slid into her seat. "Good-bye, Daddy."

"Bye, baby." He shut the passenger door behind her, then walked around to the driver's side, where

Ali was fitting the key into the ignition. "Alison, you drive carefully. Call me when you stop for the night."

"I will." Ali lifted her face for his quick kiss. "You guys be safe, too, and have a wonderful time. I hope you catch dozens of fish."

She started the car, and she and her daughter drove off for their grand adventure.

As road trips went, it proved to be one of the most pleasurable Ali had ever experienced. She and Caitlin shared a similar traveling style. They agreed on what music and audiobooks to listen to. They both wanted to stop every two hours, and they liked driving late into the night and sleeping in the next morning—just the opposite of Mac's preferences. What Ali enjoyed most were the hours on end spent in conversation with her only daughter. They talked about everything under the sun—family, friends, old memories, new dreams, wishes, and desires. Ali knew that she'd remember and treasure for the rest of her life this time spent with Caitlin.

Eventually the conversations ended. The trip ended. Four days after leaving Denver, in a slightly different version of the scene Caitlin had had with her father, Ali told her daughter good-bye in the parking lot outside her dorm. They hugged, they kissed, and they declared their love for each other, but Ali could tell her daughter was distracted. Her suitemates were waiting for her to go shopping for their coordinating bathroom accessories.

Ali made it three whole blocks before she burst into tears. She pulled into a convenience store parking lot and buried her face in her arms against the steering wheel. She cried long, hard tears, pouring out her sadness and her grief, sobbing out her sadness and her sorrow.

Finally, when she'd drained her tears and used all the tissues in the box, she went into the store and used the facilities, then picked up a new box of tissues and a packaged brownie. For a long moment she eyed the selection of tall-boy beers. Sighing, she chose a Coke instead, paid for her selections, then resumed the long drive home.

An hour into her trip, she tried to call Mac, but of course his phone went to voice mail. Her men were out in the wilds of Alaska, where cell phone coverage wasn't exactly grizzly-to-grizzly. She tried to call her father, but his phone, too, went to voice mail, and she recalled that he had a golf vacation this week. Charles Cavanaugh didn't carry a cell phone in his golf bag.

She drove another fifty miles, then dialed one of her friends in Eternity Springs. She had a nice long conversation with Sage Anderson, recently engaged and planning a Christmas wedding. Afterward, Ali tried Mac again.

Silly of her, really. Mac wasn't there. Mac was rarely there anymore.

"Don't be snotty," she scolded herself. Mac had an important job that kept him extremely busy. Hadn't she known from the very first that this was what she could expect if she shared her life with Mackenzie S. Timberlake?

When she'd met Mac her freshman year at Notre Dame, he'd had a well-defined plan for his future. He'd not deviated from his plan in all the years since—well, except for the surprise they had named Stephen. Following his undergrad years, Mac had gone to Stanford for law school, then on to private practice at her father's law firm. While the family connection had landed him the job, he'd earned his partnership all on his own with hard work, a brilliant mind, and excellent instincts. He'd achieved his goal of a federal court judgeship three full years ahead of the timeline he'd outlined to her on their second date. A man didn't accomplish so much at such a relatively young age without a full share and more of discipline.

Of course, she'd had a plan for her future, too, but the surprise currently attending law school had altered her plan permanently. She'd graduated from college with a degree in business she didn't want, the dream of culinary school in mothballs because of the baby already on the way. While Mac built his résumé, she'd wiped snotty noses, organized PTA fundraisers, and spent a good portion of her day in a minivan toting kids from one event to another.

She'd loved it. She might never have fulfilled her own workday dreams, but she'd settled comfortably into her role as a stay-at-home mom, and the entire Timberlake family had thrived.

And, eventually, outgrown her.

That's okay, she told herself. It wasn't like she didn't have a life of her own separate from the kids. She'd still keep busy. She had her volunteer work. Her classes at the gym. She thoroughly enjoyed her occasional trips up into the mountains to Eternity Springs. She'd find plenty to do to fill the hours now empty of baseball games or debate matches or dance recitals.

Maybe she'd leap headlong into the whole quilting thing. She could join a guild in Denver. Meet a whole new group of friends. Except Ali already had lots of friends. She didn't want more friends. She wanted her family.

She was a stay-at-home mom who'd completed her job. Lost her job. A thundercloud of self-pity built in her emotional sky, but she fled from it, tried to outrun it, by lecturing herself aloud. "You haven't lost your family. They just don't live with you anymore. In lots of ways, that's a good thing."

She'd no longer have sweaty gym socks stinking up the boys' rooms or a clutter of makeup spread all across the upstairs bathroom vanity. Those were good things. She wouldn't have to lie awake in bed worrying until her kids made it home by curfew—or not. Another good thing. And one of her friends had told her that the best thing about having an empty nest was that now she and her husband could have sex on the staircase if they wanted. Personally, Ali couldn't imagine that being too comfortable, but hey, she was willing to try anything once.

"I'll just put that on the calendar," she decided, feeling marginally better.

So she'd finished the stay-at-home mom years of her life. Big deal. She hadn't lost her family. She still had Mac. Maybe they could use this time to reinvigorate their relationship. Enjoy an empty-nest honeymoon of sorts. Spend time and energy on each other instead of the kids. Why, this could be the best time of her life. Of their lives.

Thank goodness she still had Mac.

"The Desai case?" Mac repeated, one week after his return to work following his Alaskan vacation.

Desai was a high-profile case of attempted domestic terrorism. "I thought that went to Judge Harrison."

The court clerk nodded. "It did, but Judge Harrison had a heart attack this morning on his way in. We heard fifteen minutes ago."

"Oh, no. How's he doing?"

"It's serious. His son took my call and said he's not out of the woods entirely, but they do expect him to survive."

"That's good news."

"Yes, but the son also said the doctors are talking about retirement."

Mac hated to hear it. Harrison was a brilliant jurist and an affable colleague. He'd be missed.

"The case has been reassigned to you, Judge Timberlake. You have a hearing that starts in twenty minutes."

"Twenty minutes! What sort of hearing?"

"The U.S. attorney wants a search warrant executed today. We have FBI, DEA, and the Denver police headed in." The clerk handed over a file. "It's a good thing you had your vacation. This thing is liable to have you tied up for months."

Mac stared down at the bulging file and sighed. He should call Ali and warn her that he might be late. He thought she might have dropped the word *special* when she'd referenced dinner tonight.

As he headed for his office to make the call, his secretary, Louise, stopped him with a problem. From that moment on, the Desai case consumed him, and he didn't leave the courthouse until well after 10:00 p.m. It wasn't until he walked into his dark house and smelled the faded aroma of his favorite, veal parmigiana, that he remembered that he'd never made that phone call, and his stomach dipped.

Next he recalled the possible special plans reference, and his stomach dropped even more.

Sure enough, when he peeked into the dining room, he saw the table set for two with her mother's china. *Oh, hell.*

Mac rubbed the back of his neck and inwardly groaned. He'd screwed up. Big time. He knew this was a difficult time for his wife, and he'd been trying to be extra sensitive to her wishes and desires. Luckily, she'd appeared to be happier since he returned from Alaska and she returned from Tennessee. He had hoped that Ali would find the anticipation of Caitlin's departure for college more upsetting than dealing with the actual aftereffects of it, and so far, it appeared that would be the case.

But letting her down like this tonight sure didn't help the situation. "Timberlake," he murmured, "you're an ass."

He slipped off his jacket and loosened his tie as he climbed the stairs to their bedroom. The room was dark, the figure in the bed unmoving. Attempting to be as quiet as possible, Mac readied for bed, then slipped between the sheets.

He breathed in the familiar lavender scent of the lotion she habitually smoothed over her skin before bed and edged closer to her warmth, trying not to wake her as he put his arm around her, seeking, and finding, that sense of homecoming she offered him even after all these years.

"You're home," she said.

Mac closed his eyes. *Damn.* "Sorry I woke you. I'm sorry I'm so late. I know I should have called."

"Where were you?"

She said it like a question, not an accusation, so he breathed a little easier. "I had a hearing. A new case. We ended up ordering in dinner."

"Oh. Okay."

She sounded tired—very tired—so he decided to wait until the morning to offer any further details. He kissed her shoulder and spooned her tight against him. "Goodnight, babe. Sleep well."

"You too."

Mac waited for her to continue their usual night-time ritual, but her regular breathing told him she'd fallen back asleep. Disquieted, he drifted off plagued with a sense of foreboding.

When was the last time they'd gone to sleep together without exchanging the words *I love you*?

TWO

❦

The pressure in her chest began the moment Ali awoke. She didn't need to open her eyes and see the undisturbed covers on Mac's side of the bed to know that he had never come upstairs. She was freezing. Cold clear to the bone. It was as if she'd lain exposed to the chilly early spring air throughout the long night.

Come to think of it, that aptly described what had happened. Mac radiated heat like a furnace, and for most of their marriage she'd slept comfortably snuggled up against him with only a thin cotton blanket on their bed. But his body heat didn't do her a darn bit of good when he slept on the sofa downstairs, now did it? How many nights in a row was it now? Five? Six? Sporadically before that?

And yet maybe she was wrong. Maybe she could blame it on hormones. Maybe her body's thermostat was all screwed up. She was forty-three, after all. Instead of hot flashes, could a woman suffer cold spells? Frigid spells? Was that the problem?

That was probably what Mac would say. She'd

seen the accusation in his eyes, though he'd never said that *F*-word out loud.

Holding her breath and hoping, Ali sought warmth by slowly stretching a leg across the wide expanse of their king-sized bed. Inch by inch she searched. She encountered nothing but cold, crisp Egyptian cotton.

The pressure in her chest intensified. Despair oozed through her like a cold, dark cloud. She yanked her leg back and curled into herself. Burying her head beneath her pillow, she willed away the tears that threatened. She was tired of being cold. In her bed. In her home. In her marriage. So cold that it hurt. It was as if the Colorado winter had moved inside and surrounded her.

She lay shivering and miserable, looking within herself for the will to meet the day, until finally the lure of a hot shower enticed her from her bed. A glance at the bedside clock revealed red numerals glowing 6:03 a.m., a good hour before her customary time to rise. In the master bathroom, she glimpsed her reflection in the mirror and winced. The dark circles beneath her eyes complemented the Medusa thing she had going on with her hair. Black mascara streaks on her cheeks accentuated the look.

"I wouldn't want to sleep with you, either," she said to her image before turning away and stepping into the shower. The fact that she'd neglected her makeup removal routine last night bothered her. As did the reality that she was overdue for a haircut, and she'd been MIA at her standing manicure appointment for weeks now. Okay, months. The last time she'd had a pedicure was the mother-daughter spa day she'd indulged in with Caitlin the week before they left for Tennessee.

As the hot water warmed her, Ali's spirit rebounded. It wasn't like she'd let herself go, because she hadn't. So what if she weighed eight whole pounds more than she had on the day they'd married? She'd given birth to three of his babies. That was only 2.67 pounds per child, and frankly, they didn't look bad on her. And if her breasts weren't as perky as they used to be, well, she'd nursed those three babies, too. What did he expect?

Sure, she had a few lines on her face, but her skin wasn't leathery from a lifetime of worshiping the sun. Maybe she'd noticed a few gray hairs creeping in. So what? Since she was blond, they weren't all that noticeable. And she still had a darn fine butt. She wasn't going to allow Mac Timberlake's lack of attention make her doubt her femininity.

If she said it often enough, maybe she'd eventually believe it.

Nevertheless, her little pep talk had helped. At ten minutes to seven, wearing the armor of fresh makeup, styled hair, her favorite slacks, and a cashmere sweater, she made her way downstairs to the kitchen and the coffeepot, which Mac always programed to start brewing at 6:30 a.m. As she grabbed a mug from the cabinet, she glanced out the kitchen window into the backyard where the Honorable Mackenzie S. Timberlake was swimming his morning laps in the heated pool.

At the sight of her husband, Ali's melancholy came rolling back in. It was hard to be married to Mr. Perfect.

That was an apt description of the man. His dedication to his exercise regimen offered a good example. How many Monday mornings had she declared a new beginning to an exercise routine of one sort or another? Too many to count. She would do fine for a week or two, sometimes even a month, but then something would happen—one of the kids would get sick or their schedules would change—and she'd miss one day, then two, and her good intentions would go right down the drain.

Mac, on the other hand, never let illness or schedules stop him. In all the years they'd been married, he'd missed his daily workout no more than a dozen times. Even that stupid Desai case that had consumed his life from September to February hadn't stopped him from getting his exercise. He'd get up an hour early, cut his lunch short, or even hold a meeting at the health club to fit it in. A part of Ali admired that tremendously. Another part of her thought it was a bit . . . well, she wouldn't use the word *anal* because the term offended him, as she'd learned one time when she'd called him that to his face. The term she'd adopted to describe her husband was *über-disciplined*, and it fit Mac Timberlake to a T.

These days, she found it so annoying.

Outside, he finished his laps and stood in the shallow end, his arms resting on the side of the pool. He gave his head a shake and sent water droplets flying, then levered himself up and out of the water. Watching him as he reached for a towel, his swim trunks hanging low on his hips, Ali couldn't deny that his exercise regimen paid off. At six foot four and 220 pounds, the man could have made his living as a model had he not chosen law. He had thick, mahogany-colored hair, gray eyes, and a square jaw. His broad shoulders tapered to a slim waist, and his belly remained almost as flat as it had been the day she'd met him. After more than twenty-two years of marriage, he still made her mouth water when she saw him naked.

Not that she'd seen him naked lately. Not for weeks. Okay, a month. Months.

As he toweled off in the cold morning air, Ali indulged in a little fantasy where she exited the house, crossed the yard, and pushed him back into the pool. She'd done that very thing a few years ago when the kids were up in the mountains on a church youth group camping trip. She'd caught Mac by surprise and he'd teetered at the edge of the pool, his arms windmilling as he fought for balance. He'd fallen backward with a huge splash, and she'd been laughing when he'd surfaced, sputtering. His eyes had flashed. He'd scrambled from the pool and she'd started running.

Of course he'd caught her. They'd both been laughing when he'd tossed her fully dressed into the pool, then jumped in after her. Before they were done, they'd made love once in the pool and again in the hot tub.

Ali knew that if she pushed him into the pool today, she wouldn't be playing, wouldn't be laughing when he surfaced. It would be an act of meanness, plain and simple.

"What happened to us, Mac?" she murmured.

Tears stung her eyes and she tried to blink them away, but she had little success. Nothing new there. Lately she cried at just about everything—sappy commercials, country songs on the radio, and the color yellow. The yellow thing was a bit weird, she would admit, but yellow was just so . . . happy.

Maybe, though, she should go for some yellow. Try to make some happiness happen.

As he started toward the house, she stepped away from the window and decided to make an effort this morning. They could share a cup of coffee, a conversation, maybe even a meal. When was the last time they'd sat down for a meal together that didn't involve either his work or one of her philanthropic interests? She honestly couldn't remember.

Ali grabbed a second mug from the cabinet—a yellow mug—and filled both cups with coffee. She added a teaspoon of sugar to Mac's, then stood near the door just as he walked inside, a damp royal blue beach towel draped over one shoulder. Seeing her, he stopped abruptly. "Oh." She heard surprise in the word. "Hi."

"Good morning." She handed him a mug with a smile that, despite a sincere effort, probably didn't reach her eyes.

"Thanks." He glanced at the clock as he sipped his coffee. "You're up early."

She hesitated. She wanted to tell him that the cold woke her up, but she wasn't ready to toss the issue out into the open like a bad piece of fish. One couldn't ignore bad fish, and Ali wasn't prepared to face the stink. Not here and now, anyway. It wouldn't be . . . yellow.

She cleared her throat. "I have a busy day ahead of me."

"Oh? What's on your docket?"

She didn't miss the surprise in his voice, and for some reason it raised her hackles. The words *Nothing you'd respect* hovered on her tongue.

This morning she had a meeting planned with her friend Celeste Blessing to discuss window drapes. Celeste had decided to redecorate her private suite of rooms at Cavanaugh House, the mansion once owned by Ali's silver-baron ancestor and now the centerpiece of the Angel's Rest Healing Center and Spa property in Eternity Springs. Recalling that Ali recently had chosen new draperies for her father's Victorian home, Celeste had asked to see them next time she visited Denver. That was today, so draperies were on Ali's docket.

Unlike Mac, Ali didn't spend her days deciding the fate of criminals or corporations. Justice might be blind, but in Mac's case it was also arrogant. He considered drapery design little more than fluff.

So as he set down his coffee mug and opened the laundry room door, she shrugged and responded to his question about her plans for the day by saying, "Shopping."

"Of course."

Of course? What did he mean by that? Was it a snide observation or just filler because he didn't care to talk to her?

He lifted his robe from its hook and slipped it on. When he turned his back to her as he shucked off his swim trunks, the tightness returned to her chest. They were the only two people in the house. Since when did he feel he had to hide himself from her?

Anger and despair swirled inside her, and she blurted out the question. "Did you sleep well on the couch?"

His shoulders subtly stiffened as he belted his robe. He hung up his wet trunks, then turned and reached again for his coffee. He stared down at the mug and spoke with an apology in his tone. "No, I didn't. I intended to come up, but then time got away from me. I didn't want to disturb you."

She clamped her teeth against a sarcastic *How considerate of you, dear.* She was supposed to be making an effort here. "What were you working on?"

"Just reading a brief." He avoided her gaze and drank deeply from his mug, then crossed to the refrigerator. Opening the door, he gazed inside. "I think I'll have an omelet this morning. Would you like me to make one for you, too?"

Ali froze. Had he really asked that? She couldn't eat eggs; she'd never been able to eat eggs. They gave her a horrible stomachache. Mac darn well knew that.

Hurt sliced through her, a sharp, deep pain that lodged right beneath her breastbone. Ali shut her eyes, shivered, and shriveled. He knew eggs made her ill, but he simply didn't think, not about her, not anymore. She was of no more consequence to Mac Timberlake than the puddles of water he'd left pooled on the laundry room floor.

He pulled his breakfast ingredients out of the fridge. Eggs, milk, butter, cheese. He never glanced her way or gave any sign of listening for a response to his stupid, careless question. As had become the pattern of late for her, on the heels of hurt came anger.

Fuming, Ali set down her coffee mug and left the kitchen without a word. Forget yellow. Never mind sharing a meal or conversation. She'd forgo her usual yogurt and fruit this morning, stop off at Archie's and buy a hot glazed donut. And maybe a jelly donut, too. Shoot, she'd go for broke and add an éclair to her order. All that grease and fat and cholesterol. Yum. At least she'd enjoy her breakfast before it made her sick. That ought to make him happy.

The thought wasn't exactly fair. Ali knew very well that his offer had been thoughtless, not mean, but she didn't care. That single question summed up all the slights and hurts of the past seven months and left her furious. Marching toward the entry hall, where she'd left her purse and keys on a console table, she paused at the door to his home office and stared into the room.

Ali might have chosen the drapes, furnishings, and paint colors, but it had always been his space. Woe be the family member who invaded it without invitation or permission. She'd not had a problem with that. She'd always agreed that the room and its contents should remain off-limits to the children. Wasn't she forever going in search of scissors that had "walked off" from her own desk in the den?

"But it's supposed to be your office," she muttered, taking in the tableau. "Not your bedroom."

His shoes sat on the floor next to the couch, socks tucked neatly inside, the big, square pillow moved from the window seat to one end of the sofa, the afghan mussed and thrown over the back cushions. Like he'd just climbed out of bed.

Ali's temper rose. His sleeping downstairs was an insult. A slap in her face. The need to strike back at him was a living, breathing thing inside her.

She stepped into his office. His inner sanctum—*his new bedroom*—and strode toward his desk. There she brazenly committed a sin of significant magnitude and booted up his computer. She opened the browser. With her pulse thrumming, her heart pounding, she typed in her favorite luxury retailer's Web address, then navigated to bedding. After a brief search, she made her selection, filled in her credit card and delivery information, then defiantly clicked the button to confirm the purchase. She was breathing as if she'd run a marathon.

"What do you think you're doing?"

It wasn't the question that prodded her temper but the tone. Clipped and condescending and challenging, all in six little words.

"I'm looking up omelet recipes," she returned in as snotty a voice as she could manage. Then she snapped her fingers and added, "Oh, no, wait. That wasn't it. I almost forgot. Eggs make me deathly ill. Actually, I was looking at porn. You see, my sex life has been lacking of late."

"Alison!" He stood in the doorway looking shocked, unhappy, and annoyed.

Her chin came up. "Guess that wasn't funny, was it, Mac? Okay, fine. What I really did on your computer just now was buy a down blanket for my bed to keep me warm at night. You can sleep on the couch forever for all I care."

"What is *wrong* with you?" He took a step into the room, his gray eyes a winter storm bearing down upon her, bitterly cold and dangerous.

"What is wrong with me?" she repeated. In that moment, she finally found the strength—or maybe surrendered to the weakness—and stepped out from behind the desk, folded her arms, and confronted the elephant in the room. "You don't sleep with me anymore. We haven't made love in months. I don't know, Judge Timberlake. You're the one with all the answers. What *is* wrong with me?"

"Oh, for God's sake," he said with disgust and a scowl. "Have you been taking your hormones?"

Ali sucked in an audible breath. At that moment, she truly hated him.

She rushed toward the door. When she passed near him, Mac reached out and grabbed her by the arm just above her elbow. Not hard enough to bruise, but firmly. Flames of anger had replaced the coldness in his eyes.

Ali looked down at his hand. "Let go. You're hurting me."

He dropped her arm as if scalded and stepped away. When his gaze dropped to the spot where he'd held her, Ali wanted to smirk. She knew the man. He thought she'd accused him of physically hurting her. Was he worried she would call the cops? Charge the irreproachable judge with domestic violence?

As furious as she was at him, she would never do that. Mac Timberlake was many things, but he'd never been the least bit physically abusive. Not with the kids and not with her. The man never, ever lost control.

The devil in her urged her to push him, to prod him, to make him lose control. She'd like to make him lose control. At least that would mean he still cared.

Even as she debated her response, the anger left his face and he schooled his expression into an increasingly familiar passionless mask. Standing with his hands relaxed at his sides, he said quietly, "I don't want to fight with you, Ali."

With that, the temper drained from her, too, leaving her exhausted, weary, and worn. Defeated.

In that defeat, she needed to know exactly how much she had lost. *Ask him. Get it over with. Find out once and for all.* She licked her lips. "Are you having an affair, Mac?"

His head jerked up and his gaze met hers, steady and piercing. "No."

Those gray eyes didn't waver, and she believed him. He was telling her the truth. It wasn't another woman after all.

She waited to feel a sense of relief. During the past few months, for the first time in their marriage, she had worried about his fidelity. However, relief didn't come. If not another woman . . . "Then what's wrong, Mac? What is wrong with *us*?"

His square jaw hardened and he closed his eyes. "I don't know."

That she did *not* believe.

Now that she'd finally lobbed the stinky fish onto

the table, she had to try again. They had to acknowl-edge the problem and confront it in order to fix it. "People say you're one of the most brilliant minds in the country. I've even heard murmurs that depending on the way the political winds blow, you could be headed for the Supreme Court. I can't buy the con-cept that someone so smart could be clueless about what's happening in his own life." Taking a chance, she reached out and touched him. "What is it, Mac? Why are we falling apart?"

His jaw relaxed, and she sensed an opening. He was finally going to talk to her!

She drew in a bracing breath, aware that whatever he said was likely to wound her, but knowing that it needed to be said nonetheless.

But instead of talking, his eyes shuttered. His shields went up and he shut down, locking her out. "We're not falling apart."

Her hand fell away from him and she took a step backward. Sadness bigger than any she'd known be-fore washed through her, and the tears she despised welled within her once again. Why wouldn't he help? They were broken and she couldn't fix them by her-self. She couldn't fight this fight by herself.

She couldn't bear to hurt this way any longer.

She exhaled softly and closed her eyes, making a decision on the spot. Celeste wanted her help for more than simple decorating. "I've been offered a job, Mac, and I've decided to take it."

It obviously threw him for a loop. He gave his head a little shake as if he'd heard her wrong. "A job? You mean another volunteer thing?"

Ali told herself not to be annoyed at his reaction. After all, she had not held an outside job in all the years of their marriage, and Mac had been the one to always say that she worked just as hard as a volunteer as he did as an attorney.

"No, a paying job. I'm going to run a restaurant in Eternity Springs."

His lips twisted in a smirk. "Right."

Ali bristled. "The Bristlecone Café has been closed since its owners moved to Florida last fall, and Celeste Blessing rented it because tourism is so good that the town needs it. She offered me the position of manager." She named a salary that made his eyes go gratifyingly wide, then added, "I'm going to accept."

He stared at her for a long moment, then shook his head. "Eternity Springs is four hours away. You can't commute that far."

"You're right. I can't." Ali drew herself up and swallowed hard. "I can't bear it here, like this, any longer. I'll be staying there, Mac. At least for a little while, I'll be living in Eternity Springs."

With that, she turned and walked calmly upstairs.

Once in her bedroom, she went a little crazy. She kicked the pillow that had fallen to the floor, then yanked open the closet door and tugged out her biggest suitcase. She paid scant attention to what she packed, grabbing this and grasping that and tossing it all into the suitcase in careless disarray. When she went into the bathroom to fill her cosmetics case, a glance in the mirror revealed the tracks of tears on her cheeks. She angrily wiped them away. She was done with crying. Done with being sad and lonely and alone. Done with hurting.

Done with him.

She won't leave.

Mac told himself that as he returned to the kitchen, cooked his omelet, and sat down to eat with the newspaper and a second cup of coffee. This was just another one of her ridiculous dramas.

After more than two decades of marriage, he certainly knew what those looked like. The time a month after they'd met when her father forbade her to fly to Paris to attend cooking school over summer break, the panic around her pregnancy with Stephen, the boycott she instituted at Mother's Day Out, the Little League fund-raiser revolt, the middle school tennis banquet incident, the high school drama club debacle . . . It just went on and on and on. Not that she hadn't been right most of the time. Not that she hadn't been effective. But Alison Michelle Cavanaugh Timberlake, American princess, had a way of turning an issue into an Issue. That's what she was doing this morning.

She wouldn't really leave.

Finished with his breakfast and unable to concentrate on his newspaper, he stood and carried his dishes to the sink. As he topped off his coffee, he heard her footsteps on the stairs, along with the *clunk clunk clunk* of a rolling suitcase.

Okay, so she'd actually packed. She still wouldn't leave. She might haul the suitcase downstairs, even go as far as throwing the thing in her car, but she wouldn't back out of the driveway. This was a grand gesture, an infantile attempt at manipulation. Ali was a master at that.

His temper simmered. She wanted to talk, did she? Now, on her timetable? Wasn't that special. Never mind that he'd tried for months to get her to talk to him. Finally he'd quit trying.

What a crock.

He fought to keep a neutral expression as she allowed the bag to bang its way down the staircase, step after step after step. She was mad, was she? Well, fine. He was plenty angry himself. In fact, he was furious. He was sick to death of the roller coaster she'd had him riding for months now. Sick to death of the games.

Mac's grip tightened around the handle on his coffee mug. Let her go. In fact, he hoped she did go. Maybe he'd carry her bag to the car. Start the engine for her.

At the entrance to the kitchen she stopped and stared at him. Her blue eyes were red-rimmed and wounded. The sight of them fed his fury. He wasn't a villain. He was sick to death of being stared at with wounded, suffering eyes. She'd been doing it for months, looking at him as if he were the source of all the ills on earth, and he didn't deserve it. What did she have to feel wounded about?

Something mean rolled through him. It must have shown in his eyes because hers widened slightly and registered caution.

Good—she should be wary of him. The emotions that churned inside him at the sight of her with suitcase in hand, her expression accusing him of all sorts of nefarious deeds, were as ugly as any he'd felt in years. He didn't as a rule go around analyzing his own psyche, but really, did she think this injured-party business was a one-way street? He had plenty of scrapes and cuts and bruises and breaks, thank you very much.

So, now what? Did she expect him to drop to his knees and beg her to stay? Well, forget that. He was calling her bluff.

Masking his thoughts, he calmly lifted his coffee cup to his mouth for another sip, then pulled out his three aces. "What about the kids?"

At that, her eyes went big and round. *Aha—hadn't thought of your children, had you? And you, the poster child for great motherhood.*

She grimaced and cleared her throat. "I guess I should call them."

"I guess you should." He'd like to eavesdrop on those conversations, hear her attempt to explain this nonsense. However, he knew good and well that those phone calls wouldn't happen because any minute now she'd come up with an excuse to stay.

"What about the governor's dinner?" he added, throwing her a bone. He was slated to speak at a dinner honoring the recipients of the Governor's Award for heroics in law enforcement in a few weeks. He had two seats at the head table, and he knew Ali was looking forward to the event. "Shall I ask . . ." The words "a date" hovered on the tip of his tongue, but when it came time to say them, he couldn't be that cruel. Instead, he substituted their daughter's name. ". . . Caitlin to take your place?"

Ali pursed her lips. "That's so close to the end of the semester. Cait might have trouble getting away. I don't want to interfere with her studies." Then she lifted her chin and declared, "I'm not cancelling my commitments, Mac. I'll attend the dinner."

Well, lucky me. He'd expected her to lob out some sort of excuse that would allow her to attend, but this particular one touched an old nerve. Same song, ten thousandth verse. He loved his children. Truly, he did. But why did their needs invariably come before his with her? "Don't do me any favors, Alison," he snapped. "Maybe I don't want you there."

He saw the blow land as she sucked in a breath. Then she tilted her chin even higher and said, "Are you asking me not to attend?"

With that, he lost patience. "Give it up, Ali. You're not taking a job in podunk Eternity Springs. You're not leaving."

Her eyes went to ice. She removed her sunglasses from her shoulder bag, then slipped them on. In a voice as cold as January, she declared, "Just watch me, your honor. Just fucking watch me."

Mac gaped at her. Had he heard right? Had his wife just dropped an *F*-bomb? His Ali? The woman never cursed. Ever! It was one of her most precious principles. And to start with that particular word? Whoa.

For the first time since she'd stormed upstairs, he wondered if she might actually leave him after all.

Needing something to do, he took another sip from his coffee mug. She gave her hair an angry toss, then strode toward the door leading to the garage. She opened it, stepped outside, then had to yank her suitcase hard when it got hung up on the threshold. She reached back into the house for the doorknob, shot him one last furious look, and slammed the door shut.

Mac heard another shocking curse, followed by the sound of the garage door going up. He remembered then that she'd forgotten to move her car into the garage last night, leaving it parked in the center of the circular drive in front. He moved to a window that gave a view of the front yard and watched with an unusual sense of detachment. By the time she dumped her suitcase into the trunk of her BMW and slammed the lid, it was as if he was staring through window glass ten inches thick.

He saw her climb into the driver's seat, and for some weird reason he recalled bringing Caitlin home from the hospital. When Ali started the car and pulled out of the drive, he remembered Chase pedaling his Big Wheel in that same drive. When she punched the gas and fishtailed her way down the street, he thought of the day Stephen got his driver's license and made his first solo trip to the grocery store to buy a gallon of milk for his mom. He watched the vapor from her tailpipe evaporate on the crisp morning air. Then she turned the corner at the end of the street and was gone.

Gone. Okay. Well, good. I'm glad.

She'd come right back.

He waited and watched the grandfather clock in the hall. Two minutes. Five. Plenty of time to drive around the block.

Mac looked out the window once again, but the street remained empty. *Okay. Well, then. Fine. Just fine.*

Mac brought his coffee mug up to his mouth. *Just fucking watch me.*

He jerked his arm back and sent the mug flying. Dark liquid splashed against butterscotch paint as the mug slammed against the wall, then fell to the tile floor and shattered. "Damn her."

Mac stood with his fists and his teeth clenched, breathing hard. Breaking the mug wasn't enough. He wanted to hit something, to put his fist through the wall, to break something else. His body trembled with need of it.

His gaze swept around the family room and focused on the collection of photographs that sat in crystal frames atop the baby grand piano. He was seconds away from sweeping the pictures to the floor with a violent swipe of his hand, but common sense prevailed. Just because Ali was acting like a fool didn't mean he should.

She'd left him. He couldn't believe she'd actually left him.

He glanced at the clock and winced. He was running late for work. But instead of shifting into overdrive with his morning ritual, he stayed in the shower long enough to drain the hot water tank, then took twice as long as usual to shave. He felt numb.

She hadn't believed him when he claimed not to know the source of their problems, but he had told her the truth. Some difficulties in their marriage were obvious—sex being the prime example. However, their lack of sex wasn't the problem; it was a symptom of the problem. The underlying disease was more difficult to diagnose.

It would be easy to blame it on his job. He'd worked long hours during the Desai case, and it was true he'd neglected Ali from time to time throughout, but that wasn't anything he hadn't done in the past when he'd had a big case. She'd always been understanding in the past. She'd seemed to be understanding this time. Yet after the Desai case ended and his overtime hours disappeared, life hadn't returned to normal. Somehow, somewhere, they'd gone from being united to being apart.

They had little in common anymore. They hardly spoke and rarely touched—even casually, much less sexually. Maybe he shouldn't be surprised that she intended, apparently, to physically move to the mountains. She'd been there mentally for months. It was as if sometime last fall Ali had taken up residence on the summit of a high peak surrounded by unscalable cliffs and deep snow that defeated him anytime he tried to reach her. He would lie beside her in bed, aching with want for her, sensing she wanted him, too, but knowing that the Ali he loved was beyond his grasp.

He didn't like making love to a shell. It left him feeling as empty as she.

And angry. So freaking angry. *How dare she freeze me out. How dare she walk out!*

He'd been a good husband to her. He'd been faithful. He'd been a good father to their children. He'd loved his family. He'd loved her. He didn't deserve this.

She didn't deserve what you did to her, either.

Mac clenched his jaw against the old guilt that

never completely went away, despite his efforts to re-
deem himself. That sin was more than twenty years
old. He'd done his level best to make it up to her.

*Have you, really? After all, you've never confessed
to it.*

Staring at his reflection in the bathroom mirror, he
said with a sneer, "Well, I can't do much about that
now, can I? She's left me."

So, now what? What are you going to do about it?

"I'm going to get dressed and go to work. I have a
meeting at ten."

He strode into his bedroom and grabbed underwear from the bureau. He'd go to work and do the
job he'd worked so hard to get, and maybe she'd be
back by the time he came home.

Just fucking watch me.

He sighed heavily. Or maybe not.

Standing at his closet door a few moments later, he
stared at the row of suits and found himself frozen
with indecision. Blue? Gray? Solid? Pinstripe? What
color shirt? Which tie?

Whoa. This wasn't like him at all. Overwhelmed.
Incapable of making a simple decision. Not a good
situation for a man in his line of work.

He pivoted and crossed to a telephone, called his
office, and claimed a sick day—his first in more years
than he could remember. He no sooner replaced the
receiver in the cradle than the phone rang. Checking
caller ID, he winced. Caitlin. Should he answer it or
not?

Mac found this choice no more easily made than
the last. Had Ali already phoned the kids? Was
Caitlin calling to rag on him? Or was this simply one

of her usual, multiple daily calls to her mother? He allowed the answering machine to pick it up, then sat on the edge of the bed to listen.

"Hey, Mom. You there?" his daughter's voice asked. "I remember you're going shopping with Mrs. Blessing sometime today, but it's early yet. Hello?" After a pause, she continued, "Okay, maybe you're in the shower. Well, I'll just talk to the machine until my bus comes—I'm on my way downtown to pick up a new tire for my bike. Some Einstein got the idea to hang all the bikes in front of the dorm in the trees overnight and when the campus cops took it down, the tire was history. Speaking of which . . . I got my paper back in history and made an 86, which blows because I needed an 88 to bring my grade up to an A. In more interesting developments, I met the cutest guy at the library last night. His name is Patrick and he's a psych major. He wants to go to law school. I think . . . Okay, here's my bus. I'll call your cell later, Mom. Love you. Tell Daddy I said hi and give him a kiss for me. Bye."

Mac closed his eyes. Caitlin would flip when she heard her mother's news. The boys wouldn't like it, but Caitlin had her mother's drama queen gene. She'd probably cut her classes and book a flight home. She'd cry a river and hire a pop psychologist to come to the house and counsel her off-their-rocker parents, and they'd all make their television debut on a reality show.

"Ah, Ali, what have we done?"

At that point, Mac had to get out of the house. He pulled on jeans, a T-shirt, and sneakers, then grabbed his wallet, keys, and cell phone and headed for the garage. He'd take a nice long drive and clear his head. He'd go east. Away from Denver, away from the mountains. Away from Alison.

While she drove west, away from him.

THREE

Twenty minutes after leaving her house, Ali turned into her father's neighborhood. How lucky that she'd arranged to meet Celeste this morning at her dad's house. She needed a dose of comfort, and she knew she'd find it there. This was her Dorothy moment—there's no place like home.

She couldn't believe what she'd done. It was as if the Medusa thing that had begun with her hair had spread and taken control of her body. *I've been offered a job, Mac. I'm going to take it.*

"My oh my oh my."

She'd left her husband. She'd packed a bag and driven off in a flurry of temper and trauma and drama, and Mac had never asked her—or told her, or begged her—to stay.

The jerk.

Ali had halfway expected that she'd lose her nerve and turn around. Yet, deep down inside, she'd known that wouldn't happen. She'd spoken the truth when she told him she couldn't bear it at home any longer. She didn't know how long this journey would take, where it would end, or with whom, but her first stop would be Eternity Springs. Well, after a detour to her daddy's house.

She parked in the driveway of the three-story Victorian mansion that had been the family home for three generations. Ali loved the place. Her father and his ancestors had taken great pains not to ruin its historic charm while adding modern conveniences. Celeste Blessing had used the same approach while converting her Victorian in Eternity Springs to the Angel's Rest Healing Center and Spa.

It was one of the reasons Ali had visited there so often during the past couple of years. At Angel's Rest in Eternity Springs, she felt at home.

Celeste believed the valley in which the little town nestled held a special healing energy, so when Eternity Springs faced an economic crisis a few years back, she'd stepped up with a solution—her Angel Plan, she'd called it. She'd set out to revitalize the town by establishing a first-class healing center and making Eternity Springs the Sedona of Colorado. So far, so good. Angel's Rest was bringing new prosperity and new opportunities to the citizens of Eternity Springs.

Ali opened her car door and reached for the coffee cake she'd stopped to buy on her way, emotional trauma being no excuse for being a poor hostess. Thankfully, her semiretired father golfed on fair-weather Tuesday mornings, so she wouldn't have to face any uncomfortable questions. She used her key and let herself in. In the kitchen, she put on a pot of coffee. Just as the appliance beeped a signal that brewing had ended, the doorbell rang. Ali returned to the front of the house, pasted on a smile, and opened the door.

Celeste stood on the front porch. A widowed, retired schoolteacher from South Carolina, she had purchased the Cavanaugh estate in Eternity Springs about three years ago and transformed it into Angel's Rest. She was a delightful woman, and Ali had liked her from the moment they'd met. Her lovely blue eyes always seemed to twinkle, and her soft southern accent made Ali think of sweet tea and front porch rockers. Celeste kept her silver-gray hair cut in a fashionable bob, demonstrated a fondness for angel-themed collectibles, and rode a Honda Gold Wing motorcycle for fun. Ali had decided she wanted to be Celeste when she grew up.

Celeste took one look at Ali, then offered a sympathetic frown. "Alison? What's wrong?"

"Oh, Celeste." Tears swelled and burst free as Ali stepped into her friend's waiting arms.

The story spilled out, everything from her missed manicures to the frozen tundra of her marriage bed. At some point during the telling, Celeste guided Ali into a chair at the kitchen table and set a cup of coffee, a piece of coffee cake, and a box of tissues in front of her.

Ali grabbed a tissue and blew her nose, then confessed, "I know you weren't serious about the job, Celeste, but I told him you were. I made up a salary figure. I lied to him. I never lie! But I knew I had to leave there, and I couldn't run away. I had to run *to* something, and Eternity Springs just seems like the place I need to be. Does that make any sense?"

Celeste clicked her tongue. "Now, Alison. I don't condone lying, but I am happy to have you help me with the Bristlecone. I do need a manager, someone to hire a staff and oversee the menus. Glenda Hawkins was kind enough to share her recipes with me, but I wouldn't mind making a few changes. You can have the job for as long as you like, but I don't want you to feel bad about leaving when it's time for you to go home. You can stay in the carriage house apartment. It's lovely. If, that is, you are certain about this?"

"I know I have to go. It's the only thing I *am* certain about, Celeste." She closed her eyes, rubbed them, and said, "The children. I have to call them. I told Mac I would."

Frowning sadly, Celeste shook her head. "You poor dear. What will you tell them?"

"Honestly? I don't know. How can I explain what's happening when I don't even understand it myself?" Ali glanced at the clock. It was only ten o'clock, and the morning already seemed like it'd been ten hours long. "I should call them now. Neither Cait nor Chase has class today until after noon. I don't know what Stephen's schedule is, though."

"Do it. The task will weigh upon you until it's done."

"I know." Ali picked up a fork and cut a bite of the coffee cake in front of her, but she didn't eat it. Nor did she look at the phone. "I'm glad you're here, Celeste. I don't think I could do it alone."

Celeste reached for her hand and gave it a quick, comforting squeeze. Ali's knees felt a bit wobbly as she rose and lifted the phone handset from its cradle on the counter. She started with the boys first. Stephen answered his cell on the second ring. "Hello, Granddad," he said before Ali said a word. "I was going to call you later. My prof said you were right about that interstate commerce question."

"Stephen, it's Mom," Ali interrupted.

"Mom?" Her son paused a moment, then asked, "You're calling from Granddad's house. Is he okay?"

"Yes. Your grandfather is fine. He's on the golf course this morning. I . . . um . . . have other news." Ali closed her eyes and reached deep inside herself for the right words. "I don't quite know how to say it. I'm not sure how to start."

"Mom? You're scaring me."

"No! Don't be scared. You absolutely don't have to be scared. It's just that . . . well . . . your dad and I are experiencing a rough spot in our marriage right now, I'm afraid. I think it's best that we spend some time apart. I'll be living up in the mountains for a little while. I've been offered a job—can you believe it?"

She bit her lower lip as she waited for his reply. It was a long, torturous moment in coming. "I knew something was wrong," he finally said.

Her eyes flew open, her gaze seeking Celeste's as she asked, "You did?"

"Yeah. It was obvious at Christmas." While she tried to process that piece of news, he added, "Are you okay, Mom? Do you want me to come to Colorado?"

This was her baby, her firstborn. He was a fine young man of good character with a huge, loving heart. A sensitive heart. It didn't escape her notice that he avoided asking why she'd taken such drastic action. Stephen would expect the answer to be painful for them both, so he wouldn't ask it. Instead, he asked in his own way if she needed him.

It would be so easy to lean on him now, but she wouldn't do it. It wouldn't be fair. It was important for the whole family that she stand on her own two feet through this mess.

"I appreciate the offer, but the last thing I want is for this situation to interrupt your schoolwork. I'm going to be okay, honey, although I'll be honest and tell you that right now I'm a little shaky. I'm excited about the job, though."

She spent a few moments telling him about the restaurant, and then he responded, "Well, I think you'll be excellent at the job. You are a fantastic cook, and you certainly know how to manage a kitchen. You oversaw all those dinners for Dad's firm and catered some of them yourself. This is perfect for you, Mom. So you're going to get the place up and running, and once that is done, you'll come home?"

Now it was Ali's turn to pause at length. "I don't know, Stephen. I just don't know."

"But it's possible?"

She heard the unspoken question. *The problem isn't so bad that it can't be fixed?* "It's certainly not impossible. I don't know what else to say to you, Stephen, other than I love you and your father loves you and we'll get through this. All of us."

After saying good-bye, Ali let out a heavy sigh. "That went better than I thought."

"Good," Celeste said. "Maybe that's a sign."

Or maybe not, Ali thought a few minutes later when she gave the same rough-spot-in-their-marriage-and-moving-to-the-mountains explanation to her son Chase. His first reaction was "You left Dad and got a job? Right. And I'm making an A in physics, too."

She didn't respond to that, and after a full ten seconds, he said, "Mom? You're kidding, right?"

"No, Chase, I'm not."

After another pause, he demanded, "What happened? What did he do? Did he cheat on you? Did he—"

"Chase! Stop!" Ali grimaced and rubbed her forehead as she attempted to reach past her middle child's anger. He might look like Mac, but he certainly didn't have his father's temperament. Chase had always been the hothead of the bunch, the most independent, the most reckless and daring. He didn't wear his heart on his sleeve, but she never doubted the loyalty and love in its every hard, strong beat. "Your father is not cheating on me."

He paused a beat, then said, "Ah, jeez. You're having an affair? Mom, how could you? Dad's a great guy. What is this, a middle-aged crazy sort of thing?"

"Michael Chase Timberlake! Would you please listen rather than make snap judgments? I realize that, being twenty-one years old, you think the entire world revolves around sex, and I ordinarily would never speak of such personal matters, but it's not the problem in your parents' marriage." *It's a symptom of the problem.*

"Then what *is* the problem, Mom? Why would you go and leave Dad if he's not cheating on you? He's not abusive. I know that. Is it his job? Are the hours too much?"

Again Ali closed her eyes. The kid had always been persistent, too. One of her nicknames for her middle child was "Terrier." She should have anticipated this reaction from him. "Chase, it would be nice if problems in life were simply black and white, but unfortunately, that's not the way it is. Relationships are complicated, and complications in relationships are even more complicated. If they weren't, I wouldn't be on my way to the mountains today."

When he finally responded, his voice was tight with pain. "This sucks, Mom."

"I know, baby. I'm sorry."

He let out a sigh, then asked, "Do you have a place to stay?"

"I'll be at Angel's Rest."

"Well, that's good. You have friends there to lean on. You and Mrs. Reese can take turns crying on each other's shoulder because your little girls are off at college."

Ali smiled sadly. "Yes, I guess we can do that."

"Okay, then. Well, I've got to go. I need to study. Talk to you later."

The sound of the dial tone echoed in her ears. "I love him dearly, but that child can make me crazier than just about anyone else on the planet."

"You've told me previously that Chase has his father's drive," Celeste said. "He's liable to set the world on fire. You just wait and see."

"As long as he doesn't do it literally. I'll never forget a certain fireworks incident when he was seven." Recalling the wild child he'd been made her shake her head in bittersweet memory. Parenting Chase had been a challenge from the day he was born. Actually, he'd been a trial since before he was born, considering that she'd gone into premature labor with him and had spent six weeks confined to bed. Those years with three children under the age of five had been enormously difficult. But, oh, how she missed those days! Life had been full and exciting and brimming with laughter and love. "Time goes so fast, Celeste. How did I get from my twenties to my forties?"

"Oh, honey, just wait. One hundred is the hard one." When Ali shot her a disbelieving look, she chuckled and added, "So I'm told."

Ali's mouth quirked in a faint smile, then her thoughts returned to the matter at hand. "Think I could wait to call Cait?"

"Only if you want her to hear the news from her brothers."

Ali dialed her daughter's number and heard it ring one time, then two, before it switched over to voice mail. Coward that she was, she couldn't help but feel a measure of relief. Yet no sooner had she left a message for her daughter to call her grandfather's house than the phone rang again.

"Mom? Sorry, I was on the other line. How is this for karma? I was talking to Daddy when Stephen called, then Chase called, and finally you called. Is that weird or what? We have our own Timberlake family psychic network. So, what's up? Did you get my message?"

"What message?"

"Messages, actually. I left one at home and I've called your cell a couple of times."

"Is there a problem?"

"No. Just wanted to chat, catch you up on my love life. I met a hottie at the library and he's asked me to the basketball game Thursday night. His name is Patrick Talley and he's from New York. When I couldn't get you, I called Daddy."

"A new guy. That's exciting." Ali licked her lips. "What did you and your dad talk about?"

"Nothing important."

Caitlin launched into a story about bicycles in trees and a tiff she'd had with her roommate. Ali could hardly listen. So the boys had called their sister. She'd bet they were calling their father now, too. The last thing Ali needed was for Chase to call again and Caitlin to click over before Ali could stop her.

"Cait," Ali interrupted. "Listen to me. I have some hard news. Dad and I have . . ." She snapped her mouth shut against the word *separated*. *Think, Alison. Choose your words carefully.*

Warily, Caitlin responded, "What? Dad and you have what?"

Ali couldn't use the same words she'd used to tell Stephen and Chase. She and Caitlin had a different relationship. A female relationship. It required a different kind of communication, and in many respects it made this particular conversation that much more difficult.

"Mom?"

"Baby, this is so hard. Dad and I really aren't getting along these days, and it's very confusing to us both, I think. He hasn't done anything awful and neither have I, but it hurts more to be together than to be apart right now. So, I am going to move up into the mountains for a little while. By myself." She told her about the job and how much she liked Celeste and her other friends in Eternity Springs. "I feel peaceful there, Cait. I feel okay when I'm there."

After that, she paused and waited for Caitlin's reaction. Ali knew her daughter. Caitlin did enjoy drama, and under other circumstances Ali would expect her to launch into tears and wailing and demands. But with something so serious, so central to the fabric of her life, Caitlin's thoughts and emotions would go deeper than drama. Ali's baby girl would be afraid.

The silence of Caitlin's response proved that Ali's instincts had been spot-on. So she drew upon more than two decades of maternal experience and said, "It will be okay, Caitlin. I promise you that. We will still be a family, no matter what. We will love you and you will love us—that won't change."

"But . . . you and Dad. You don't love each other anymore?"

"No, I do still love Dad." Saying it, Ali knew it was true. "I love him very much. And sweetheart, I think that's probably why I had to do this."

"That makes no sense."

As she spoke with her daughter the vague thoughts and feelings that had circled in her mind all day began to congeal. "I know what love is. I know what loving and being loved is. It's wonderful, Caitlin. It fills me up and sets me free and brings me indescribable joy. I had that with your dad. We had it together. But somewhere along the way, we lost it."

"So you're what? Just giving up? Throwing it all away?"

"I hope not. I hope we will discover a way to find it again. I hope we will *want* to find it again. But that's something your dad and I need to figure out on our own. For some time now, Dad and I have been settling for less. I don't want to settle."

"But how can you possibly fix something if you're living apart?"

"I'm not saying I have all the answers, Caitlin, because I don't. But this is what my heart is telling me to do. I don't know what I'll find in Eternity Springs. I just know I need to go there."

Seated across from her at the kitchen table, Celeste reached across and squeezed Ali's arm in support. Ali smiled tremulously and continued, "I recognize that this is difficult for you and your brothers, and I feel terrible about that. But sweetie, like you are always quick to tell me, you're an adult now. Your dad and I have raised three wonderful children who are smart and strong and make me so very, very proud. I know you want your parents to be together. I know you want nothing to change. But honey, things do change. Life happens. Children grow up and leave home. And sometimes families change."

"This really stinks, Mom."

"Yes, I know, baby. I'm sorry."

After a long moment, Caitlin asked, "I wish I'd gone with you on one of your visits to Eternity Springs when you asked. Now it feels to me like you have a whole other life I don't know anything about."

That was how Ali felt about Caitlin's life at college. "You can come visit me over Easter break."

"Maybe. I just have a long weekend."

"Whatever works for you is fine with me. I just want you to know that you're welcome."

"Unlike Daddy?"

Ali let that little dig pass without comment. "What is meant to happen will happen, and it will be okay, Cait. Have faith in that. I do. We may have a few bumps in the road, but in the end we'll be okay."

"In Eternity Springs, Colorado?"

"Absolutely. People all over the country are coming to Angel's Rest to heal. Maybe the magic will work for me."

Mac downshifted and gunned the engine, and the sweet little Porsche 911 took the mountain curve like a dream. One side of his mouth lifted in a crooked grin. As spontaneous gestures went, this one rocked.

When he'd left the house this morning in his sedate Lexus LX10, he'd had no particular destination in mind other than to head east. He often took a similar drive when problems weighed upon him. Ordinarily he'd head away from Denver and the crowds, working through the issues that plagued him on long stretches of straight, flat roads. He would drive in silence for an hour or two or however long he needed to clear his mind, then he'd tune his radio to a classical music station, turn around, and head back to town.

Today he'd taken an unexpected path. Something had happened as he'd stopped for a traffic light in front of the Porsche dealership. His wife's challenge had echoed in his memory one too many times, and his prudence and judiciousness flew right out the window. When the light changed, instead of going straight he'd turned into the lot, and half an hour later he'd purchased the car right off the showroom floor.

"Just effin' watch me," he murmured as he navigated a switchback at nine thousand feet. Rather than head east, he'd gone west into the mountains and tested his new ride on two-lane roads. Instead of riding in silence in order to think, he'd played Rod Stewart on the stereo. Loud.

He'd tried not to think at all.

When he finally turned back toward Denver, he'd made no decisions, discovered no answers, but while driving in the mountains he had found a sense of calm. He could almost see why Ali chose to escape to Eternity Springs. Almost.

As he returned to their home, he wondered if he'd find her car parked in the garage, her suitcase back in her closet, her homemade red sauce simmering on the stove. It would be her peace offering to him. His wife habitually tried to solve problems with food. It was a wonder that his family members didn't have serious weight issues.

She had no way of knowing that each time she plied him with a delicious meal after one of their fights, she reinforced his doubts about their marriage. His unhappiness continued to grow with every meal until finally her spaghetti made him nauseous. Never mind the fact that the taste of it was right out of the Italian neighborhoods of heaven.

He idled at the intersection for a moment, bracing himself before he turned onto his street. Glancing toward his house, he spied a vehicle in his driveway, though it wasn't Ali's car. His son Chase's truck was parked in the circular drive where Ali's BMW had sat earlier that day. Mac muttered a curse beneath his breath.

The young man sat on the front porch steps bouncing a tennis ball on the strings of a racket. It was typical Chase. He spent every free minute in a competition of one sort or another, made with whatever objects were at hand. How many times could he bounce the tennis ball without missing? How many pebbles could he toss into that target drawn in the dirt? The boy had been born to compete, and he liked nothing more than to win.

Unfortunately, his competitive drive came with a quick temper. At twenty-one he still allowed it to rule him too often. Mac sighed, sensing that he was about to see an example of that temper.

He pulled the Porsche into his drive and parked behind Chase's truck. The young man slowly rose, his eyes rounding as he saw his father climb out of the sports car.

"Dad, why are you driving a Porsche?"

"Hello, son."

"Is it yours?" Chase stepped away from the porch and walked toward Mac, his gaze shifting from Mac to the car, then back to Mac again. "Did you buy it?"

Calmly Mac answered, "Yes, as a matter of fact, I did."

Temper flashed in Chase's eyes, and at his side his fists clenched. "Mom covered for you, didn't she? You *are* cheating on her! You've betrayed my mother. So who is she, Dad? Some hot young defense lawyer looking for a bit of judicial action?"

Mac walked toward the front door. "Let's spare the neighbors and go inside to do this, Chase."

"Fine by me. I tried to go inside already, but my key

didn't work. I've been waiting on the porch for two hours. You must have called a locksmith the minute Mom left. Guess it'd be embarrassing to have your wife and children walk in on you and the new honey."

"Stop it!" Mac shoved the key into the lock and gave his wrist a hard twist. After the morning he'd had, he wasn't in the mood for his son's lip. Opening the door, he stepped inside and waited for Chase to follow.

Then he slammed the door after the boy. Hard. As Chase's eyes widened in surprise at his father's show of temper, Mac snapped, "I know you're upset, but you need to watch your tone. Your mother lost her keys last week at the mall. We had the locks changed then. There's a key for you in the kitchen."

He led the way to his office. If Ali were having this conversation, she'd do it in the kitchen, in her territory. She'd pour her son something to drink, put a plate of cookies in the middle of the table. Then she would sit and stare down into her coffee cup as she told Chase how horrible her life was, lifting a teary, martyred gaze from time to time.

Mac went straight to the liquor cabinet, poured himself a scotch, and waved a hand toward the bar fridge, kept stocked with bottled water and juice.

Chase obviously hadn't come to Denver to share a drink with dear old Dad, and he apparently hadn't listened to his father's warning a minute ago, either, because he braced his hands on his hips and demanded, "What's the deal, Dad? Why did you step out on Mom?"

The temper vanquished by Mac's long drive came roaring back. He banged his tumbler down on his desk, glared at his son, and demanded, "Did she tell you I cheated on her?"

"No. Actually, she denied it. I guess covering up for you is a habit."

"Covering up for me? When has your mother ever covered up anything for me?"

"Well, she left you, didn't she? Out of the blue? She had to have been covering up something."

Mac just shook his head. "If you have any desire to know the real truth, sit down and be quiet and I'll tell it to you. But if you already think you know everything, then get your new house key from the kitchen and lock the door on your way out. It's been a long day. I'd like to see it end relatively soon."

Turmoil rolled across Chase's expression, and Mac had a flash of memory of when the family dog, Draper, had slipped the leash and run out in front of a car. Chase had worn the same expression as he waited for the vet to tell them if his pet could be saved. Despite Chase's outward stoicism, Mac knew his son well enough to be aware that inside, the boy— now the man—was filled with dread. He wanted his daddy to reassure him that all would be well.

That Mac simply couldn't do.

He took a bracing sip of his drink, then said, "I don't quite know what to say to you. I haven't cheated on your mother. I haven't been violent toward her or done any other villainous thing you might consider. Has your mother told you otherwise?"

"She didn't tell me anything other than the fact that she'd moved out," Chase responded, his voice subdued. "What is going on here, Dad? I don't understand."

"To be perfectly honest, I don't understand, either. All I know is that your mother hasn't been happy for a long time now."

"Is *she* having an affair?"

Mac started to respond no, then hesitated. Was that what this was all about? Another man?

He'd never considered that particular possibility, but maybe that was naive of him. She certainly had the opportunity to cheat. He had never worried that she would do it. Still, he couldn't believe it. Ali was lots of things, but sneaky wasn't one of them. "No, I don't believe so."

"Then why did she leave us?"

"She didn't leave you, Chase," he replied, his lips twisting in a sad smile. "She left *me*."

"She left our family. Why? What did you do?"

The question stirred his simmering anger. What had he done other than love her and support her and take care of her since the day they got married? "Honestly, I don't know. That's something you'll have to ask your mother."

"This is crazy." Chase marched around the room, raking his fingers through his hair. "I know she really likes Eternity Springs. I do, too. But why would she want to leave Denver? This is where her home is. It's where her life is. And Stephen told me that she's going to run the Bristlecone. Why in the world would she want a job? She doesn't need money, does she? She hasn't developed a gambling habit or something weird like that, has she?"

Again Mac hesitated before denying it. Ali could be involved in something that might surprise him. He didn't know much about her life these days. "I have no evidence that your mother has taken up any unhealthy habits. Look, Chase, you're asking the same questions I'm asking, and I haven't found any answers. Not yet. It would be easier to fix the problem if I knew what caused it, but I don't. I don't think even your mother knows for sure."

Chase walked to the window and gazed out into the yard. Quietly he asked, "Do you want to fix it, Dad?"

"Of course I do." *Don't I?*

Mac's mouth settled in a grim line. Was that yet another question for which he had no answer? In all honesty, he hadn't been any happier than Ali of late. He loved his wife, but he was tired of being lonely. He was tired of being with her but being apart. "That said, I'm not sure that her idea of fixing it will coincide with mine. Or that ours will coincide with yours or your siblings'."

Chase twisted his head and scowled at him. "What are you saying, Dad? You want to fix it by getting divorced?"

Leave it to Mr. Impatient to use that particular word first, Mac thought with a wince. He wanted to lie and deny the possibility, but he always tried to be honest with his children. "I don't know, son. That's certainly one possibility."

After a long moment, the young man declared, "This sucks. Totally."

Mac moved to stand beside his son at the window. "For what it's worth, I'm sorry, Chase."

They stood for a time in awkward silence. Finally Chase shrugged and said, "That car is awesome. Is it a Cabriolet?"

Mac grabbed at the change of subject like a lifeline. "Yes. A 4S."

"Sweet. How many horses?"

"Three hundred eighty-five."

"Whoa. What's the zero-to-sixty?"

"Four-point-seven seconds."

"Dude. That's totally sweet. Say, I've got a date tonight. You gonna let me borrow it?"

"Absolutely not."

"Didn't think so, but it was worth a try."

"Always worth a try." Mac sipped his drink, then casually asked, "You want to drive it?"

Chase's head whipped around, and for the first time during the visit, a smile touched his face. "You mean it?"

"I'll let you take it around the block."

"Score."

"Too bad you have a date or we could go for a spin, stop and get some dinner before you head back to Boulder."

"I don't have a date. That was just a ploy to get my hands on your Porsche."

"I figured as much," Mac replied, his lips sliding into a half smile. He tossed the keys to his son and said, "Give me ten minutes here. I have a call I need to make. You can check out the engine—just don't drive off."

"Excellent!"

Moments later, after deciding to let Chase do the driving this evening, he poured himself another drink, sat in his desk chair, and dialed his wife's cell phone. She answered on the third ring, a cautious "Hello?"

He pictured her sad blue eyes. "Are you in a place where you can talk a minute?"

"I'm in the car. Let me pull off. Hold on a sec." He could tell from the sounds that she'd dropped the phone into the console. It reminded him that he'd been planning to buy her a new car, one that came equipped with hands-free calling. She spent too much time on the phone while she was driving for it to be safe. While he brooded about that, she came back on the line. "All right."

Mac's hand tightened around the receiver, but he kept his voice modulated as he said, "Chase came home from school."

"He did?"

"He's . . . concerned. We're going out to dinner, and I thought you might like to join us."

Following a long pause, she spoke in a tight voice. "Mac, I'm almost to Eternity Springs."

He exhaled a breath he'd been unaware of holding. *She's really going through with this.*

"I see. Okay, then." He shoved his fingers through his hair. "I'm at a bit of a loss here, Ali. What do you want from me during this separation? Are there rules? Do you want me to call? Are we to see each other?" Then, because he was feeling raw, he added, "Are we to see others?"

She responded with a laugh that had tears in it. "Are you asking my permission to date other women, Mackenzie?"

Frustration rolled through him. "I'm confused, Alison. Your children are confused. How are we supposed to fix our marriage if you're living half a state away?"

"How can we fix it if we don't know what's wrong?" she fired back, a bite in her tone. "Unless you've had a great revelation in the past nine hours. For instance, have you figured out why you can't find your way to our bed at night?"

Maybe because it's the coldest place on earth. Mac set down his drink, closed his eyes, and rubbed his forehead. "This isn't helping anything."

He sensed, rather than heard, her sigh. "The governor's dinner is in a few weeks. Perhaps it would be best if we didn't speak again until then. I'm angry, Mac. I need some time to cool off."

"Well, fine. That works for me. I just wanted to know the plan." He hung up without saying goodbye and sat staring at the phone, feeling as lost and alone as he had the day he walked into the first of his foster homes.

Mac didn't hear his son enter the room and approach him. It wasn't until Chase's hand gripped his shoulder that Mac's thoughts returned to the present.

"C'mon, Dad," his son softly said. "Let's go for that drive. You might want to get a sweater, though. That is too sweet a car not to break it in as a convertible. We're going topless."

Topless. The memory of an anniversary trip to St.

Barts and a beautiful but bashful Ali flashed through his mind, and he grimaced. Not since that day in an Oklahoma courtroom had he felt this powerless. To borrow his son's vernacular, this sucked.

Totally.

FOUR

Exhausted, heartsick, and dehydrated from shedding an ocean of tears, Ali went straight to bed upon her arrival at the Angel's Rest carriage house in Eternity Springs. For the next week she rarely left it.

As a rule, she wasn't one to lie around feeling sorry for herself, but this time she had no energy for anything more. She slept, then slept some more. When she woke up, she'd stumble to the bathroom, then return to bed and fall back to sleep. Sometimes she'd managed to make her way downstairs to the kitchen, where she scrounged for coffee and choked down a couple of handfuls of dry cereal from the box, but she ate because she felt she should eat rather than to sate an appetite. She didn't have an appetite. All she wanted to do was sleep, although the nearly constant ringing of her phone made that difficult.

Each of her children called—again and again and again. She didn't pick up the phone, but she did, finally, send them each a text message reassuring them of her health and asking them to lay off the phone for a bit. Her father called, and since she didn't have the gumption to talk to him, either, she waited until a time when she knew he wouldn't be home to phone and leave a message on his machine.

Mac did not call.

Finally around noon, a week to the day following her arrival in Eternity Springs, she awoke with enough energy to thumb the button on the television remote and caught part of a local newscast out of Denver. She paid more attention to the anchorwoman's outfit—was showing that much cleavage on a morning show really necessary?—than the news until the buxom blonde mentioned the high-profile athlete arrested for importing drugs the previous year. The Sandberg trial was set to begin on Monday, presided over by the Honorable Mackenzie S. Timberlake.

Ali sat up in bed and glared at the television set. So it was about to start. Another high-profile trial right on the heels of the first. She folded her arms as her pulse spiked for the first time in days. She'd known he'd been assigned another flashy case because he'd groused about it. He'd never mentioned it was about to start. Since the Sandberg trial would consume his life for the next five or six months, you'd think he would have said something, but no. She had to hear it from the news.

Commence round two. After living through the Desai case, Ali knew that high-profile cases added an extra burden to an already difficult job. Seating a jury would be a chore, witness lists would be a mile long, and the media would do their best to turn the trial into a circus. Mac would spend a lot of time dotting *i*'s and crossing *t*'s. He had excellent clerks, but Ali knew her husband. In this case, he'd be detailed in his oversight and his ordinarily long hours would stretch into marathon days.

With the Sandberg trial looming, he most assuredly wasn't lying around their bedroom today feeling sorry for himself because his marriage had imploded.

"So why am I?" she murmured.

The more she thought about it, the more annoyed she became. What in the world was she doing? She hadn't come to Eternity Springs to fall apart and feel sorry for herself. She'd come here to work. To help make the Bristlecone something special again. She should get started today. Celeste had given her the keys. She would begin by making a complete inventory of the Bristlecone's kitchen.

Actually, she should start with a shower. She really needed to start with a shower. And a toothbrush.

Twenty minutes later, clean and dressed and feeling marginally human once again, she exited the bedroom. For the first time since her arrival, she took a good look at her surroundings. On her other visits, she'd rented a room up at the main house. She liked the idea of having more space during an extended stay. The remodeled Victorian carriage house truly was a darling little place, with two bedrooms and a bath upstairs plus a kitchen, a living room, and a half bath on the ground floor. The furnished rooms were tiny but welcoming. "You will be happy here," she told herself, trying hard to believe it.

She grabbed a banana and an apple from the bag of groceries she'd left on the counter upon her arrival, then stepped outside. The day was still and quiet but for the bubble and rush of the waters of Angel Creek a stone's throw away. Cool, pine-scented air swirled around her as she stepped off the porch and down into the yard. She lifted her face toward the sunshine, and in that moment she experienced a glimpse of the peace that she had come searching for in this valley. Surprising herself, Ali smiled.

A rumble of thunder caused her to look around. Behind her, a thundercloud was building up over Murphy Mountain. Maybe she should grab her umbrella out of her car before walking over to the Bristlecone.

She'd covered half the distance to the garage when suddenly a male voice called from behind her. "Stop. Don't go any farther."

Ali gasped a breath as she froze in midstep. Before she could manage a word, the man continued. "Sheriff's office, ma'am. A bear went into the garage a few minutes ago. We need to give her some time to find her way out."

"Oh." Surprise widened Ali's eyes. "Okay. I'll just go back inside the carriage house."

"That'll be good. I'll let you know when the coast is clear."

Ali retreated to the carriage house and stood watching the garage while she ate first her banana and then her apple. She'd seen deer in the middle of town on prior trips and heard stories of a mountain lion who had parked herself in the middle of Aspen Street one time, but she hadn't given much thought to bears. If she was going to be living here, maybe she should give the bear-sighting flyer available in the tourist office a glance.

Almost ten minutes after the sheriff stopped her, she saw a large black bear wander out of the garage, then disappear up the hill behind Angel's Rest. A moment later, a knock sounded on her door. She answered with a smile. "My hero. You saved me."

He grinned and extended his hand. "Zach Turner."

"Ali Timberlake."

They both said simultaneously, "You're Sarah Reese's friend."

Sarah was a single mom with a daughter Caitlin's age. She owned the local grocery store and was a caretaker for her mother, an Alzheimer's patient. Ali knew she had dated Zach Turner some, before they decided they worked better as friends.

He was younger than she, probably mid-to-late thirties. He wore a khaki uniform shirt, complete with badge, tucked into worn jeans with a handgun holstered at his hip. He had thick brown hair, a handsome, angular face, and drop-dead gorgeous blue eyes. He was definitely a sexy man. *Sarah, what's wrong with you?*

"I saw you at Sage's wedding," Zach observed. "I got called away before the reception, so I missed the chance to actually meet you. I'm glad to have the chance to do so now."

"I'm happy to meet you, too, Zach. This is my first trip back since the wedding. I'm here to help Celeste get the Bristlecone Café reopened."

"Oh, yeah? That's great news. I ate there twice a week before it closed. The town needs another full-service restaurant."

"Well, our plan is to get it up and running ASAP. Celeste is convinced we'll find a cook and be able to reopen and get all the kinks worked out before the tourist season hits in force. I'm reserving judgment on that until after I've seen what I have to work with. In fact, I was on my way to grab my umbrella out of my car and walk over there when you and your furry friend stopped me."

Zach glanced up toward the sky, where the dark clouds continued to build and thunder continued to rumble. "Looks like you'll probably need that umbrella. I'll walk with you. You can tease me with more details about the new Bristlecone. Are you changing the menu?"

Ali offered up what few details she knew as she retrieved her umbrella, then headed for the Bristlecone, which was right across Angel Creek on Cottonwood. The restaurant faced the creek and offered a lovely view of a grassy slope leading down to clear, bubbling Angel Creek and, across it, the charming structures of Angel's Rest nestled between the water and forested mountain behind.

During new construction at the healing center, Celeste had ordered a footbridge to be built that offered convenient access to local businesses for healing center guests. As they neared the footbridge, Ali spied Celeste approaching from the direction of the mansion. Seeing them, the older woman waved and called, "Good morning. Isn't it a lovely day?"

Zach Turner frowned. "It's about to storm, Celeste."

"I know." The older woman beamed. "I just love thunderstorms in Eternity Springs. The echoes of thunder reverberating off the mountains are God's exclamation points."

Ali smiled at the thought, then as a particularly

loud clap of thunder sounded said, "He's exclaiming a lot today. I hope you brought your umbrella."

As Celeste pulled a compact umbrella from her bag, the hair on the back of Ali's neck rose and a forked bolt of lightning flashed out of a dark cloud above them. Thunder cracked. She smelled ozone. Instinct had her diving for cover, dragging Celeste along with her.

"It hit the Bristlecone," Sheriff Turner said, grabbing the radio on his hip. He started running for the footbridge, shouting into the handset, "Fire! Fire at the Bristlecone."

"Oh dear." Celeste sighed. "I do seem to have a bit of bad luck where fires are concerned, don't I? You do know that Cavanaugh House caught fire the first year I moved here, don't you? Luckily, our wonderful volunteer fire department was able to save it and limit the damage." She clucked her tongue, then added, "I hope I have as much luck this time."

An hour later, Celeste declared herself one lucky woman. Ali wasn't certain she'd have gone that far. The Bristlecone Café had been saved, but damage was extensive. Gabe Callahan estimated that repairs would take months.

Ali's job had just gotten a whole lot bigger.

The summons came two weeks after Ali had left him. Mac had finished his morning swim, showered and dressed, and sat down to breakfast when his phone vibrated to announce the arrival of a text message. There were only a handful of people in this world to whose tune he jumped, but Charles Cavanaugh was one of them. The man had been his employer, his mentor, and his confidant for more than twenty years. Mac owed him more than he ever could repay. Yet when he read the message asking him to present himself at Charles's home posthaste, Mac seriously considered ignoring it. Charles might be his mentor, but he was first and foremost Ali's father.

This wasn't going to be pretty.

Mac decided to take his old pickup instead of the Porsche for this particular meeting. No sense inviting trouble.

He arrived at the Cavanaugh home in Denver to find his ordinarily dapper father-in-law dressed in dirty jeans and a chambray shirt, indulging in another hobby of his—backyard vegetable gardening. Mac shoved his hands into his pockets, took a bracing breath, and approached. "Lettuce is looking good."

Without looking up from the row he was weeding, Charles said, "Third row needs weeding. Hit your knees, son."

Okay, so that's the way this will be.

Respect took Mac down onto his knees, and he went to work on the weeds. The men didn't exchange a word during the next few minutes. As he tugged thin blades of grass and dandelions from the rich brown soil, Mac made mental bets with himself as to how Charles would begin this discussion. Would he bring up the firm first? The Sandberg case? Maybe ask about the kids? Or would he go straight for the jugular, asking what horrible thing Mac had done to Ali?

When Charles finally got around to talking, his

choice of subject took Mac by surprise. "Alison's mother believed in family dinners. She said that having supper together as a family each night was the best thing we could do to build bonds and foster positive relationships between us all."

Mac had no clue as to how he was expected to respond, so he didn't.

"I tried to continue that practice for both Alison and myself after we lost her mother, but sometimes I think she developed a stronger relationship with our cook than she did with me."

"Alison feels close to you," Mac protested.

"Does she?" Charles rolled back on his heels, rested his hands on his thighs, and stared directly at Mac. "Then why is she dodging my phone calls, and why do I have to learn that she is divorcing you from a secretary at the firm?"

Divorce? Mac's gut clenched. "What?"

"I guess I should be glad that I learned from Serena rather than cable news," Charles continued. "I hear your name a lot these days, since the Sandberg case is on every channel."

"You heard wrong, Charles. No one has said anything about divorce."

"Alison has left three messages on my machine in the past two weeks. She talked about a lot of things, but she never mentioned the fact that she's left Denver and you. Do I have that fact wrong?"

Mac couldn't believe this. He'd thought for sure that Alison would have called her father. In fact, he'd been counting on it. He'd thought Charles might talk some sense into the woman.

"Mackenzie?"

"We're just going through a rough spot." Mac stood and brushed the dirt from the knees of his jeans with a little more force than was necessary to get the job done. Divorce. That was nothing but law office gossip. Somebody had heard about Ali's new project and . . . Mac frowned. How had anyone at the firm learned about Ali's new project? He hadn't told a soul.

"Who started the rumor at the firm? Has someone been talking to Ali?"

His father-in-law shrugged. "I believe she contacted Bob Renwick's sister. She is—"

"Ali's favorite interior designer," Mac concluded with a sigh. He'd hoped Ali would come to her senses and come home before the news got out. So much for hope.

"Who is her lawyer?" Charles asked.

The question caught Mac off guard. "Bob's sister's?"

"Alison's."

Mac's chin came up. "I'm her lawyer." When Charles chastised him with a look, he added, "She doesn't need a lawyer. Look, any talk about divorce, even legal separation, is premature."

"I suspected that would be your response. Just so you know, I've retained Walt Prentice on Alison's behalf."

Mac sucked in a quick breath. Prentice was the best divorce attorney in Denver. If Mac were in the market, Prentice was the man he'd choose. The fact that Charles had hired the lawyer for Ali didn't make him angry. It was what he'd expect—if Ali needed a divorce lawyer, which she didn't. Still, he was surprised at his own reaction to the news. He was . . . hurt.

His relationship with Charles Cavanaugh was complicated. He figured if he ever landed on a psychiatrist's couch, the doctor would rack up big bucks on that subject alone. Since the day Ali introduced them, Mac had worked to earn Charles's approval. Then, professional interests had driven him. He'd wanted access to Charles's connections in order to land a prime clerkship. Later, he'd wanted a position in the firm and eventually a partnership.

Just when his desire to please became personal, he couldn't say, but somewhere along the way he'd developed a desire to make Charles proud. Was it because Mac had never had a father of his own in his life? Or was it due to the fact that he admired Charles more than just about any man he'd ever met? Whatever the reason, Mac had waited to hear the words *I'm proud of you* from Charles for more than twenty years.

It had finally happened at the reception following his swearing-in ceremony. Almost, anyway. While he'd been accepting the congratulations of family and friends, he'd overheard Charles tell the district attorney, *Yes, we're proud of him.*

So proud that he'd hired a divorce attorney based on office gossip.

"Fine. You do what you feel like you need to do."

"I will." Charles Cavanaugh used the hoe lying nearby for balance as he climbed to his feet. "You know, Mac, when I gave you an opportunity at the firm, my daughter asked me to refrain from inserting myself into your private life, and up until now, I have done so."

Mac couldn't hold back a snort at that. Charles Cavanaugh had never resisted the opportunity to butt into Mac and Ali's personal life. Oh, he did it subtly, Mac would give him that, but the fact remained that the man had managed to make his opinion known on subjects as wide-ranging as where Mac and Alison should buy a house, attend church, and shop for groceries to what video games the boys were allowed to play when they were young and what brand sneakers Caitlin should wear while running.

"However," Charles continued, "in light of this recent development, I felt compelled to act. That's why I also hired a private investigator to look into your affairs."

That bit of news hit Mac like a punch to his gut. An investigator? Holy hell. How far back would the guy go?

Bristling with anger and a measure of fear, Mac snapped, "For God's sake, Charles. Why didn't you just call and ask me? I don't have affairs. I'm not cheating on her. I never have. You should know me better than to think that."

"I didn't know what to think, and I've been a lawyer too long to take anybody's word about anything. I wanted to know if you were running around on my girl or hiding assets, or if you had committed some other nefarious act that might damage my daughter or grandchildren if it became public knowledge."

His blood running hot, Mac folded his arms and glared at the older man. "So, tell me. Just what did your investigator learn about my . . . *affairs*?"

Please, God, don't let him have looked all the way back.

"Apparently you don't have any, not that the investigator could find, anyway." Charles harrumphed. "It was a relief to me, I must say. I hated to think I had misjudged you so completely. I admit I had my doubts about you at first. The fact is, I resented you. You took my Ali away from me."

Mac blinked. This was as frank a talk as any he'd heard from this man, and it took him aback.

"Intellectually, I knew that was the way of it, but emotionally, I didn't handle it well. After we lost her mother, all we had were each other. I depended on her as much as she depended on me. When you came along, she began shifting her allegiance to you, and I didn't like it."

Mac opened his mouth, but he didn't know what to say.

His father-in-law continued, "Oh, I wanted her to marry and have children. I expected that. What I didn't anticipate was that she'd find a man who suited her as well as you did. When the two of you became a couple, you became a unit. A unit in which I had no place. I was jealous of you. And selfish."

This shocked Mac. "Charles, I don't know what to say. I just—"

The older man shook his head. "Let me finish. I seldom put my pride on the chopping block like this, so allow me to get it behind me. When Alison asked me to offer you my professional support, I wanted to refuse, but as you undoubtedly know, I've seldom been able to refuse my daughter anything, so I grudgingly gave you my backing. Right from the start, you proved worthy. You were smart, hardworking. Your peers respected you. You became a damn fine lawyer and an asset to the firm. I knew you'd be an exceptional judge."

Mac's mind was spinning. Just how had they gone from an investigator delving into his bank accounts to a pat on his judicial back? He dropped his arms to his sides, then slipped his hands into his pockets. "Uh, thank you."

Charles drummed his fingers against the garden hoe's wooden handle and continued, "More important, you've been a good husband to Alison and an excellent father to her children. I'll also admit that you've been a fine son-in-law to me. I want to see you and Ali work this thing out. Unless . . ." He paused and cleared his throat. "Has Allison done something unforgivable?"

Yes. She left me. Months ago, she left me. "No, Charles. Like I said a few minutes ago, we're just going through a rough spot."

"Is there anything I can do to help?"

Mac rocked on his heels. This whole exchange was a bit surreal, and it had left him at a loss for words. On one hand, he was overwhelmed at finally hearing praise from Charles Cavanaugh. On the other hand, he was annoyed to hear it now. Why did it have to take Ali leaving him to drag a kind word out of the man's mouth? And while he was glad to have his father-in-law's support, it chapped his butt to know that he'd had him investigated. How was he supposed to respond?

Finally he settled on the truth. "I appreciate the offer, Charles, but right now I don't know how you could help. The kids have asked the same thing. The fact is that Ali and I created the problem, and Ali and I are going to have to fix it."

If they both wanted to fix it, that is. He couldn't forget that somehow the word *divorce* had entered the picture. Could Ali be thinking along those lines already?

"Very well, then. Know that I'm here if you need me."

Mac's mouth twisted wryly. "You and Walt Prentice?"

Charles shrugged. "She'll always be my baby girl."

"Fair enough." Mac drew a deep breath, then exhaled in a rush. In the bare-your-soul spirit of the moment, he decided to lay it out as plainly as possible. "Look, Charles, I don't know what's going to happen with me and Ali. I'm not sure what I want to happen, and I don't know what's best. Neither of us has been happy for a while now. Could be that Ali was right to leave. Maybe we need this time apart."

"How does being apart solve anything?"

I'm not as lonely.

It was true. Somehow it was a whole lot less lonely to be apart from her physically than to be with her in the same room while being emotionally light-years away. "Maybe you can ask your daughter that question next time the two of you talk. In the meantime, I need to be going. I have a pile of work waiting for me on my desk that I want to get through today."

He was halfway across the lawn when Charles called out, "Just a minute, Mackenzie. There's one thing I'd like you to think about. When you get to be my age, you begin to realize just how short life really is. Don't waste the time you have. Don't let this situation drag on too long, but also don't settle for less than what life should be. If you love my daughter, then love her with your whole heart and demand the same from her. But if the two of you can't make each other happy anymore, then be honest with yourselves and let each other go. If Alison doesn't have the guts to make that break, then you need to man up and do it for her. For both your sakes."

Mac replayed the strange conversation in his mind as he drove home. Charles Cavanaugh had certainly surprised him. He'd given Mac more compliments in a twenty-minute conversation than he had in the past twenty years. As he pulled into his driveway and parked the truck, he wished Ali were home so he could tell her about it.

But Ali wasn't at home. No one was home. He was alone. Totally alone.

With that thought, Mac's throat went tight. Dear Lord, he was tired of this. Feeling lonely. Feeling empty. Feeling old and used up.

He shifted into park and switched off the motor. Shutting his eyes, he let his head drop back against the headrest. He thought he just might cry. He hadn't cried since Judge Roscoe Whitcomb sentenced his mother to jail the first time, but here in his very own driveway on a sunny Saturday in springtime, tears were welling up inside him. How pitiful was that?

Screw this.

He sat up straight, twisted the key, and started the engine once more. If he wasn't mistaken, the animal shelter was open until two. "I'm gonna go get me a dog."

FIVE

On a day during Ali's third week in Eternity Springs, she awoke to birdsong and sunshine, a to-do list about a million miles long, and a phone call from her eldest. "Hello, Stephen."

"Hey, Mom. How are you doing?"

"Pretty good, actually," she said, glancing at the bedside clock. "You're up early."

"Yeah, I have a bit of a problem. Do you have a few minutes?"

She thought of all she had waiting for her and stifled a sigh. "I always have a few minutes for you. What's up?"

After ten minutes of advising her son about wardrobe choices for an upcoming round of interviews, she showered, dressed, and grabbed a bagel on her way out the door. Her spirits were light as she traversed the stone path, looking forward to her workday. So far, she loved her job. She was busy from morning until night.

Ali now agreed with Celeste's declaration that the fire could be considered a blessing. Fast action by Zach and the Eternity Springs Volunteer Fire Department had prevented serious structural damage, but cosmetically, the place had been a mess. This had given Celeste an excuse to completely remodel the restaurant, which gave Ali the opportunity to outfit the space with what she believed to be the best. She was having too much fun.

Each morning she met with Celeste at Cavanaugh House to go over the previous day's accomplishments and plan upcoming tasks. They'd spent days on restaurant design and development, and more days after that hashing out a list of staff positions to be filled along with a projected start date for each of them. Ali realized soon into the process that a primary part of her job would be keeping Celeste's feet on the ground when it came to her wishes for the new Bristlecone.

The woman dreamed big. While Ali supported big dreams, she also believed that laying one brick at a time made for a stronger structure. She continually reminded Celeste that Rome hadn't been built in a day; neither had Sedona, Arizona. Eternity Springs needed a restaurant that served the needs of local people like Zach Turner, not just well-heeled visitors from around the globe.

As her path took her near the bank of Angel Creek, she was surprised to hear Celeste call her name. Looking around, she saw her friend and employer standing with a fisherman at the little boulder-sheltered pool that Ali herself had discovered earlier this week when she'd decided to fish after work one evening.

"Good morning, Celeste," Ali called, changing the direction of her steps when Celeste waved her over. It wasn't until she drew closer and the fisherman turned to face her that she realized just who the man was. "Dad?"

He waved. Yes, it was her dad. *Oh, for crying out loud.*

Unhappiness rolled through Ali. She didn't need this. He had no business coming here. She was an adult. An adult with adult children of her own. She shouldn't have to answer to her father about the decisions she made about her marriage!

"Well, well, well," he said. "Imagine running into you here, sweet pea."

"Yeah. Imagine. Dad, what are you doing here?"

"I'm fishing. I've already pulled in two pretty rainbows. Thought maybe you and I could share them for breakfast."

Once the initial flash of annoyance passed, Ali's head started spinning. This was not good. She had made a tactical error in going with the message-on-the-machine avoidance strategy. She should have known her dad wouldn't let her get away with it. "Gee, Dad. That would be nice, but my job—"

"Isn't a problem," Celeste interrupted. "I was on my way to the carriage house to tell you we're taking the morning off when I stopped to visit with this lovely gentleman who, coincidentally, is your father."

Ali wrinkled her nose. "Celeste, there is nothing coincidental about his visit to Eternity Springs."

"Oh, quit grumbling, dear. You should have had this talk weeks ago." She held out her hand to Ali's father and said, "It's been a pleasure to meet you, Charles. Now, I'm off to my rock-climbing class. Enjoy your visit with your daughter, and best of luck with the fishing."

"Thank you, Celeste. I will give your suggestion serious thought. You're an angel."

"You'd better believe it. And isn't this just a heavenly day?" Celeste's happy laughter tinkled like church bells across the morning air as she headed back toward Cavanaugh House.

Ali frowned at her father. "What suggestion?"

"She suggested I sponsor a section of the healing center's garden in your mother's name."

Ali made the connection immediately and warmth filled her, dispelling some of her annoyance. "The Peace roses. I mentioned to her that you've said how much my mother loved Peace roses."

"They were her favorites." He lifted a wistful gaze toward Murphy Mountain. "She loved the mountains, too. I think your mother would be proud that you're involved here."

Ali certainly hadn't anticipated that sort of reaction from her father. Encouraged, she asked, "Did Celeste mention my work at the Bristlecone?"

"She did. It's an ambitious project, what with the fire damage."

Just as Ali began to relax, he added, "Though I'm not sure that you are the right person to make it a reality."

She bristled. "You don't think I can do the job?"

"Oh, I know you can do the job. What I doubt is that you *should* do the job. Not if it means putting the job before your marriage." He reeled in his fishing line, and when a bare hook emerged from the water, he said, "Hand me my tub of night crawlers, would you, hon?"

She did as he asked, then, knowing her father, found a comfy spot to sit. She had avoided this conversation as long as possible. Might as well get it behind her. "This job has not caused trouble in my marriage."

The trouble was already there. In fact, if anything, this job might save her marriage.

He waited to respond until he'd baited his hook and dipped it in Angel Creek, but when he did, he cut right to the heart of the matter. "I'm disappointed in you, Alison."

Go ahead and stab me through the heart, Dad. "Why? Because I took a job doing something worthwhile?"

"Because you've attempted to avoid me during this, the biggest crisis of your life."

The biggest crisis of her life? Ali had always known that she came by her flair for drama honestly. "Dad, there is no crisis. Who have you been talking to? Caitlin? Chase?"

"I've discussed the situation with Caitlin, Chase, Stephen, Mac, Louise, and Walt Prentice."

Oh. She didn't know why she was surprised. She should have anticipated this. Of course he'd talk to the family, to Mac's secretary. "Who is Walt Prentice?"

"The best divorce lawyer in Denver."

Divorce lawyer! Ali's knees went weak. She was glad she was already sitting down. What had Mac said to him? Was that the real reason her father had made this trip? Bracing herself, she asked, "Dad, why did you talk to a divorce lawyer?"

"Insurance on your behalf."

Whew. So Mac hadn't asked him to do it.

"Although the contact with Prentice took place before I received the private investigator's report that cleared Mac of any serious wrongdoing."

"Oh, Dad." An investigator, too. Ali closed her eyes and dropped her head back, lifting her face toward the heavens. *Dear Lord, give me patience.*

"Which brings me here today. Alison, running away seldom solves anything. I believe you have made a mistake."

That was all it took to bring the doubts and the guilt roaring back. Ali respected her father's intellect and opinion. She knew that for her dad, she would always be the most important person on the planet, and that he truly wanted only the best for her. And how could she defend herself to him when she couldn't explain herself to herself?

She didn't know if she'd done the right thing by leaving. She just knew that in that moment, she'd had to leave. "Dad, it's complicated."

"Life is complicated, sweetheart. You are a bright young woman with a loving heart. That's really all you need to find your way back home."

"I'm not ready to go home. However, I do intend to attend the governor's dinner. Maybe by then things will be clearer to both me and Mac."

Apparently that was enough to satisfy her dad, at least for now, because he said no more until he pulled another trout from the water a few minutes later. Wearing a gleeful grin, he asked, "Breakfast?"

She returned his smile and rose to her feet. "Breakfast."

"Excellent. After that, I hope you will offer me a tour of the Cavanaugh manse. I'd like to see that part of the family history."

Once her father had added the trout to his creel, he picked up his fishing gear and they headed toward the carriage house. As they approached the front steps, he paused to enjoy the view. "Beautiful place, Eternity Springs. I like the fact that our ancestors had a hand in building it. Your friend Celeste said this valley has a special healing energy. Do you feel it here, honey?"

Ali considered the question as she, too, looked at the mountains surrounding them. "I think so, Dad. I want to believe it. I know that I'm here looking for answers."

He reached out and pulled her to him for a hug. Then he kissed her forehead and said, "May I offer you one last piece of advice?"

Ali grinned. "Could I stop you?"

"Probably not." He gave a strand of her hair a gentle tug, a gesture he'd made all her life when he wanted her to take special notice. "You have it within your power to simplify your situation. Just be sure that every decision you make, every choice you make, is motivated by love. If you do that, what is meant to be will be."

Ali smiled wistfully. "How did you get to be so smart?"

"Your mother's influence."

Ali touched his face. "I'm sorry I was chicken and called when I knew you'd be playing golf, Daddy."

"That's okay, baby. This time. Don't let it happen again."

"Yes, sir. I won't. Now, let me get you a knife and a pan and you can clean your fish. After breakfast, before I show you the house, we'll take a tour of the grounds. I'll show you the rose garden and we can talk about just how you could honor Mama."

Charles Cavanaugh's eyes glistened briefly and he cleared his throat before responding, "It's perfect."

"Then while we tour Cavanaugh House, you can stop by Celeste's office and write a check."

Mac had named his dog Gus. He had no particular reason for the choice. The brown and white springer spaniel mix just looked like a Gus to him. He weighed about forty pounds—thirty of which must be hair, based on how much he shed. Mac thought about Gus as he waited for the tech guys to fix whatever was screwing up the video the lawyers were trying to play. He wondered what Ali would say when she discovered that he'd gone and adopted a dog. A dog that shed.

Guess he would find out tomorrow when she came home. Over the past three weeks, Mac had kept a list of things he wanted to say to her. Last night he'd organized his thoughts into a clear and thorough summation. His points were well considered and to the point. With a little cooperation from Ali, they could work their way through the list in ninety minutes. He'd even built in time for some theatrics. With any luck, they'd have the situation settled before they left for the governor's dinner, and that night she would be home where she belonged.

"Your honor?"

Mac jerked his attention back to the courtroom.

The tech guys were gone and a sea of lawyers looked his way expectantly. "Yes, proceed."

For the next two hours he dealt with motions and procedural issues while making an effort not to allow his disdain for the ballplayer to show. Josh Sandberg was an idiot. He'd had a beautiful wife, three great kids, and a career that boys all across America dreamed about. No matter how this trial ended, his reputation, his life, would never be the same. He could have avoided every bit of it if he'd just been truthful with his teammates and his family.

Mac left the courthouse at the end of the day amidst the lights, cameras, and microphones of media and paparazzi alike, and when he heard his own name called, he scowled and forged ahead. Judges didn't talk to buzzards, but that didn't stop them from trying. Would they never learn?

He was tired of the nonsense already.

Later as he drove home, he found himself thinking about celebrities and the public's fascination for them. Personally, he just didn't get it. He'd never understood the whole hero worship thing over actors and singers and sports stars. Cops and firemen, yeah. Soldiers, absolutely. He appreciated and admired a great athlete's abilities, but just because a guy had the eye-hand coordination to swing a bat and hit a ball didn't make him a hero. Neither did riding a bull in a rodeo.

In his experience, more often than not, those God-given talents ended up making people jerks.

And jerks attracted some women like moths to flame.

Red neon light flashed through the half-drawn curtains of the run-down hotel room in Oklahoma City. He sat on the corner of the bed and watched as his mother stroked cherry red lipstick across her mouth while she stared into a cracked and dusty mirror. "Just imagine. The championship buckle. How exciting is that? Now, you be a good boy and don't get into any trouble while Mama's gone. You hear?"

He was seven years old. She didn't come back for three days.

Celebrities. Mac exhaled a long, heavy sigh. What he wouldn't give for a good embezzlement trial.

He hit the garage door opener as he pulled into the drive, which served as the signal for Gus to go wild. Barking, running, jumping—the dog did everything but flips when Mac let him inside. Grinning, he sat in one of the kitchen chairs and let Gus plop his paws in his lap as Mac scratched him behind the ears. "I'm glad to see you, too, boy. Just . . . whoa. Keep the tongue to yourself, okay?"

He reached into the treat jar he kept on the table. "Here you go, boy."

Gus gulped it down in seconds, then came back at him with a dog kiss he wasn't quite fast enough to dodge. The weird mood from earlier returned with the rough scrape of Gus's tongue and he was back in that hotel room, this time with bright yellow sunshine beaming through the window.

"But Mama, please? I'll take care of him. I'll feed him and water him and he won't be one bit of trouble." Mac had named him King, and they'd become pals—best friends—in the days his mama had been gone.

"*Don't be ridiculous, Mackenzie. He's a stray. You can't go picking up strays.*"

"*Why not? You do.*"

It wasn't the first time she'd hit him. Nor was it the last. It was, however, the last time he asked for a dog. When they left Oklahoma City the next day, King didn't go with them.

And when Louise brought him his mail today at the office, he'd had a letter from his mother, the first contact he'd had with her since he'd turned eighteen.

Damned celebrities. Damned paparazzi. Damned Court TV.

A month after running to the mountains, Ali returned to Denver. As she pulled into line for valet parking at the Brown Palace Hotel downtown, she told herself she should have dressed in feathers for tonight's events. Heaven knows she was just as much a chicken as what was likely on the menu for this evening's meal. The dress she'd purchased specifically for the awards dinner still hung in her closet at home. Rather than face Mac alone at home for the first time since she'd left, she'd chickened out, stopped at her favorite boutique, and bought a new outfit, from earrings down to shoes, then sent him a text saying she'd meet him downtown.

Nerves had her drumming her fingers against the steering wheel. She wished she'd never committed to attend this dinner. She'd been dreading it like a bikini wax since she told him she'd be here. Just thinking about Mac was hard these days. She sensed that seeing him, speaking with him, would be just short of torture.

The last few weeks in Eternity Springs had been packed full from morning to night. Being so busy had enabled her to think about something, anything, other than the sad state of her marriage, and with each day that passed, her heart grew a little lighter. She knew she wasn't solving anything by ignoring reality, but she thought she'd needed this breather. Her heart was wounded, and she'd needed a little R&R before joining the battle once again. But when the valet opened the door for her and she exited the car, Ali knew she wasn't ready to resume hostilities after all. Had someone not called her name at that very moment, she'd have ducked back into her car and sped away.

Instead, she pasted a smile on her face and turned to greet Trudy Hartsworth, the society editor for the *Denver Post*. "Hello, Trudy."

"My oh my, don't you look divine! That's a new look for you, isn't it? I hope you're seated out of Mac's line of sight during his speech or he's liable to babble like an idiot."

Ali summoned up a confident smile. The boutique had been low on inventory in her size this afternoon, but she hadn't had time to try another shop. The dress she'd chosen was a filmy, flirty sundress with a plunging halter neckline in emerald green. She wore strappy jeweled sandals, dangling earrings, and a matching locket that nestled between her breasts.

Trudy was right. It was a different look for her, one she probably wouldn't have tried had she not been desperate and running out of time. But the minute she put the dress on, she'd loved it. She'd wanted it. The dress made her smile. It made her feel pretty. It made her feel sexy.

And yes, she wanted Mac to take one look at her and babble like an idiot. Swallow his tongue. Drool with desire. Go from soft to stallion in 2.3 seconds.

Or at least, that's what she had thought she wanted. Now that the moment was upon her, second thoughts consumed her. She knew better than to let it show, however, so she smiled brightly and said, "Thank you! I thought it was time to shake things up. I've become just a little too dependent on twin sets."

"Darling, that is no twin set." The writer glanced around, then asked, "I assume you're meeting Mac here? I'm hoping he'll introduce me to Sandberg's defense attorney, Christina Fiore. I'm sure she'll be here tonight. That's not inappropriate now that he is a judge, is it? I certainly don't want to do anything untoward."

Untoward? Trudy Hartsworth had built a career on untoward.

"I'm sure Mac will do whatever is right," Ali said as they walked into the luxurious hotel lobby and made their way toward the Grand Ballroom, where the dinner was being held. Trudy saw someone else she knew and flittered off, disappointing Ali, who had hoped to have the woman at her side when she approached Mac.

"This is stupid," she murmured beneath her breath. He wouldn't make a scene in public. Mac didn't make scenes in private. *Just walk up to him and say hello and get this behind you.*

Ali stepped into the ballroom and glanced toward the reserved tables in the front of the room. She didn't see him, but it was still early and most people had yet to take their seats. Mac was always on time and usually early. His height ordinarily made him easy to spot in a crowd.

She moved through the room making her way slowly toward the front. Halfway there, she again heard her name, and she turned toward the sound. This time, the person doing the speaking was a complete surprise. "Zach?"

He offered her an easy, welcoming smile. "I can't tell you how glad I am to see a friendly face in this crowd."

"I didn't know you were going to be here."

"Yeah. I couldn't get out of it." He grimaced and rubbed the back of his neck. "Things like this are so not my cup of tea."

Ali wouldn't have guessed it. Zach looked perfectly at ease in his charcoal pinstripe suit and an aqua tie that complimented those amazing eyes of his.

She liked Eternity Springs's sheriff. She'd spent time with him on a handful of occasions since their first meeting, and she found him to be intelligent, industrious, and a lot of fun. He was certainly the most laid-back, charming lawman she'd ever met. "Are you here with a date?"

"No. I'm stag tonight." He gestured toward one of the bar stations set along the wall. "Can I get you something to drink? Champagne? A gorgeous woman like you wearing a stunning dress like that . . . You need a glass of champagne in your hands."

She couldn't help smiling. "Thank you, Sheriff

Turner. You're too kind. I don't ordinarily drink at events like these."

"Well, this time is different. I insist." He made a show of looking her over. "The dress demands it, and besides, you can't say no to me. I'm one of tonight's stars."

"You're a speaker?"

"No, I'm an award winner."

"You are?" Ali beamed a smile at him. "I didn't know that! How did I miss this news?"

When he simply shrugged, she persisted. "I know that Alton Davis has seven Twitter aliases. I am aware that Marlene Lange auditioned for *American Idol*. For heaven's sake, I know that Dale Parker is going in for a colonoscopy tomorrow, so how in the world did I miss the fact that Eternity Springs's very own sheriff is being honored as a hero by the governor's office tonight?"

He shrugged. "I didn't tell anyone."

"He didn't tell anyone," Ali repeated, gazing up toward the ceiling and shaking her head in frustration. "So spill it, Turner. Why are you being honored?"

He winced. "They're gonna yammer on about it later. Truly, it's not that interesting. Now, let's get that champagne and I'll tell you something you'll really want to know. A prime bit of Eternity Springs news." He placed his hand at the small of her back and guided her toward the bar.

Despite his relaxed attitude, Ali could tell he wasn't comfortable. She didn't know him well enough to know if he simply didn't like the attention or if it was the incident itself that bothered him, so she let it drop. "Something I want to know, hmm?"

"Yep." He ordered two glasses of champagne from the bartender, handed one of them to her, then saluted her with his glass. "To new friends."

"New friends," she replied with a smile, toasting him back. "And interesting news."

He clinked their glasses, bent his head toward her, and murmured, "I have the scoop—pun intended—on the new ice cream flavors being unveiled next week at the opening of the Creamery."

"How did you manage that?" Ali asked, arching her brows. "Did you confiscate the truck?"

She knew that the opening of the Taste of Texas Creamery for the summer season was a highly anticipated event and that speculation over the season's flavors lasted for months. There was even a betting pool at the Red Fox Pub to guess the flavors.

Ali's friend and the town veterinarian, Nic Callahan, had explained what all the fuss was about. The ice cream shop's owner, Jared Kelley, taught at a small private college in Texas during the school year, but for the past few years he'd spent his summers in Eternity Springs. Because he had a passion for the ice cream made in a small south-central Texas town, he'd had a summer supply shipped to him each May. After three consecutive years of running out of the creamy concoction by mid-June, Jared made the decision to open Taste of Texas. He owned his own refrigerated truck and made the fifteen-hour run to the factory whenever required.

"Confiscate the truck? Are you kidding? Someone

would knock me down, steal my gun, and shoot me if I tried to do that."

Ali laughed. "I have this sudden mental picture of Reverend Hart doing a kung-fu kick and—"

"Alison," a chilly and familiar voice interrupted from behind her. "It's time we took our seats."

SIX

❦

Mac couldn't recall the last time he'd been this furious.

He'd waited for his wife for twenty minutes beyond the time when they'd needed to depart their home in order to reach the Brown Palace with a comfortable cushion. It wasn't until he'd grabbed his phone and car keys from the console by the front door where he'd left them an hour earlier that he'd found her text message. He'd listened for the phone to ring but had ignored notice of incoming texts—a reasonable act considering that Ali had never once sent him a text before today.

He'd stewed about the situation all the way downtown. He'd wanted to hash out their problems in private before they faced the public. She would have known that, too.

Communication between the two of them had been next to nothing since she left. No phone calls, just a brief exchange of terse emails over a couple of issues with the kids, a question he had about her credit card bill, and one she had about the warranty on her tires. He'd pictured her having a blowout on a hairpin mountain curve, and he'd wanted to ask why she needed the warranty information, but he'd refrained.

Logically, if something too bad had happened, she wouldn't be asking for information.

The fact that he'd had to worry about it at all annoyed him, and it was one of the items on the list of things he wanted to tell her. Only she hadn't come home. She'd outmaneuvered him, and he wouldn't have the opportunity to talk to her before he had to see her and pretend. That totally chapped him—as did the fact he could have been late to his own speech because of her.

When he'd pulled the Porsche up to the valet parking area, he'd tipped the driver well and asked, "Have you parked a red BMW convertible tonight? Good-looking blonde driving?"

"I haven't, but my buddy did," the young man responded. "We noticed both the car and the babe."

He'd been relieved to hear it. At that point he wouldn't have put it past Ali to stand him up. A check of his watch as he'd entered the ballroom showed he'd made it with ten minutes to spare. Barely enough time to glance through his notes for his speech.

He'd stopped just inside the ballroom and scanned the room looking for his wife. She wasn't at the reserved tables in the front, and it didn't help that he didn't know what she was wearing. Nevertheless, he expected to find her in something simple, stylish, and black. His gaze gravitated toward that look.

He didn't see her anywhere. He took a slow walk through the center of the ballroom, his gaze skimming over the crowd, until the unmistakable sound of her laughter amidst the din of conversation stopped him short. He turned toward the sound, but he still didn't see her. Then a flash of emerald caught his eye and he identified his wife.

Her shoulders were bare. Her dress was short. Her heels were high. And there was another man's hand at the small of her back.

Son of a bitch.

Mac didn't exactly storm across the room, but he definitely marched with steely determination. "Alison, it's time we took our seats."

He watched her spine straighten as she went rigid. The free-handed man she was with moved his mitt away from her waist and extended it and a lazy smile toward Mac. "Judge Timberlake, it's a pleasure to finally meet you. I'm Zach Turner, formerly of Prowers County. I understand that you were instrumental in my being nominated to receive this award tonight. I want to thank you. It's a great honor."

It took Mac a couple of seconds to process the information. Zach Turner. He'd been attached to a federal task force and worked undercover in Oklahoma. Went into a burning trailer to rescue a couple of children when a meth lab exploded. *He* was the guy with his hands on Mac's wife? *Great. Just great.*

"Yes, of course." He accepted the man's handshake. "I was glad to be of help. Your actions were the definition of heroism. You deserve the recognition. I'm just sorry it's taken so long for you to get it."

Mac could tell that Turner's revelation had caught Ali by surprise, so he asked, "How is it that you know my wife?"

Ali finally found her voice. "Zach is the sheriff in Eternity Springs."

"Really." Mac placed his own hand at the small of

his wife's back. "Small world, isn't it? Now if you'll excuse us, Alison and I need to take our seats."

Sheriff Turner lifted his champagne glass in a salute that Mac considered a shade mocking. "Enjoy your evening, your honor. Ali."

"You too, Zach," Ali replied. "And congratulations on your award."

Mac guided her through the milling crowd toward the head table. Though she hid it well when greeted by friends and acquaintances along the way, he knew she wasn't happy. Shoot, if her spine grew any stiffer, she just might break in two.

Not that he cared. He was plenty torqued himself. If her game had been to make him angry, she was racking up some score.

The head table was actually two reserved rounders, each set for six, at the front of the room. They found their places just as the emcee for the evening stepped up to the podium and asked those gathered to take their seats. Before he could exchange a private word with Ali, they were joined at the table by an honoree and his guest. Mac inwardly winced when he spied Sheriff Turner ambling their way.

The dinner proved to be a trial. Mac had attended countless events such as this throughout his career, but he couldn't recall ever being quite so uncomfortable. The company was affable, even interesting. Ali had always been a master at directing conversation in such circumstances, and tonight was no different. Yet tonight was completely different.

It was almost as if Ali were here with Turner and Mac was the one who'd attended solo. Throughout the meal, he and Ali communicated sparingly, avoiding each other's gazes. In contrast, his wife and the sheriff gave the impression of being longtime friends. Mac heard more than he'd ever wanted to know about the curious personalities of Eternity Springs.

He brooded over his steak and would have missed his cue to rise for his speech had Ali not elbowed him sharply in the ribs. He was glad to escape the table, and he put his personal troubles out of his mind as he gave the talk about heroism that he had worked hard to perfect in recent weeks.

He managed a jab at the celebrity-worship phenomenon while he spoke about qualities found in heroes, of courageousness and determination, of selflessness and sacrifice. It had occurred to him while writing the speech that once he'd have ascribed such attributes to his wife. Their children certainly had recognized it. How many times had he heard one or another of them say, *Thanks, Mom, you're my hero?*

That wasn't what the kids were saying about her now, and Ali needed to know that. Here, tonight. He'd be damned if he'd give her the chance to dodge him again.

After concluding his speech and introducing the video prepared about each of the honorees, Mac slipped outside the ballroom and made his way to the lobby, where he rented a room. He returned to the dinner just in time for the award presentation, and he tried not to begrudge Zach Turner the enthusiasm Ali displayed on the sheriff's behalf when they announced his name. The man truly was a hero.

Of course, that didn't mean Mac had to like it when he caught said hero enjoying the view presented by Ali's plunging neckline.

The emcee thanked everyone for attending and announced the date for next year's awards dinner, then the lights came up and the crowd rose from their seats. Individually, Mac and Ali took a few moments to personally congratulate each of the honorees. They both saved Zach Turner for last.

Mac shook the sheriff's hand and thanked him for his service. Then he placed his hand at the small of Ali's back and waited, letting both Ali and Turner know that he wasn't going anywhere without his wife. Except for the slight firming of her spine, Ali ignored his presence when she spoke to the sheriff.

"The story of that rescue was amazing, Zach," she said. "I am in awe of your bravery, your courage, and your compassion. I'm so glad I was here tonight to hear about it." Adding a teasing note to her voice, she added, "Especially since it'll give me cachet at the next Patchwork Angels quilters meeting."

Turner grimaced and scratched his cheek. "Any chance I could bribe you to keep quiet about this? Maybe a sample preview of the Creamery's new flavors?"

"That is definitely a tempting offer, especially since the information is bound to come out whether I say anything or not. I saw a reporter for the *Denver Post* here tonight, and Celeste reads the newspaper religiously. Besides, if I'm smart about it, I can leverage this news for something from Sarah's oven. The Creamery's ice cream may be good, but it can't possibly top Sarah's desserts."

"You're right, I'm afraid."

Ali glanced toward the crowd of others waiting to

speak to Turner, then said, "Again, congratulations, Zach. Have a safe trip home."

"Thanks." Following a quick glance at Mac, the sheriff added, "You too."

Ali turned and walked toward the exit. Mac stayed right behind her. Upon reaching the lobby, she opened her evening bag and withdrew her valet ticket. Mac grasped her elbow and tugged her to a halt. "We need to talk, Alison."

She closed her eyes. "Yes. But not now. Call me and—"

"Now. Upstairs." He reached out and plucked the ticket from her hand. "I rented a room."

Ali gaped at the valet ticket now clutched in her husband's fist. He'd swiped her ticket. She couldn't believe it. Mac didn't do things like that. "What are you doing? Give me my ticket."

"No."

He grasped her upper arm in a firm grip and propelled her toward the elevator. He wasn't rough, and he didn't hurt her, but he also didn't give her a choice. This was crazy. Mac didn't act this way.

At the elevator bank, he pressed the up button and a door immediately opened to their left. He dragged her into the empty elevator, and the minute the doors slid shut, she yanked her arm free and whirled on him. "This isn't necessary."

"True." He punched the button for the fifth floor. "We could have had this discussion at home. But then, you didn't come home, did you?"

She didn't respond to that. She couldn't. She didn't

have a legitimate defense. Okay, fine. He wanted to talk? They'd talk. She folded her arms and they both remained silent, watching the floor numbers light as the elevator climbed. She caught a whiff of his after-shave, the same woodsy scent he'd worn for the past dozen years, and her heart gave a little twist of sadness. The last time the two of them had ridden an elevator to a downtown Denver hotel room they had been on a romantic escape from the kids. It had been a night of fun and fantasy and toe-tingling sex. That had been, what, three years ago? Five?

What happened to us, Mac?

He'd reserved a suite. Ali wondered at the extravagance until she realized that he probably didn't want the bed sitting in the middle of the room like a big old accusation while they argued. Crossing to the window, she tossed her evening bag into a chair, opened the window curtains, and stared at the lights of downtown without really seeing them.

"Okay, Mac. What is it you want to talk about?"

After a moment of silence, he said, "I ordered a bottle of scotch. Do you want a drink?"

"No."

She heard the clink of ice cubes against glass, then the splash of pouring liquid. She waited. This was his game. He needed to make the first move.

Finally he cleared his throat and asked, "Last time we talked, you said you needed time to cool off. Are you still angry? Is that why didn't you come home this evening?"

"No." Now that he'd broached the subject, guilt snaked through her, along with a measure of resentment that she felt guilty to begin with. Blowing out a heavy sigh, she turned to look at him. "I was afraid."

"Of me?"

"Of facing you. Of facing our home." When her throat tightened, she swallowed hard. "It's full of pain, Mac."

He reached up and tugged on his tie to loosen it. "That's an awful thing to say."

"But it's true. You know it is. It's full of hurt and anger and misery, and I wasn't ready to face all that again. Not yet."

"So I guess that means you haven't found whatever answers you went looking for in the past month?"

"Not really." She licked her lips. "Have you?"

"I know that it's lonely without you there."

"It was lonely when I was there."

He shrugged. "I got a dog."

Ali's mouth gaped. Years ago, one of the kids accidentally let their dog Draper out. He'd been hit by a car and his back injured, paralyzing his hind legs. With the kids then busy preteens, care of the high-maintenance dog had fallen on Ali's and Mac's shoulders. When Draper died five years ago, Mac had sworn he never wanted another pet. "I'm surprised."

Again he shrugged. "He's a friendly dog. A springer spaniel mix. He's good company."

Unlike me. She filled her lungs with air, then said, "That's nice. I hear you bought a car, too."

"Yeah. Don't quite know what got into me, but I like it. Midlife crazy, I guess." He frowned down into his scotch. "Ali, the kids have been calling me. A lot. They're frustrated because you're not communicating with them."

"What?" That annoyed her, and she folded her arms. "I'm not ignoring them."

"Caitlin said you've told her not to call."

She didn't like the accusation in his tone. "I told her not to call during business hours unless it's an emergency. That's the same rule you've had all these years."

"Well, she feels like you're abandoning her."

"What?" Annoyance grew into anger. "That's ridiculous. I have a job now. Caitlin needs to learn to respect that. She was calling me ten times a day."

"Look, I'm just telling you what she's said to me. It's understandable that she'd think that way. You've always been there for her, Ali, and now you're not."

"I'm still available to my children, just not between the hours of eight and five. I don't think that's too much to ask. You shouldn't think it is, either, considering I'm simply following your example."

He finished his drink and set down his glass. "When Caitlin called me this morning, she said she'd decided not to come home for the summer."

That bit of news took Ali aback. "Does she want to go to summer school?"

"No. She wants to get a job."

"Caitlin? *Our* Caitlin?"

His mouth quirked wryly. "Yeah."

For the first time in months, and for just a moment, they shared the same wavelength. Caitlin had never been one to concern herself overmuch with working. She wasn't lazy—far from it—but she'd always managed to arrange her life in such a way that she managed to earn the funds they'd required her to contribute without working a traditional job. She'd babysat, she'd tutored, she'd set up an easel in the park and drew portraits for money. Only once in her life had Princess Caitlin ever held a job—as a clerk at a clothing store in the mall. She'd lasted one week.

"She thinks she can get a job at a fast-food joint near campus that is open around the clock," Mac said. "She said they're always needing workers for the late shift. I don't want her doing that, Ali. It's not safe."

"Then tell her to look for something else. You're still holding the purse strings. You still have control."

"I want her home. The boys both came home between their freshman and sophomore years. Cait should, too."

Ali shrugged. "Then tell her that."

"But you're not home to be there with her."

The comment irritated her. Caitlin was eighteen, almost nineteen. An adult. She'd have her friends, her social calendar. It would be no different from last summer, when she did little more than sleep at home. If Cait truly needed her to be at home this summer— if she had a real problem that she needed a mother's help dealing with—then of course, Ali would be there for her. She'd be there for the boys, too. But that wasn't the case here. Odds were the new boyfriend planned to remain in Nashville over the summer. Mac needed to open his eyes.

"Our daughter is an adult now. I don't have to be there to babysit. My work is done. I've raised my kids, and I think I . . . we . . . did a pretty good job of it. No one is on drugs, no one is in jail, no one had children of their own when they were still children. They're good people and they don't need me anymore."

"That's ridiculous," he scoffed, scowling. "Of course they need you. You're their mother."

Okay, he was right about that. Her kids would always need her, just like she would always need them. But for once, during this particular moment in time, she needed to work on herself. She needed to find herself, define herself. She needed to figure out who she was going to be in the next part of her life.

She tucked a loose strand of hair behind her ears and stood tall. "You're right. I am their mother, but don't you think it's time that I got to be more than simply that? More than simply the Timberlake kids' mom—and, frankly, more than your wife? What's wrong with that?"

"Nothing's wrong with that." He set his glass down on the bar. "I don't understand why you've decided you have to go to the mountains to do it!"

Ali closed her eyes and counted to ten before quietly asking, "Be honest with me, Mac. Isn't it easier for you, too, if I'm not there?"

A full minute passed before he replied, his voice low and gruff. "In some ways, yeah. But Ali, this is no way to conduct a marriage."

Her mouth went dry and she licked her lips. "Actually, I think it may be the way we save our marriage."

He shot her a sharp look but waited for her to say more.

"I think that you and I have been angry at each other for a long time now. It's been an undercurrent in our lives for months. Now it's out in the open. That's a positive step."

Mac didn't deny it. He rubbed the back of his neck. "Okay, then, spell it out for me. This is more than a few weeks' vacation from each other. Is that right? Are we officially separated?"

Now her stomach took a sick roll. Was that what she wanted? A clean break into the single life? During all this time, he had never once asked her to come home. Instead, he'd asked, *Are you coming home?* Big difference there. "Could we call it a trial separation?"

"Fine. Now, if this is what we're doing, I suggest we discuss a few important matters in order to avoid misunderstandings. First, are you comfortable keeping it informal or do you want to get lawyers involved? I think your father would like you to seek advice from Walt Prentice."

Her stomach pitched and rolled. "I don't want a lawyer. We don't need to do that, do we?"

"I'd prefer not to involve anyone else as long as you and I are on the same page. Finances aren't a problem with us, and child custody isn't an issue. It would help me if we had a time frame to work with. I need to know what to expect. What are you thinking? Two months? Three? I'll probably be tied up with the Sandberg trial through the end of the summer."

That was absolutely the wrong thing for Mac to say. She'd be hanged before she'd schedule her separation around his trial. She'd done that with vacations for more years than she could count. Reacting from emotion more than thought, she said, "I've made a commitment to Celeste and to my job. I'll need to stay until the restaurant is open and running smoothly."

"How long do you expect that to take?"

"Four to six months." That was longer than she truly anticipated, but she didn't want to go home before that darn trial was over.

Mac's jaw tightened. "All right, then. I'll agree to a six-month separation. Do you want to see each other from time to time, or are you thinking a complete break?"

He had shifted into negotiating-lawyer mode now, and Ali didn't like it. It felt cold and clinical when the subject was thick, hot emotion. Her instinct was to lash out, to say she didn't want to see him until Christmas, thank you very much, but she stopped herself. Barely. "I'd think it'd be good for us to see each other some. Maybe you could visit me in Eternity Springs."

"I'll be busy with the trial." When Ali snapped her mouth shut, he hastened to add, "I could probably come in the fall."

"Maybe we should leave that question open," she suggested, a bite to her tone. Once again his needs came before hers.

"All right, then. There's just one other thing I think we should put on the table in order to avoid misunderstandings." He pinned her with a laser gaze she simply couldn't read. "What about sex?"

"Excuse me?"

"How far do you want to take this separation? Do

you want to date? Do you want to sleep with some-body else?"

Now she could read the emotion in his eyes. It was accusation. Ugly and mean, and it made her blood run cold.

"Maybe you have your eye on the sheriff?" Mac continued, his tone biting. "He certainly has his eye on you."

"That's enough." Ali picked up her purse. "You've obviously reached your limit of civilized behavior. I'm leaving. Since you've rented this lovely room, I suggest you stay here tonight. I'm going home for the night. I need to pack more clothes. Don't worry about the dog. I'll see to him."

"Ali . . ." Mac grimaced, closed his eyes, and ran his fingers through his hair. "Look. I'm sorry. It's just . . . our sex life . . ."

"Sucks," she finished, speaking past a lump the size of a baseball in her throat.

He shoved his hands in his pockets, looked down at the floor for a moment, then glanced up to meet her gaze. "You looked so beautiful tonight. But that dress, those shoes. It's not you. This job isn't you. I feel like I'm losing you. It scares me."

As she reached for the doorknob, she said, "We may be separated, Mac, but we're still married. As far as I'm concerned, our wedding vows are still in effect. For both of us."

She opened the door and took one step into the hallway before pausing to look back at her husband. "Do you remember the last time you told me I was beautiful, Mac? I do. It was a year ago last Valentine's Day."

The hotel door shut behind her and Ali braced a hand against the wall as her knees went weak and watery. From inside the room, she heard a thwack and then the crash of breaking glass as Mac, Mr. Control, threw his glass at the door.

SEVEN

❦

Ali spent a restless night in her and Mac's bed, where his scent clung to the sheets and created a hollow sense of grief inside her. She'd lain awake fretting that he would come home after all, while at the same time worrying that he wouldn't.

He didn't. She couldn't decide if that made her happy or even sadder.

As dawn broke, she abandoned her attempt to sleep, washed, dressed, and prepared to pack the items she wanted to take with her. That meant a trip to the guest room closet for a large suitcase. There her gaze snagged on the box that stored her wedding gown, and she sucked in a deep breath.

The quilting bee she'd joined in Eternity Springs made quilts out of donated wedding gowns. The finished products were simply stunning. *Should I . . . ?*

Ali tugged the gown box down from the shelf. She hadn't looked at the dress since the dry cleaner packed it away after the wedding. Once upon a time she'd imagined that Caitlin would want to wear her gown when she married. By the time Cait turned twelve, Ali knew that wouldn't happen. Even if she'd wanted to wear Ali's timeless, sophisticated Scaasi gown when she married, the girl had her father's height and stood four inches taller than her mother. The gown would never suit.

"Yes, I should. No reason not to," Ali murmured. Celeste wanted wedding gown quilts for all the bedrooms at Cavanaugh House, so the Patchwork Angels could certainly find a use for it.

An hour later, suitcases, boxes, and wedding gown in her car, Ali left her house, left her husband, for the second time.

Back in Eternity Springs, the days passed swiftly as she worked with Gabe Callahan fine-tuning the remodel design and discussed colors and appropriate art with Sage Rafferty. She shopped catalogues and the Internet and anguished over appliances purchases. Had it been her own money she was spending for a restaurant of her own, she'd have been much more comfortable with her choices. In her experience, stoves and ovens were such personal things to those who used them on a daily basis. This was like buying a mattress for a stranger.

On a Tuesday evening in late May, she put her wedding gown box in her car and drove to Nic Callahan's house for a Patchwork Angels meeting. Ordinarily the group met in the attic workroom at Angel's Rest, but Celeste had decided to refinish the floors, so they'd temporarily relocated to Nic's. Ali looked forward to the weekly meetings of the quilting bee. She enjoyed the camaraderie and treasured the friends she'd made in Eternity Springs—Nic, Sarah, Sage, and recently Sage's sister Rose. And, of course, Celeste. Ali liked these women very much. They made her laugh—not an easy feat these days.

Nic lived in a charming Victorian on the edge of

town. Her cozy library had been transformed into a sewing room. Tonight's group was small, but conversation was lively. Very lively—Ali feared fisticuffs might break out at any moment. She hadn't had this much fun in months.

"You are so wrong!" Nic said, waving her rotary cutter in Sarah Reese's face. "It's Princess Grace by a million miles."

Sarah wrinkled her nose. "So says the woman whose idea of style is to wear jeans 360 days a year. Look, we're talking about the dress itself. You're giving it extra points for the whole prince-princess thing. When you take the dress and only the dress, Liz Taylor's gown wins by a mile."

"You have to be more specific, Sarah," Sage pointed out. "Liz Taylor had a lot of wedding gowns."

"Fine. I'm talking about the gown she wore to marry Conrad Hilton."

Nic fired back, "You're wrong. Princess Grace's gown would have looked gorgeous on lots of women. Liz Taylor's gown needed a body like Liz's to pull it off. That narrows the field considerably. Face it, you're just a Liz fan because of your eyes."

Sarah batted thick, luscious lashes over her gorgeous violet eyes.

Grinning, Ali decided to join the fray. "You're both wrong. Jackie Kennedy's wedding gown was the most gorgeous celebrity gown ever."

There was a moment of quiet while the group considered it. Then Nic said, "This is useless without pictures. I'm going to get my laptop."

"I'll get it, Nic," Gabe said as he walked into the

room. "I want to look in on the girls. They're too quiet."

"They're asleep. They're supposed to be quiet."

"I don't trust it."

As Nic rolled her eyes at her husband, a knock sounded on her front door and she rose to answer it. Celeste walked in with LaNelle Harrison, the master quilter who had taken the group of novices under her wing. "Hello, my dears," Celeste said. "Sorry we're late. I took LaNelle on a quick spin on my Gold Wing, and we had such a good time, we went farther than we'd intended."

"I thought I'd be afraid, but it was so exhilarating," LaNelle said. "I've driven the Alpine Trail many times, but it's different on the back of a motorcycle. She took me by Heartache Falls. I haven't been up there in years. It's almost like you are in a corner of heaven. Nothing in nature is quite so beautiful as an alpine meadow in springtime."

Celeste nodded. "Makes me want to put on a wimple and run across the fields singing."

Sarah and her daughter, Lori, home following her first year off at college, shared a look and a laugh. Lori explained, "Mom and I used to do that all the time. I so fell in love with *The Sound of Music*. I'd wrap the napkin from our picnic basket around my head and twirl my arms around and sing. I wanted to be Maria in the worst way."

"She can carry a tune," Sarah explained. "Unlike me. I wasn't much help with 'Climb Ev'ry Mountain,' but I did love my character's name: Mother Superior."

Lori gave an exaggerated roll of her eyes, and as

Gabe entered the room carrying a laptop, Ali sang, "'How do you solve a problem like Miss Lori?'"

"Whoa there, Ali," Gabe said as he handed the laptop to his wife and the women clapped and smiled. "You have a set of pipes."

"Thank you." She dipped her head to the applause. "They're rusty pipes, I'm afraid."

Celeste said, "Such a lovely, lovely voice. Are you professionally trained?"

"No." Ali shook her head. "My dad wanted me to take voice lessons, but I had another artistic passion. I wanted to go to cooking school in Europe."

"Me too!" Sarah said, her voice turning wistful as she added, "It was one of my biggest dreams. I planned it from the time I was in fifth grade. I had files stacked to the ceiling—financial aid, travel budgets, tuition, living expenses. It was . . ." Her voice trailed off, then she shrugged. "Not meant to be."

"Because she got knocked up with me," her daughter, Lori, drawled. "I'm a dream killer."

"Not hardly. I found my dream when the doctor laid you in my arms, young lady."

"Ah, that's so sweet," Sage said.

Lori rolled her eyes, but Ali could tell that the young woman was touched. As Sarah blinked away tears, Nic diverted everyone's attention by asking, "How about you, Ali? Did you find your dream? Did you make it to Paris?"

"Rome. Our cook when I was growing up was Italian." Ali picked up her sewing needle and smiled wistfully. "No. I've traveled to Europe, but I never made it to cooking school."

"What happened?" Sage asked.

"Not what happened, but who. Mac Timberlake happened. I fell head over heels in love."

Sarah nodded knowingly. "Gave up your dreams for a guy, huh?"

"I don't know that I'd say that. My dreams changed. I was happy with Mac." She paused a moment, then repeated softly. "We were happy."

Starry-eyed, Lori Reese asked, "You met him in college?"

"I did."

"Tell us about it."

A tender smile played upon Ali's lips. She hadn't thought of that time in so long. "I was dating someone else at the time, but I noticed him around campus. He was hard not to notice. Mac played baseball—he was at Notre Dame on an athletic scholarship—and he had shoulders that took a girl's breath away. We never had a conversation until I saw him and his dog at the park in my neighborhood one afternoon.

"I was dog-sitting for a friend for a couple of weeks, and I took her corgi to the park in the afternoons." Ali shook her head and added, "I think I fell in love with him because of Dusty."

The crispness of autumn hung in the air as Ali ambled through the park, allowing Crandall the corgi to sniff his way along a dirt path covered in fallen leaves. Someone in the neighborhood had steaks on a grill, and she teased herself by drawing a deep breath as her mind fluttered back to this morning's economics exam. "I should have studied the graphs better, Crandall. Need to remember that next time."

The corgi halted in his tracks and lifted his head. For a second Ali thought the dog had reacted to her comment, but then she saw the little dust mop of white fur trailing a bright red leash race toward her— on three legs.

Crandall started barking and straining at his leash. The dust mop loped forward, amazingly graceful on only one foreleg. Ali was only vaguely aware of foot- steps pounding up the path behind the little dog; she couldn't take her eyes off the poor thing. It ran right up to Crandall, who quit barking, and the two said hello by sniffing each other's butt.

"Would you grab the leash for me, please?" a voice called out.

Ali bent down, scooped up the leash, and rose to greet . . . that too-cute guy she'd noticed on the steps of the student union.

"Thanks." He flashed her a grin. "I was beginning to worry I'd never track her down. I don't know how a three-legged dog can run so fast."

He took the leash from her then held out his right hand. "I'm Mac Timberlake."

"Ali Cavanaugh."

"Nice to meet you, Ali. I'm lucky you and . . ." He gestured down at the corgi. "Who is this?"

"Crandall."

"I'm lucky that you and Crandall were here to stop Dusty. Otherwise I think she might have run for days."

"She's amazing." Ali knelt down to scratch the dog behind her ears, receiving puppy kisses on her wrist in return. "What happened to her leg?"

"I don't know. She was that way when I adopted her."

Ali looked up at him, amazed. "You adopted a disabled dog?"

His grin turned rueful. "As embarrassing as it is to call that little thing a dog, yeah. I went into the pound looking for a Lab. I'm still not sure how I walked out with a dust mop."

Ali went all warm and gooey inside. He must have a tender heart.

"These two are getting along good. Mind if we walk with you for a bit?"

"That would be nice," Ali said. "I'm dog-sitting for a friend who has another dog in addition to Crandall. Someone else is watching that dog, so Crandall is lonely."

"We don't want that."

Ali looked up the path, then down, and asked, "Which way do you want to go?"

He stared into her eyes and smiled. "Whichever way is longest."

Ali Cavanaugh, coed, shivered.

Ali Timberlake, estranged wife, sighed. "He took so much ribbing about that dog, but she was such a sweetie. When the kids came along, Dusty made the best pet. I really think it made them look at special-needs people differently than other children their ages did."

"I thought you said your family dog needed a wheelchair," Sarah observed. "Was that after Dusty got older?"

"No. That was our second disabled dog, Draper."

"You had two disabled pets?" LaNelle asked.

"We did. I admit it got to be a pain. That's why when we finally lost Draper, Mac swore he was done with pets."

But that vow hadn't lasted, had it? He had a new dog. A springer spaniel mix. Vows didn't seem to mean as much to Mac Timberlake as she had believed.

More than ready to change the subject, Ali addressed Nic. "Have you found a photo of Jackie Kennedy's wedding gown, yet?"

"Oh, yeah. I found it and Princess Grace's and Liz Taylor's. *People* magazine did a best-and-worst wedding fashion issue, and it's archived. So here you go." She turned the laptop screen around so that the other women could see. "I still say I win."

"What's the contest?" Celeste asked.

Sage gestured toward the box at the end of the table. "Ali brought her wedding gown to donate for the cause, and it started an argument about which celebrity had the most beautiful wedding gown."

Ali expected Celeste to join the other women in viewing the photographs and debating the question. Instead she walked to the end of the table and lifted the wedding gown from its box. "Oh, Alison, this is lovely."

It was yards and yards and yards of satin and Chantilly lace and tiny white pearls. The style appeared dated today, but twenty years ago she'd been on the cutting edge of fashion. "I knew it was mine the moment I saw it."

"Tell me about that day."

"Oh, Celeste, I don't want to—"

"Indulge me, dear."

What was this, trip-down-memory-lane day?

Celeste fluffed out the dress, spreading out the train. "Where did you buy this?"

"Marshall Field's on the Miracle Mile in Chicago. One of my sorority sisters went with me and we made a day of it, shopping for my gown and the bridesmaids' dresses. She was my maid of honor at our wedding. She told the salesclerk to bring something sophisticated but romantic. I knew the moment I saw it that it was my dress. I put it on and I felt as glam as Jackie, Liz, and Princess Grace put together."

"You were happy."

"I was so very happy." *That day, and for a long time afterward.*

Celeste touched her arm. "Are you certain you want to donate your gown to our quilt project?"

"I'd love to see us make something beautiful out of it. It's hopeful, in a way. That something old and tired can be transformed into something new and wonderful. Does that make sense?"

"It makes perfect sense." Celeste squeezed her hand. "The wedding gown quilts the Patchwork Angels have made reflect the positive energies of Eternity Springs, this special place where we are blessed to live. When I place a wedding gown quilt on a bed in Angel's Rest, it's as if the fabrics we used, the stitches we made together, offer love and hope and dreams, friendship and laughter and compassion to those who come to this valley in pain."

"That may be a little too much symbolism for me, Celeste. My marriage is in serious trouble. I don't know how much hope the fabric from my wedding gown has to offer. In the other quilts we did, the fabric represented marriages that lasted forty and fifty years."

"You don't think a marriage that has lasted more than twenty years has value? You don't think that a marriage that lasts forty or fifty years has rough spots?"

"I . . ." Ali snapped her mouth shut. All marriages had rough spots. She knew that.

"You need to remember . . ." Celeste's voice trailed off as she looked inside Ali's gown and pursed her lips. "What do we have here?"

She reached inside the bodice and pulled out a little stick-on green shamrock. Seeing it, Ali caught her breath in surprise.

The scenery in Rocky Mountain State Park took one's breath away. On this last full day of Mac's first visit to Denver, she'd taken him up to Estes Park for a drive through Rocky Mountain National Park. At his suggestion, she'd packed a picnic basket and they'd found a spectacular, clover-covered meadow on which to spread their blanket and enjoy their lunch.

"It simply doesn't get any better than this," he said, stretching out and resting his weight on his elbows, his long, denim-clad legs crossed at the ankles. "Beautiful scenery, beautiful weather." He glanced over and gave her a steamy look. "Beautiful woman."

Ali grinned. "Don't even think about it," she warned. They'd been sleeping together for more than a year now, and she recognized that look. "This meadow only seems isolated. We could be overrun by a station wagon full of tourists looking to get an up-close and personal look at nature."

"Hey." He rolled over onto his side and allowed his gaze to slowly trail over her. "What's more natural than a big horny goat in a mountain meadow?"

"That's bighorn sheep, city boy."

"No." He reached out and traced the vee at her neck with an index finger. "I'm definitely a goat."

Ali shivered at his touch and considered cutting the tour short and finding a room to rent near Estes Park. "I wish I were going back with you tomorrow. I should have gone to summer school."

"No, it's good for you to have this time with your dad. I like him. It's clear that he loves you a lot." He hesitated a moment, then asked, "What has he said about me?"

The nervousness in his expression touched her. "I think he likes you. I know he enjoyed debating the death penalty with you at dinner last night."

"When he wasn't eyeing his steak knife as if he wanted to plunge it into my heart."

Ali laughed. "You have to understand that he's very protective of me, and he's always been a little chilly to the guys I've dated."

"Chilly? I'd say icy better described it." Mac took hold of her hand and brought it to his mouth to press a kiss against her palm. "That's okay. I can't blame him. It's only natural for him to resent me because I am the luckiest man on earth."

"Lucky?"

"Yep. Don't look now, Ali, but we didn't spread our blanket in just any old field of clover. These are four-leaf clovers."

"Oh, really?" she replied, playing along.

"That's right. Perfect setting for a guy to get lucky, don't you think?"

"Stop right there, Timberlake. I already told you that you're not getting lucky here."

"See, this is why I'm gonna be the lawyer. Whereas you are considering only one definition of the phrase, I have something else in mind. For now, anyway."

Mac kissed her palm again, and then the sensitive skin on the inside of her wrist, as he stared deeply into her eyes. "I love you, Alison Michelle Cavanaugh. I love your strength and your compassion and your wisdom. I love your heart. I love your beauty, inside and out." His lips twitched as he added, "God knows I love your body."

"Oh, Mac." Ali melted at both his words and the emotions shining in his eyes. "I love you, too."

His expression grew both serious and intense as he rolled up onto his knees. Keeping hold of her hand with his left hand, he reached into his pants pocket with his right.

Ali's breath caught and her heart began to pound as he knelt on one knee before her. "Ali, be my wife, my lover, my lucky charm." He pulled a lovely diamond solitaire from his pocket and said, "Ali, will you marry me?"

When she said yes, Mac Timberlake got lucky in a field of clover high in the Colorado Rockies—in every sense of the word.

In Nic Callahan's house in Eternity Springs more than two decades later, Ali Timberlake fingered the little shamrock and sighed. "Mac used to give me shamrocks. It was kind of our special symbol. He talked my maid of honor into putting that there so it would be next to my heart when we said our wedding vows." She paused a moment, then added, "I haven't thought of shamrocks in a very long time."

"Perhaps you should think about that while you're working on our next quilt." Celeste patted her arm, then handed her a pair of scissors and addressed the group. "I'd like to suggest for our next wedding gown quilt that we use the pattern called Hopes and Wishes."

"That's a lovely choice," LaNelle said.

Hopes and Wishes and shamrocks. Ali slipped the point of the scissors into the seam at the waist. Definitely something to think about.

The Patchwork Angels meeting continued, drawing Ali into the pleasure of friendship, and it wasn't until the meeting broke up and Lori Reese approached her with a question that returned her thoughts to topics less pleasant. "Ali? Could I talk to you for a few minutes? About Chase?"

"Sure, honey," she said, though she swallowed a sigh. She was having enough love-life trouble of her own. She really didn't want to get tangled up in the romantic foibles of her children. Yet she knew that was exactly what she had to deal with now. "I drove over tonight since I had so much to carry. Want to go for a ride with me?"

"In the Beamer? Of course! Can we put the top down?"

"It's definitely a ragtop evening." Ali waited while Lori spoke with her mother, explaining the plan. Lori had dated Ali's son Chase during the two summers he'd spent in Eternity Springs working on the Double

R Ranch. Last fall when Chase returned to Colorado University and Lori went away to college in Texas, the two agreed to date other people. From what she'd observed and Sarah had shared, both kids were okay with the arrangement. This summer Chase had an internship out of state, so he wouldn't be spending his break in Eternity Springs. She hoped Lori wasn't brokenhearted. She adored Lori, but she already had enough heartache on her plate.

On the way out to the car, she tossed Lori the keys. "Will you drive?"

"Woo-hoo!" the teenager said. "Okay if I take the scenic route?"

"Sounds great."

Ali decided to let the girl take the conversational lead, so she settled back into the leather seat, rested her head against the headrest, closed her eyes, and enjoyed the evening air as Lori made the drive around Hummingbird Lake. She relaxed and was feeling quite content because Lori kept the conversation to innocuous subjects such as Ali's car, Sarah's latest hairstyle, and the contest taking place at the Mocha Moose to pick the birth date of Sage Rafferty's first child—never mind the fact that Sage wasn't pregnant.

It wasn't until Lori pulled the car to a stop in front of her own house that she broached Chase's name. "So, Ali, about Chase."

Ali stifled a groan. Just barely.

"He asked me to remind you that you thought the intervention you guys had with Sage a while back was a good idea." Lori grinned, stepped out of the car, and finger-waved. "Bye."

"Wait!" Ali called after her. "What are you talking about?"

"See you tomorrow, Ali. Thanks for letting me drive your smokin' car." The young woman all but ran into her house to escape any further inquisition.

Yet as Ali drove back toward the carriage house, she knew what she would find. Her maternal instinct on high alert, she parked her car in the Angel's Rest garage and walked toward the carriage house.

"Surprise!"

The sound of Chase's voice was no big shock. Hearing both Stephen's and Caitlin's voices stopped her in her tracks. An intervention? *This is bound to be fun,* she thought wryly.

Nevertheless, she opened her arms and said with complete sincerity, "My babies! I am so happy to see you."

EIGHT

Mac drew down the zipper of his judicial robe as he walked into his office at the end of a long work day. He was tired both in body and in spirit. As the trial had dragged on, he'd realized he didn't like celebrity lawyers any more than he liked celebrity ballplayers. He didn't like celebrity trials, and he absolutely didn't like the paparazzi and tabloid reporters who apparently didn't believe in the word *no*.

Nor did he like going home to an empty house.

He hung his robe on the wall tree, then loosened his tie and walked past the large cherry worktable piled with his books. He sank into his leather office chair just as a knock sounded on his door. "Come in."

The door opened and Mac's clerk, Mike Reed, entered with Gus. Mac eyed the dog and felt a little of his tension ease. "Hey, boy. Did the vet get you fixed up?"

Mike released the leash, and the dog slowly ambled over to Mac—a stark contrast to his ordinary dash and bound—then plopped down at his feet. "Gus has a respiratory infection. I have medicine. He's good for tonight, so start it in the morning." Setting two blue plastic prescription bottles down on Mac's desk, he added, "Doc says he should be just as good as new next week, but if he's not, bring him back."

Mac scratched his pet behind his ears. "Thanks for taking him for me, Mike. Not exactly in the job description, I know."

"Hey, my dogs are my children. I'm glad to help. Poor boy was downright pitiful." Jerking his thumb over his shoulder, he said, "I saw Louise headed out the front door. She said we're done for the day?"

"Yes." Mac picked up one of the prescription bottles to read the label. "I think we all need a night off to recharge. Go do something fun and relaxing, then show up here ready to work at eight."

"Yes, sir!"

Once his clerk had departed, Mac discarded all his judicial demeanor and sat on the floor beside his sick dog. Gus put his head on Mac's thigh, and Mac allowed his head to clear as he stroked his ailing dog's soft fur. "I was worried about you, boy."

He'd been worried and just a little bit annoyed, to be honest. He'd been in a bind this morning when he realized Gus was sick and needed to see the vet, and he'd hated asking for help. Up until now, Ali had always been there to take the dogs to the vet, the kids to the doctor, the cars to the shop. It was a pain to try to do everything that everyday living involved in addition to overseeing the Sandberg case. It would have been a lot more convenient for him if she'd waited to have her meltdown until this case was over.

Regarding meltdowns, he wondered how many times Caitlin had called him today. Not a day went by that she didn't phone at least three times. He loved his daughter. She was the light of his life. But for crying out loud, the girl needed to cut the cord. She definitely needed to learn that he didn't want to hear an endless litany of wonderful about this new hairy-legged boy she was dating.

Mac eyed the center drawer of his desk, where he kept his cell phone during court, and made a silent bet with himself. Ten. He'd have ten phone messages or more from his children and at least fifteen texts. He knew they worried about him. He understood they thought they needed to check on him every day—even though he'd told them checking in once a week or so would be plenty. Frankly, they were wearing him down.

Mac scratched Gus behind the ears, then said, "Okay, boy. I might as well just get it over with, don't you think?"

He opened the drawer, pulled out his phone, thumbed it on, and checked his missed calls and messages. "Stephen, Caitlin, Caitlin, Chase . . ." Mac's voice trailed off as he began to count.

Chase had called three times, but he'd sent seventeen text messages. That wasn't like Chase. He pulled up the first text message: *Dad, call me*. The second message: *Dad, call ASAP*. The third: *Dad, pls call*.

Mac's heart began to pound and he rose to his feet. Dear Lord, what had happened? Was he hurt? Bleeding? Had he done something stupid? He immediately dialed Chase's number, and as he waited for the call to go through, he told himself that his son wasn't dead—dead people didn't text. Nor did people having major surgery. Nor was Chase in jail, since no one had taken his phone away.

As the phone rang, Mac thought desperately, *Please, Lord, let nobody have died.*

"Hello? Dad?"

"Chase, are you all right?"

"Dad. Thank God you called."

Mac gripped the back of his office chair hard. "What's wrong, son?"

"Hold on. I can't talk here. Let me get outside."

Mac heard music playing in the background, then the loud squeak of springs and the bang of a door. Screen door, he figured. Seconds later, the background noise faded and his son said, "Dad, you have to do something about Mom."

Oh. With that, his fear for his child faded and he tensed with dread, sensing he'd rather not have this conversation. He delayed it by asking, "Where are you?"

"Eternity Springs."

"What? I thought you were in D.C. Don't you start your internship this week?"

"I was there. I came back. Family emergency."

Mac closed his eyes. *Oh, great.* "Okay, then. What's the emergency? Why all the texts?"

Chase explained how he, his brother, and his sister had traveled to Eternity Springs to try to talk some sense into their mother. *You guys should have asked me before you went to the effort. I could have told you that was a waste of time.*

Chase said, "I thought we made some progress. She did seem to listen and what she said reassured us. Stephen and Caitlin had an earlier flight than I did, so they took off early. I went to visit with Lori, then breezed by the Bristlecone before I left town. Did you know there was a fire at the restaurant? They're repairing and replacing, and right now she's painting the walls in the kitchen."

"Your mother is painting?"

"Yep. And not by herself. Some guy is helping her. Dad, she's making a fool of herself."

Guardedly he asked, "How so?"

"It's unusually hot today, granted, and the Bristlecone doesn't have a working air conditioner, but Mom is wearing shorts and a tank top. He doesn't have a shirt on. In my opinion, Dad, it's way too cozy. As I walked into the restaurant a little while ago they were throwing movie quotes at each other. Mom was saying, " 'I'm alive. Maggie the cat is alive.' "

As his son continued to talk, Mac's gaze settled on the baseball displayed on a shelf of his office bookcases that held personal mementos. He recalled the first time he'd heard Ali recite those lines.

He'd glanced around for Ali as he stepped down from the team bus to a cheering crowd of students and supporters of the Fighting Irish as the team arrived home from the regionals, where they'd defeated Michigan to advance to the College World Series. The baseball he'd hit to score the winning run was tucked carefully into his backpack—he wanted to show it to her and share the biggest sports-related moment of his life. Not spying her, he frowned. Ali almost always met the team bus. What could she be . . . oh. The play. Ali was starring in an off-campus production of Cat on a Hot Tin Roof. *The first performance was tonight.*

Mac checked his watch. Ten after seven. Well, he'd be a little late but he knew she would like him to be there. She'd been stoically supportive when the tournament schedule was released and they realized he'd probably not make it home tonight. However, thanks to some awesome pitching on both sides, the game had moved more quickly than anyone had anticipated, and here he was. Slipping through the crowd, he mentally reviewed the contents of his wallet and decided that this time he'd splurge on a cab ride.

He entered the theater in time to see Ali, playing Maggie the Cat, strip down to her slip, and then he lost himself in the power of her performance. Her talent floored him. Her raw sexuality seduced him. When the play ended with Maggie and Brick sharing a passionate kiss, jealousy and a bone-deep desire to claim her for his own washed through him.

He waited for her in the alley outside the stage door, leaning back against the red brick wall, his arms crossed over his chest. When she exited the building laughing with a pair of girlfriends, he pushed away from the wall and stood with his legs spread, his hips flexed forward. He locked his gaze on her but didn't say a word.

Her friend noticed him first and stopped abruptly. Ali turned her head and upon seeing him, her eyes rounded and her smile slowly died. "Mac. You're back!"

Now he let his arms drop to his sides and he advanced slowly toward her. "Uh-huh."

She licked her lips. "Did you get to see any of the play?"

"Oh, yeah, Ali-cat."

His blood ran hot and thick, fueled by her performance on the stage and his own on the diamond, and he shifted his direction, cutting her from the herd just as slickly as any cowboy on the clock.

"Um . . . ," one of the girls said. "We'll, uh, catch you later, Ali."

"Did you win?" Ali asked, a little bit breathless, her stare locked on his.

"Oh, yeah." He moved forward, backing her up against the theater's wall, his hands and forearms flat against the bricks, pinning her with his hips. "Oh, yeah."

Then he kissed her, a hard, desperate crush of his lips against hers that told her without words of his dark and hungry desire. Ali melted bonelessly against him, moaning into his mouth. Her surrender only further stoked the fires of his need.

He released her mouth in order to draw a breath, and his lips skimmed over her face to that sensitive spot on her neck just below her ears that always made her shiver. He nipped her with his teeth and murmured, "I want you, Ali. I want you so damned much."

In a thready, whisper of a voice, she said, "Okay."

Mac froze. He lifted his head and met her gaze. "What did you say?"

"I said okay. I want you, too, Mac. I'm ready."

He sucked in a breath. Ali was a virgin, and they'd been taking it slow. As much as he wanted her, as badly as he hurt, he understood the importance of the step they contemplated. "Are you sure, honey? I'm not trying to pressure you."

She smiled and wiggled her hips against him. "What do you call that if not pressure?"

Mac groaned. "Agony."

Now, she laughed. "I'm sure, Mac. I knew when I saw you here tonight that the time was finally right. I feel on top of the world. I love you, and I want to be with you."

"I love you, too, Ali," Mac replied, meaning it, surprising himself. It wasn't the first time he'd told her he loved her. She wasn't the first girl to whom he'd said those three big words, but this time, for the first time, he actually meant it. And it wasn't because she'd just agreed to sleep with him, either. "You're special. You're really, really special."

Then he stepped away from her, took her hand, and raised it to his lips and kissed it. "This is shaping up to be the best day of my life."

More than two decades later, as Mac sat in his office and tried to focus on his son's monologue, he realized that particular day had been first of many best days of his life.

And Ali had been part of each and every one of them.

"So, Dad, you are going to do something about it, right? I'm telling you, she's vulnerable. The sheriff is a stud and he's not married. And let's face it, for a woman her age, Mom is hot."

The sheriff. Mac's stomach took a sickening roll. "Zach Turner is helping her paint the restaurant?"

"Yes. Weren't you listening to me, Dad?"

Great. Just great.

Mac grimaced and massaged his forehead with his

fingers. He decided he'd heard all he wanted to hear on this subject. "I'll deal with your mom. You don't need to worry. Now, tell me about your internship."

Chase's sigh communicated his displeasure, but he knew his father well enough not to argue. He talked about the job with the Department of the Interior, the apartment he shared with three other interns, and the stultifying heat of the nation's capital in summer. He ended with another sigh and the statement, "Too many people there. I miss the mountains. Still, change can be good."

Mac eyed Gus, who lay sprawled in a sunny spot in front of the window. "Yes, change can be good."

Then, as his gaze moved back to the shelf and what he'd always called the "home-run baseball," he added, "Sometimes, though, you learn that the status quo was better."

Seated at a table for one at the Blue Spruce Sandwich Shop, Ali picked at her dinner salad, almost too tired to eat. After three days of hard work, the painting was completed. *Next time I'll let the contractors do it.*

Guilt over spending so much on kitchen appliances had caused her to look for opportunities to save money elsewhere. The paint job looked good— thanks to help from friends—but she'd never guessed the work itself would tax her so much. Her lack of gym time during the past year was showing.

The shop's front door opened, and Ali saw Sarah Reese walk in carrying a cardboard box. Sarah made the desserts served at the Blue Spruce, and Ali knew from experience that they were delicious. "Thank goodness," she said, waving toward the empty refrigerated display case. "I was beginning to worry."

"Me, too," Sarah responded as she set down the box and began to fill the case's space with cake, pies, and brownies. "Today has been one of those ugly days. Mom had a particularly difficult time today."

"I'm sorry, Sarah. Do you have time to join me? I'm buying."

Sarah considered a second, then said, "I believe I do. Iced tea, please."

As Ali gestured to her waitress to bring another glass of tea, Sarah finished unloading the desserts, dropped off her invoice in the owner's office, then joined Ali at her table. "How's the painting coming?"

"It's finally done. Thanks so much for your help. I didn't know what I was getting myself into."

"It was fun." Sarah waved the protest away, then turned serious. "It was fun. I'm glad to help you any way I can, Ali. The Cavanaugh coins have been a lifesaver for me."

Now it was Ali's turn to give a dismissive gesture. The coins to which she referred had been in a box of items Ali's father had received from the Eternity Springs side of the Cavanaugh family, and they'd been worth a fair amount of money. Once Ali had learned Sarah's big secret—the true identity of Lori's father—and realized that Lori had as rightful a claim to those coins as her own children and a much greater need, Ali had offered them to Sarah. Prideful, Sarah had resisted taking them at first, but the realities of college tuition eventually made her cave. "Family takes care of family. Or at least they should."

Sarah frowned at her. "Is that supposed to be a subtle message of some sort, Timberlake? Has my daughter been bending your ear about her father?"

"Some," Ali admitted.

"She wants to find him," Sarah said with a sigh. "We're in the middle of a huge argument about it. She wants to use the coin money to hire an investigator to find Cam and take out loans to help pay for her tuition. I refuse to do that. I've worked like a dog for these past nineteen years to support her and put money aside so that she wouldn't have to go into debt to get an education. If she does get into vet school, we'll need every penny we've squeezed out of those nickels and dollars you gave us."

Sarah's Cam was Cam Murphy, the great-something-grandson of two of Eternity Springs's founders, Daniel Murphy and Harry Cavanaugh, who was Ali's ancestor. Cam had been Eternity Springs's trouble-maker, the bad boy whose relationship with good girl Sarah Reese remained secret to this day. Sent to juvenile detention for injuring someone in a fight, he'd never returned to Eternity Springs after his release. Sarah had blamed her pregnancy on a fling with a summer tourist, and except for Lori and a few close friends, the people of Eternity still believed the lie. Nic had told Ali that Sarah had never gotten over him.

"You know," she ventured, "it might not be that expensive to track him down. The Internet has made—"

"No," Sarah snapped. "To quote one of Gabe Callahan's favorite sayings, 'That way there be dragons.'"

Trying one more time, Ali said, "High school sweethearts can have powerful connections. First love and all."

Sarah deflected by asking, "Did you have a high school sweetheart?"

"Nope. Mac was my first love."

"Powerful connections," Sarah repeated, giving Ali a significant look. "You haven't talked about him, Ali, or what's going on with you. Nic and Sage would be amazed to hear me say this, but I won't pry. I will listen if you want to talk."

Ali stared moodily into her glass. "Thanks, but no. I don't even know what to say."

"Fair enough. Just remember, I'm here if you need me."

"Thanks, Sarah."

Later, while she walked back to Angel's Rest, Ali brooded about first loves. First love. Mac.

She was lonely tonight. She missed him. She missed *them* together.

When her cell rang and she saw Stephen's name, a warmth of love rushed through her. "Hello, honey."

"Hey, Mom. Do you have a minute?"

"For you, anytime."

Five minutes later, she wished she'd left her cell phone at the Bristlecone. Stephen conferenced in his sister and the two of them explained that Chase had filled them in about seeing her painting yesterday. "With a bare-chested man!" Caitlin wailed.

Ali's children proceeded to explain that she was naive, vulnerable, and, to quote her eldest child, off her flippin' rocker. *For crying out loud.* Keeping tight control of her motions, Ali sought a calm tone as she said, "Zach Turner is my friend, Stephen. I'm allowed to have friends, even if they are male."

"But you have to be careful, Mom," Caitlin cautioned. "You're up there running around with cougars. You might just become one!"

"Excuse me?"

"A cougar. That's what they call older women who chase after younger men. Cougars on the prowl."

Ali lowered the phone from her ear and stared at it for a few seconds before saying, "For heaven's sake, Caitlin. Please."

"Mom, we know you're not up in the mountains chasing the sheriff," Stephen said, verbally stepping between mother and daughter. "It's just that if you're not careful, you might find yourself in a situation where you make poor decisions you'll come to regret."

Is it role reversal time or what?

"Thank you for your concern, but you need not worry. Thanks for calling, you two. I need to run. Goodnight."

She hung up without giving them the chance to say much more than good-bye. She continued her walk back to the carriage house trying not to obsess about the call from her kids. She wasn't aware that she'd begun to angrily kick at a stone until she ran across Sage's sister, Rose, on the grounds of the estate and Rose asked, "Ali? What's the matter?"

Ali stopped and looked up, filled with misery and heartache. "Ah, Rose. It's such a mess."

"The remodel going poorly? I'd heard you'd had some delays. My sister said she had a devil of a time getting work done when she remodeled her art gallery."

"Not the remodel," Ali corrected. "That's going fine. It's my life that's a mess."

"Oh, dear." Rose clicked her tongue and switched into comfort mode. "You look like a woman who needs a bit of girl talk." She looped her arm through Ali's. "Come upstairs and tell me about it."

Rose was a former army doctor and now the resident physician at Angel's Rest. After undergoing a hysterectomy as part of treatment for endometrial cancer, she had separated from the service and come to Eternity Springs to reconcile with Sage, from whom she'd been estranged. She'd fallen in love with both the town and the Angel's Rest suite she'd rented. Last winter, when the doctor Celeste had hired for the healing center decided he didn't like the mountains in winter after all, Rose accepted Celeste's offer of a job and the suite and became a permanent resident of Eternity Springs.

Now, as she led Ali up to her Angel's Rest apartment, Rose said, "I'll put the kettle on for tea, or I have wine."

"Don't go to any trouble."

"No trouble. Celeste often drops by this time of the evening and we have a nightcap together. Which would you prefer?"

"Do you have any chocolate? That's what I really need."

"I have an emergency stash of M&Ms. Will that do?"

Ali gave her a grateful smile. "Bless you."

Rose gestured for Ali to have a seat, and then she

pulled a big bag of dark chocolate M&Ms from the back of her pantry. She poured the candies into a big ceramic bowl, then made an executive decision and opened a bottle of cabernet. Setting the bowl and a glass in front of Ali, she said, "Talk to me."

Ali rubbed her temples with her fingertips. "I've hurt my family, and I hate that. Maybe I should just go home."

"Why don't you start at the beginning?"

After a moment's hesitation, Ali nodded. She talked about her husband, their separation, and how she'd decided she was done with the arctic winter of her marriage. She spoke of her guilt for having caused her children pain, and finished by saying, "I'm a bad mother. A bad wife."

"Why do you say that? Why does any of this make you a bad wife and mother?"

"Because I made the decision to make this huge change in my life, my husband's life, and my children's lives, and I can't articulate why."

Rose shook her head. "Don't be so hard on yourself. You're not a bad wife and mother. I think you're brave and honest."

"Because I left my husband? Left my family?"

Rose searched for the right words to convey the idea floating through her mind. "Because you won't settle for half. Not when you've had whole."

"That's what I tried to tell myself, but now I don't know." Ali sipped her wine and sighed glumly. "If Mac had offered half, I might have gone for that. Probably lots of wives only get sex four or five times a month, and I'd think intimacy would have to burn off some of the frost, don't you?"

Rose gave her a startled look. "Wait a minute. You had sex ten times a month? And you've been married twenty years?"

"Yeah. We made love two or three times a week for most of our marriage." Her wistful smile melted away when she added, "Then we stopped."

"Holy cow." Rose didn't know whether to be envious or tired at the thought. She liked sex and she really, really wished she had someone to like it with, but wow. Three times a week?

Rose considered this new bit of information. Based on her knowledge of the human condition, the usual reason a couple's sex life went south was because one of them began an affair. Ali must have seen the question in her gaze, because she shook her head. "It wasn't an affair. I was afraid that was the deal, but I finally asked him. He said no and I believe him. Mac doesn't lie."

Rose knew the polite thing would be to move the conversation on from Ali Timberlake's sex life—or lack thereof. But the woman was obviously in the mood to talk, and this *was* all primo info. "Okay, this is a really nosy question and it's totally none of my business, and if you want to change the subject just say so, but since we're already talking personal, I have to ask. Was it something physical?" In fact, she was wondering if he'd worn it out.

"No." Ali sighed heavily. "That I could deal with. But watching him roll out of bed sporting a morning erection broke my heart and crushed my self-confidence."

Rose scooped up a half dozen yellow M&Ms. For

some reason Ali had picked around the yellow ones. "So what did trigger the, um, cessation? Did you two have a big fight?"

"No. Not out loud, anyway." Ali rubbed her eyes with her fingertips. "We just . . . I don't know . . . we had this anger between us. I don't even know how it started, but at some point it became a living, breathing, freezing thing that lay right between us in the bed."

She paused a moment, then added, "Before Caitlin went off to college, I slogged my way through a few months of depression. I took antidepressants and that muted my sex drive. But Mac knew the deal; he said he understood." She sighed heavily. "My sex drive returned after I got off the pills, but by then the anger was there. I thought that if I was away from the hurt, I'd be able to figure everything out. I think it's been working, too. With the distance, I've started to relax. I've started to think about my life and about what I want to do with the rest of it. I needed this space. I still need it."

"Then don't forget the bottom line. For your children to be happy, for your husband to be happy, you need to find your way back to happiness."

From the open doorway, Celeste said, "That is excellent advice. You should listen to Rose, Ali. She's a wonderful doctor."

"I'm not a psychologist," Rose warned.

"No, but you're a friend. A good friend. That's what Ali needs around her right now. She's spent half a lifetime being there for others. It's her turn now. Her time." She joined the other two women at the table, reached out, and gave Ali's hand a comforting squeeze. "Listen to your instincts, Ali. They won't let you down."

"I hope you're right, Celeste," she said with a sigh. "I do so hope you are right."

NINE

☙

July

"Adjourned." Mac banged his gavel, rose from the bench, and exited the courtroom through the connecting door to his chambers. Striding down the small hallway past his clerk's office, he paused at the doorway to his administrative assistant's office and asked, "Anything that can't wait until Monday?"

"No, sir."

"Excellent. In that case, I'm gone." In his own office, he unzipped his robe and hung it on the antique coat tree Ali had found for him at a small shop in Colorado Springs. Loosening his tie, he took a seat at his desk and made a couple of quick notes to himself before checking his phone for messages. Good, nothing pressing.

He entered his private bathroom, where he changed into the sport shirt, jeans, and hiking boots he'd left there that morning. Five minutes later, he was out the door and headed for the garage, dialing the neighbors' house on the way.

"Hi, Donna," he said when the wife answered. "Thought I'd check on Gus before I hit the road."

"He's doing fine," she assured him. "Tim just left

the house to take him on another walk. Both boy and dog are in heaven."

"Great. Thanks. I won't worry about him, then. Y'all have a good weekend and I'll see you on Sunday."

"You too, Mac," she replied. "Tell Ali we said hello."

Mac responded with a simple good-bye. He was on his way to Eternity Springs, but he wasn't at all certain what he would do once he arrived. He had not spoken to his wife since the night of the awards dinner two months ago. Since then, all their communication had taken place by text message, email, and one voice mail she'd left on the machine at home during a time when she had to have known he'd be at work.

For a while after Chase had called to inform him about Ali's new painting partner, Mac had told himself he didn't care what his wife did up in the mountains or whom she did it with. Once when he had a free weekend, he'd driven down to Colorado Springs to play golf with a colleague. Another weekend when he could have made the trip, he'd flown to California to visit Stephen instead.

After that, events in the Sandberg trial had gone nuclear and effectively tethered Mac to Denver. It wasn't until earlier this week, when he'd come entirely too close to doing something infinitely stupid, that he'd realized the situation had to change.

It had started out innocently enough. Carla Hubbard managed the little Italian restaurant Mac passed on his way home from the office. After Ali had left him—taking her Italian-cooking talents with her—he began stopping there for dinner once or twice a week.

Carla was a lovely woman, dark and slender, with a fondness for flirtation and necklines that plunged. A couple of times when business was slow, she'd joined him at his table, and over dinner he'd learned that she, too, was separated from her spouse. The commonality created a bond of sorts between them, and to be honest, Mac had enjoyed her attention. So when he'd stopped for spaghetti Tuesday night and found her on her way to an art show opening at a local gallery, he'd accepted her invitation to accompany her.

He'd enjoyed himself. The artist was talented, the hors d'oeuvres delicious, and the company both witty and good for his ego. She'd been dressed to kill, and sexual awareness had hummed between them, adding an edge of danger to the event. She'd sent out signals a blind man wouldn't miss, and when he'd driven her home—she lived within walking distance of the restaurant—and she invited him in for a drink, he'd thought of Ali and their cold bed and her shirtless sheriff and decided, *What the hell. Why not?*

Inside, Carla Hubbard had poured them each a scotch, tasted the drink and purred, then licked her lips with a slow, seductive sweep of her tongue. Mac accepted her third invitation of the evening and kissed her. She was as intoxicating as the scotch, and he lost himself in the pleasure of having a woman in his arms. Of holding her against him. Of the sweet, soft melting of her body against the hardness of his.

He'd groaned low in his throat, then reached a hand up to cup her breast, and it was . . . different. It was wrong.

She wasn't Ali.

In that moment, bone-deep shame replaced desire. He'd released her, stepped away, made an awkward excuse, and fled the scene of the near-crime against his family. Because, separation or not, cold, empty bed or not, he was still married. It didn't matter what Ali did or did not do with her sheriff. He would not surrender the moral high ground in this war with his wife. He refused to do anything that would make looking his children in the eyes difficult. He was not a cheat.

Though he had come damned close.

It was during his drive home that night that he'd made up his mind to go to Eternity Springs. This limbo he'd been living in didn't work for him. Not any longer. Ali had asked for time, and he'd given it to her. She'd asked for space, and he'd let her have that, too. Now it was her turn to accommodate him. He needed answers. He needed direction.

He needed to get laid.

She needed to help him with that, one way or another.

So he'd adjusted the court schedule, and now, finally, he was on his way. With the top down and hard rock blaring from the stereo, he downshifted the Porsche, gunned the engine, and began the climb into the front range west of Denver. Anticipation hummed in his blood, and Mac wondered how Alison would like the surprise.

An hour outside of Eternity Springs, he stopped to put the convertible's top up, locking it into place mere seconds before the sky opened up and rain fell in sheets. This part of the state had been drenched in recent weeks, and the terrain still appeared soggy.

The rain slowed his pace and the hour left in his journey stretched to an hour and a half, but finally the sky cleared just as he drove into Eternity Springs on Friday afternoon. For some reason he didn't explore, Mac hummed the theme song to *High Noon*, the mental echo of Tex Ritter's voice entreating his darlin' not to forsake him rolling through his mind.

In the darkened Firehouse Theater, Ali laughed at the final line of the play, then stood with the rest of the audience in singing the Colorado state song. The cast took their bows and exited the stage as the lights came up. Ali clapped hard and cheered Lori's performance as a nineteenth-century ingenue, but declined Sarah's invitation to join the Reeses and their friends at her house for after-the-play dessert. She'd had a long day, a long week. She wanted a burger, a bath, and a bed, in that order.

Besides, despite the fact that she liked the Raffertys and the Callahans a lot, she wasn't in the mood to be around the happily married couples.

Her day had started before sunrise with the yoga class at Angel's Rest that Rose had talked her into. Then she and Celeste had met the contractor at the Bristlecone for an inspection of the work and afterward spent more than two hours discussing plans for the restaurant's grand reopening. Ali had kept her appointment at the beauty shop, however, because she'd spied new strands of gray hair at her temples, and she'd decided to indulge an urge for highlights and allowed her hairdresser to talk her into lowlights, too. At that point, she decided to go hog wild and get a mani-pedi.

As a result of the spruce-up, she'd perked up and arrived at the theater brimming with energy. But as the play progressed, that energy drained away and exhaustion once again lapped at the edges of her soul.

She was tired and sad. Very, very sad. And lonely. Sobbing-in-her-empty-bed lonely. Tired and sad and lonely enough that she'd lain awake for hours wondering if she should throw in the towel and go home. The effects of the pep talk Rose and Celeste had given her weeks ago had begun wearing off. She missed her favorite coffee cup. Missed her favorite radio station.

She missed her favorite man.

She could go home. He would let her. That would make the kids happy. It might even make Mac happy. It was even possible that going home would make her happy, too. At least for a little while.

Except she couldn't honestly say anything had truly changed. Mac was still ignoring her, only now the distance between them could be measured in miles, too. For her part, she still nursed a resentment against her husband that she couldn't define or understand.

Maybe she should consider going back on antidepressants. If this mood lingered, she'd make a doctor's appointment.

In recent weeks she'd been doing all right. She had found a happiness here that provided a soothing balm to her soul. She'd made friends. Bringing the Bristlecone back to life was an enjoyable challenge. Tonight, however, she had a real case of the blues. It must have shown, too, because on the way up the aisle, Sage gave her a measuring look. "You okay, Ali?"

"Yes. Just tired. I'm going to call it an early night."

Ali filed out behind Rose and the Raffertys as they

exited the theater. Thinking that a call to Caitlin might cheer her up, she was digging in her purse, not looking where she was going, when Colt Rafferty stopped abruptly and said in an admiring tone, "Now, that's a car."

His sister-in-law's tone matched Colt's. "And that's a man."

Ali looked up from her purse to see what her friends were talking about and froze. "Actually, that's my husband."

He leaned against the passenger-side door of a Porsche parked in front of the theater, his arms folded, his legs crossed at the ankles. He wore faded jeans, the solid brown sport shirt she'd given him for Christmas, cuffs turned back twice as was his habit, hiking boots, and a look in his eyes that she hadn't seen in months.

Her mouth went dry. Her pulse began to pound. Everything inside her seemed to swell. "Mac?"

"Hello, Ali-cat." He pushed off the car and stood with his legs wide, his thumbs hooked in the front pockets of his jeans, his hips cocked forward. His heavy-lidded stare locked on her.

Oh. Oh, wow. Oh wow oh wow oh wow.

She knew that look. Knew that tone. That name. She knew what he wanted—and what he intended.

The dark cloud that had hung over her for months evaporated in a hormonal burst that left her itchy and anxious and wet. He sauntered toward her, ignoring Rose, ignoring the Raffertys. His focus was on her and her alone, and Ali wanted to shout and jump for joy.

He wanted sex. With her. Now.

Hallelujah!

Halting an arm's length away, he held out his hand. "Come with me."

Wishing she'd worn perfume today, thrilled she'd made the mani-pedi decision, trying to remember if she'd shaved her legs when she showered that morning, Ali put her hand in Mac's. He tugged her toward the car, opened the door for her, then reached down to fasten her seat belt. Another time, she'd have considered that overkill, but tonight she liked having his hands on her.

He walked around the car, opened the driver's door, then slid into his seat. Without looking at her, he started the car.

She waited nervously for him to speak, but he didn't say a word. Finally the tension got to be too much for her. "Mac?"

"Wait. Just . . . wait."

When he turned the corner, she wanted to know where he was taking her, but she believed she'd figure it out soon enough. When he turned into the drive that led to the Creekside Cabins, she caught her breath. He'd rented a room. Rented a bed.

Thank you, Lord.

He shifted into park and shut off the engine. For a moment he sat without moving, then he twisted his head, pinned her with his gaze, and said, "If you don't want this, tell me now."

Despite the demands of her neglected hormones, Ali gave the question a moment's thought. Did she have reservations? Was this the right thing to be doing when they still had an ocean's worth of problems?

He'd come for her. He wanted her. It had been so long. She licked her lips. "I want . . ." *This. It. You.*

He climbed out of the car as she fumbled with her seat belt with shaking fingers. By the time she undid her belt he was there opening her door. He took her arm, tugged her up and out, then slammed the door and backed her against it, his hot gaze boring into hers.

Then he clamped his hands around her waist and lifted her, pressing her against the car, holding her there with the weight of his body, grinding his groin against her as he blistered her mouth with his kiss. In his passion, she tasted temper and frustration and need. Dark, glorious need.

She kissed him back just as hard, with just as much frustration and an equal amount of need. What followed amounted to battle.

Fast, furious, and—but for the shield of a stand of fir trees—public. She was on fire and knew she surprised him with the force of her response. She tore at his clothes even as he tore at hers. She wanted naked skin against naked skin right here, right now, or she thought she just might die.

She yanked at the button of his jeans as he ripped the front hooks of her bra and her breasts spilled from confinement. When his mouth fastened over her nipple, she cried out in sweet relief. *Dear Lord in heaven.*

Her hand found him. Thick and hard and wet at the tip. He groaned against her breast as she gripped him with one hand and tried to shove the other down his pants.

Then he tore his mouth away, muttered a curse, and grabbed her by the wrist. "Wait."

She whimpered. Now that she finally had him, she didn't want to let him go.

"Dammit, Ali. We can't." He tugged her hand out of his jeans, then scooped her up into his arms and carried her toward the cabin.

Crazily, it made Ali want to cry. It was the most romantic thing he'd done in five years. Ten years. Maybe their entire marriage.

The cabin's locked door interrupted the romance of the moment, and while she'd have loved him to make the grand gesture of kicking in the door, Mac was, after all, a federal judge. Couldn't risk a charge of public lewdness or destruction of property.

Nevertheless, he did a fine job of maintaining the urgency of the moment, shoving her against the door and going at her again as he dug in his pocket for the cabin key. When he got the door open, she stumbled back inside, losing her balance. He caught her before she fell and literally threw her on the bed.

He fell on her, kissing her over and over, all over, until she was feverish with desire. He stripped her naked; she tore his clothes away from that firm, hard body. She skimmed her hands over him until he dragged both of her arms above her head and captured her wrists in a single large hand.

His other hand went exploring where she needed him most.

Mac still knew her body as well as she did herself, and his fingers found the exact spots with the perfect amounts of pressure and speed. He knew when and where to be rough, when and how to be gentle. He knew exactly what to do to make her whimper, quiver, and surrender. "Mac, please."

Mac released her hands and rose above her, his dark eyes glittering. "Mine," he murmured as he pressed inside her, stretched her, filled her. "Mine."

Yes. Always. She wrapped her legs around him and her body clenched, gripping him hard. She met him thrust for thrust, matching his rhythm, the restless need building higher. Higher. She'd missed him. Oh, how she'd missed him.

He hissed. He growled. He groaned. He canted her hips, adjusting the angle so that he reached deeper inside her. That glorious pressure built, lifting her, sending her whirling, twirling, shooting to the stars.

All the way to heaven.

Yours, Mac Timberlake. And you are mine, too.

Mac collapsed on top of Ali, tried to catch his breath, and thanked the good Lord that he hadn't had a heart attack. It had been months since he'd been that worked up. Years. Hell, decades.

As was their long-standing habit, when he could move again, he rolled onto his side, bringing her with him, keeping her tucked against him. For the first time since he'd seen her walking out of that theater, the red haze had cleared from Mac's vision.

Beside him, Ali started to giggle. He cocked open one eye and arched a brow. She pointed toward his feet.

He was still wearing one sock. One corner of his mouth twisted up in a rueful grin, and he toed the sock off as Ali sighed and snuggled up against him. He trailed a finger slowly up and down her back and steeped in the pleasure of holding his wife in his arms again.

They didn't speak. The peace between them was something to treasure, a fragile gift, and it appeared that neither of them wanted to shatter it. She smelled familiar yet new. Fresh. He wondered if she'd begun to use a new lotion or if it was the mountain air and sunshine that made the difference.

From out of nowhere, a pang of sadness cut through him. Why had it come to this? What had happened to them?

This was the first sex they'd had in months. The first good sex they'd had in over a year. But had it solved anything other than his case of blue balls? It would be great if he could believe it had, but he knew better. There was more to this drama of Ali's than drama.

When the questions began to multiply, he shut them off. He refused to let the doubts and worries ruin this moment. Plenty of time for that later. Right now he wasn't done with her.

Mac nuzzled her neck, then sucked her earlobe into his mouth and nipped at it. She shivered in response. Ali's ears had always been near the top of the list of her erogenous zones. With the urgency out of the way and Ali cuddled against him like a kitten, he decided to please them both by revisiting each of those spots on her delectable body at a more leisurely pace. So that's exactly what he did.

When it was done, when she lay languid and sated in his arms and he drifted toward sleep, savoring the sweet exhaustion of sweaty, earthy sex, her hesitant voice asked, "Mac? Are we going to talk?"

Everything within him rebelled at the thought. "Could we wait? Could we take tonight, maybe tomorrow, too? Just, I don't know, be together?"

A long minute ticked by before she said, "I'd like that."

"Me too. I need it, Ali-cat. We need it."

She nestled against him, sighed with pleasure, and absently played with the hair on his chest. "Are you hungry?"

He thought a moment, then said, "Give me a few minutes. I'm not a young stud anymore."

She pulled his chest hair. "I meant for supper."

"Oh." He grinned, knowing that was what she'd meant all along. "I could eat something. How about you?"

"I'm torn between food and sleep at the moment."

He tucked her head beneath his chin, inhaled the citrus scent of her shampoo, and said, "How about a catnap? Then we can grab a bite to eat, and after that I'll probably be hungry again. Sound like a plan?"

"The best plan ever."

For the first time in longer than she could remember, Ali woke up warm. Toasty warm. Well, actually hot, since when she woke up her husband's mouth was tending to her breast.

When they finally crawled out of bed and showered, she grimaced at the idea of putting on yesterday's clothes. Still, she didn't want to take Mac back to the carriage house. Not yet. So she pulled on her slacks and shirt and, while he was shaving, called out, "I'll run and get us coffee and breakfast, okay?"

"Sure."

On her way, she bypassed the Mocha Moose coffeehouse and headed for the carriage house at Angel's Rest. She started stripping the moment she made it inside and went straight to her bedroom. From the bottom drawer of her dresser, she took out the lingerie she'd purchased while shopping with Sarah for Sage's wedding shower gifts last fall—a lacy, push-up, fire-engine-red bra and a matching pair of panties. They still had the tags attached. She'd had neither the occasion or desire to wear them before now, and she didn't even know why she'd brought them from home. As she pulled the tags off the panties, she wasn't totally certain she wanted to wear them today. They were thong panties. She'd never worn thong panties in her life. The whole wedgie thing had turned her off the idea, but Sarah had goaded her into buying them.

Now, faced with a choice between butt floss that just might make Mac's eyes pop out or a drawer full of plain ivory panties, she decided to go for broke and donned the new lingerie. Darned if wearing them didn't make her feel just a tad trashy.

She pulled on a clingy purple shirt and a pair of jeans, then hurried back to the Mocha Moose, where she purchased two tall coffees and two huge blueberry muffins.

Mac was waiting for her in one of the Adirondack chairs on the lawn beside the creek. Seeing her, he smiled, his gray eyes knowingly amused. "I figured you'd gone to change your clothes. Couldn't bear the idea of wearing yesterday's panties, could you?"

"No."

Accepting the coffee she handed him, he casually asked, "Didn't want me seeing your place?"

It was no casual question, she understood. "It's not that. Okay, that's part of it. I don't want to take you there this morning. I'll cook dinner for us there if you'd like."

"How about we cook dinner together?"

Happiness radiated through her like sunshine. "That would be lovely. So, what would you like to do today?"

"Well, Chase told me there's an alpine trail near here that has spectacular scenery. Apparently there's a jeep rental place in town? Weather is supposed to be good. Would you like to give that a go?"

"Absolutely. We could stop by the grocery store and get stuff for a picnic, too, if you'd like."

"Sounds like a plan."

Ali directed Mac to the outfitters, where he rented a jeep for the day. After filling out paperwork, he added a few items to the tab, including fishing poles, worms, and salmon eggs for bait. "Do you have a license, Ali?"

"Actually, I do." Noting his surprise, she explained. "My place is beside Angel Creek. Fishing is surprisingly relaxing."

"Have you caught anything?"

"I did. Once. I caught a ten-inch rainbow trout."

"Oh, yeah? What did you do then? Who took it off the hook?"

She wanted to say she'd done it herself, but she knew he wouldn't believe the lie. "I carried it over to the teenage boys fishing upstream of me. One of the boys reminded me so much of Stephen."

"What did he do, scold you with a look?"

Nodding, she sighed. "Tsked his tongue, too, and then he offered to teach me how to take the fish off the hook."

Mac smirked. "I could have told him not to waste his breath."

She opened her mouth to make her usual response, which ran along the lines of *That's why I have a husband and sons,* but thought better of it, considering she was currently living—and fishing—alone. Instead, she said, "Let me help carry some of that to the jeep."

He handed her the two fishing poles, then asked, "Are we walking to the grocery or driving?"

"The Trading Post is at the other end of town. Let's take the jeep."

At the grocery, Ali found Lori Reese manning the cash register and started to introduce the young woman to her husband, but Mac surprised her by saying, "Lori and I met last night. I was wandering around town looking for you and she clued me in on the fact that you had tickets to the play." To Lori, he said, "Thanks again for your help."

"Glad I knew the scoop," Lori replied.

"And I'm glad I finally had the pleasure of meeting you. I recall that Chase told me you want to be a veterinarian?"

"Yes, sir."

Mac and Lori discussed her freshman year at Texas A&M for a moment, then Ali asked, "Does your mom stock picnic baskets of any kind?"

"Yes, they're in the side room on the shelf beside the T-shirts."

"Excellent. We're driving the high country trail today, and we wanted to take something for lunch."

"The grapes are really good," Lori said. "We also got in a selection of cheeses you might look at."

"Thanks, sweetie." While Mac selected a bottle of wine, Ali filled her basket with fruit, cheese, crackers, and her husband's favorite guilty-pleasure junk food—Cheetos. Twenty minutes later they turned onto the narrow dirt road that took them up into the hills.

They didn't talk much while they drove, but they communicated plenty. Mac kept hold of Ali's hand, even when he shifted gears, and she thought back to college days, when he drove a secondhand Ford Crown Victoria that he'd been given by an older gentleman for whom he'd done yard work. Mac had been embarrassed by the car, but Ali had loved it. The bench seat meant she could sit beside him on their dates. After the summer when he'd interned at the Chicago firm and finally made enough money to buy what he called a real car, the Mustang he'd chosen came with bucket seats. She'd lamented the loss of the Crown Vic and explained why. That's when he first held her hand while he shifted gears.

She'd never really noticed when he'd abandoned the practice. After they married? When they had children? She guessed it didn't really matter because it was, after all, a very teenage thing to do.

Yet she felt like a teenager again this morning. She felt renewed and rejuvenated and young.

She felt happy.

"I asked the guy at the outfitters to recommend a good fishing spot along this drive," Mac said, pulling a folded piece of paper out of his shirt pocket. "He gave me this—a place called Heartache Falls. Said it's the map they reserve for locals and that it's off the beaten path, but it's a beautiful spot beside a little lake just downstream from a little waterfall. If we don't mind hiking a little ways, we should have the place to ourselves. You up for a walk?"

"Absolutely." She studied the map, glad she'd worn her boots to the theater last night. "Heartache Falls. I've heard people talk about it, but it's not on any of the tourist maps. It'll be nice to get away from the crowd."

"You call this a crowd?"

"For Eternity Springs it is. I know how important it is for us to attract tourist dollars, and since it's the height of the season, I'm glad to see the town bustling. The majority of the businesses in town make the bulk of their profit for the entire year between June and August. I admit I enjoyed the sleepy days in town before the summer people arrived."

"The town was bustling last night. So, tell me about this Lost Angel mystery. I caught the last half of the play. How much of it is fact and how much is fiction?"

"More fiction than fact, definitely. We know that the human remains found in the cellar at Cavanaugh House along with a nineteenth-century wedding dress and thirty bars of silver was Daniel Murphy's lost Angel, his bride-to-be, Winifred Smith. Pretty much everything else was conjecture."

"I expected your killer to be the lantern-jawed gardener."

"That's our banker. He says playing the villain

comes naturally to him. So were you shocked that the sweet Gertie Gallagher did the dirty deed?"

He grinned. "Yes, you definitely caught me by surprise on that one. I suspected her, then dismissed her as a red herring. It's an entertaining show. Poor old Daniel Murphy."

"He believed he lost his good luck when she disappeared."

Mac reached over and took her hand once again. "I can relate. So he drowned his sorrow in suds, lost his fortune, and had to sell his mountain, hmm? Which one is it, by the way?"

"Murphy Mountain?" Ali looked around, only just then realizing how high they had climbed above the valley that nestled Eternity Springs. "Oh, wow. Look at this view. Isn't it gorgeous?"

Rather than take in the scenery, he looked straight at her. "Absolutely."

Ali felt herself blush. She was thrilled at his attention—truly she was—and yet a part of her wondered where this attention had been for the past six months. Six years. In that moment, she experienced a stirring of unease.

Had anything changed? Anything at all?

Maybe yes, probably no. How could she know unless they talked at a level deeper than the surface? Except she didn't want to talk deeper. She was enjoying the surface. The sailing was smoother here. And smooth sailing was what she and her husband needed right now.

So stay on the surface. Let him flirt with you. Let him seduce you. Seduce him right back.

Ali believed that if they managed to fix the physical

part of the marriage, that would go a long way toward fixing the other troublesome spots, too.

She studied Mac, who had finally turned to look at the vista beyond. Maybe that was what he thought, too. Maybe that was what had brought him to Eternity Springs yesterday and lay behind his request that they hold off talking about anything more serious than the Lost Angel mystery.

Considering how she'd spent last night, Ali had to give a thumbs-up to that plan.

She pointed toward the snowcapped mountain that rose to the east of them. "That's Murphy. It's owned by descendants of Lucien Davenport, the third member of the trio who made the Silver Miracle strike and founded Eternity Springs."

"Have you met any of them? Davenports or Murphys?"

Ali hesitated. Sarah and Lori had shared the truth about Lori's paternity with her in confidence. In the past, situations like this had been the subject of debate in her marriage. Ali's opinion had been that she didn't keep secrets from her husband, any secret, that though they were a couple, they were a unit. They were one. Sharing something with one of them meant sharing with both of them.

Mac, on the other hand, could teach the CIA about keeping secrets. To Mac, a confidence shared with him was simply that, period. He would no more share it with her than a priest would break the seal of the confessional. Ali had long nursed a resentment about his stance. Unfair, perhaps, but real.

This time, however, rather than share Lori's secret, she said, "No."

Then Ali said to herself, *Surface. Surface.*

She grabbed the map to the fishing spot. "We should be getting close to the turnoff."

"All right. Help me watch for it."

Ten minutes later, she pointed toward a gate marked B&P. "There it is."

"B & P. Is that another area ranch?"

"I don't know. I haven't heard of it if it is."

Mac used the access code provided by the outfitters to open the gate, then Ali closed it behind them after Mac drove the jeep through. The road became little more than a rutted path winding its way downhill through a forest of fir, pine, and aspen. She watched for wildlife in the trees as they drove, hoping to spot elk or bighorn sheep. She'd just as soon not see any bears or mountain lions.

"The outfitters said to look for a pull-off shortly after we pass off private land into the national forest," Mac said. "We park there, then Heartache Falls is about a twenty-minute hike. You still up for it?"

"Absolutely. I have my heart set on trout for supper."

They located the turnoff, parked, and gathered their supplies. "There's the trailhead," Mac said. "You ready?"

"Lead on, Magellan."

Before they'd taken a dozen steps, a familiar voice called out, "Hello, Ali!"

"Celeste?" Ali looked around in surprise.

Celeste Blessing stood behind them on the road, her Honda Gold Wing motorcycle at her side. It wasn't running. Ali said, "I didn't hear you ride up."

"I didn't ride. Not the past hundred yards or so.

I'm afraid I failed to check my gas gauge when I started out this morning. I've run out of gas."

"Oh, no," Ali replied.

"Foolish of me, but maybe it was meant to happen so that I could run into you." Celeste beamed a smile at Mac. "You must be Mac. Ali speaks so highly of you. I'm Celeste Blessing."

While Mac stood there looking surprised, Ali introduced him to her friend. He cleared his throat and said, "I'm pleased to meet you, too, ma'am. I know Ali is excited about her work with the restaurant."

Now it was Ali's turn to be surprised. They hadn't discussed the restaurant much at all. The kids must have told him how much she loved the project. "Were you out on a ride enjoying this beautiful day like we are, Celeste?"

"Partly. I did take the long way here from town because it is such a lovely morning. However, I'm on my way to visit Bear and Patricia. He's our local mountain man, tour guide, and taxidermist. Have you seen his yurt, Ali?"

"No, I haven't."

"It's definitely something to see, and it's just up the road a little bit." She eyed the jeep, then glanced back at her motorcycle. "Could I trouble you two to give me a lift to Bear's place? I'm sure he'll have a gas can and fuel to share."

"That won't be any trouble at all," Mac assured her.

He pushed the bike safely off the road while Ali and Celeste took seats in the jeep. As Mac resumed the drive up the rutted dirt road, Ali made a connection. "The B and P on the gate. I'll bet that stands for Bear and Patricia."

"You're right," Celeste confirmed. "Bear owns a wonderful strip of property that meanders along the national forest boundary."

Ten minutes later, the older woman directed Mac onto a side road. When the jeep topped a rise, Ali spotted the yurt. It sat beside a picturesque creek and offered a spectacular view of three of Colorado's Fourteeners, mountains that rose to an altitude above fourteen thousand feet.

"What a view," Mac said, then added, "And what an interesting shelter."

"Wait until you see inside it," Celeste told them. "It's wonderful."

"Bear is one of the area's more interesting residents," Ali told Mac. "He's trapped and stuffed an amazing collection of local wildlife that he donated to the school. He lives in this yurt year-round with his wife, Patricia Robertson, who worked for NASA before moving to Colorado to live with Bear."

"She was a rocket scientist," Celeste elaborated.

"Really?" Mac looked amused.

"They're newlyweds, too. An interesting couple." Ali studied the yurt. "With an interesting home."

The yurt was a large circular tent with vertical walls and a conical roof modeled after those used by nomads on the steppes of Central Asia. Bear's yurt had what appeared to be a canvas outer shell and a wooden door frame and door. As Mac killed the ignition, the door opened and Bear stepped outside.

Mac took one look at him and grinned. Bear was the quintessential mountain man, with long hair and a full beard. He dressed in deerskin and carried a rifle. Identifying his visitors, he set down his gun, then lifted a hand in a wave and called out in his naturally raspy voice, "Peaches, it's Miss Celeste."

Peaches, Ali realized, was his pet name for Patricia, who joined him to greet the visitors. Ali introduced Mac, and Celeste explained her gasoline predicament. "Not a worry. I'll get you all fixed up," Bear declared. Noting the curiosity in Mac's gaze as he studied the yurt, he added, "Can I show you our home? It's a lot fancier inside than it used to be. Peaches fixed it up once she moved up here."

"He means I had him put in a septic system and a solar-heated bathroom," Patricia explained.

The interior of the yurt was spacious and lovely— if decorating with animal skins was your thing. It had a wooden floor, rustic handmade furniture, and a queen-sized bed that looked as plush and comfortable as any Ali had owned. A second door opened to a short corridor that led to the facilities. "She tells me not to call it an outhouse anymore since we have indoor plumbing," Bear explained.

"It's wonderful," Ali said, meaning it.

"It is. I'll be sad to leave it," Patricia responded.

"You're going somewhere?"

Patricia smiled at Bear, who gave an exaggerated roll of his eyes, sighed, then took her hand. "My woman has been offered an opportunity to teach in Brazil. She wants to do it, and I can't let her go alone."

"What will you do with your yurt?" Ali asked. "It is portable, isn't it? Will you take it with you?"

"No. I'm thinking of leasing it," Bear said. "I'm

not ready to sell, but since the short route is only twenty minutes into town, I might find someone in town who'd want to rent."

Patricia patted his hand. "We have time for him to decide. We don't leave until September."

They made small talk for a bit, and Bear invited them to stay for lunch. Celeste accepted, but Ali wanted to be alone with her husband. "Thank you, but maybe another time?" Ali said. "Mac and I brought a picnic hamper with us, and we planned to fish a bit below Heartache Falls."

Bear nodded. "It's a good spot. One side of the creek is my land, the other is Uncle Sam's. You'll have it to yourself today—since it's a Saturday in July, all the locals are working."

Ali shot her husband a saucy wink. "Mac claims he's gonna catch me a trout dinner."

Bear gave him a measuring look. "You a fly fisherman?"

"I am."

"Hmph. Try the stream right before it widens into the lake." Bear strode over to a table, opened a drawer, and removed two items. "Give these a try," he told Mac, handing them over. "They're what I call my peaches-and-cream specials, and they've brought me nothing but luck."

"Thanks. I'll definitely give them a go."

After that, Mac and Ali took their leave, and soon they were back at the trailhead. Ali carried the blanket, while Mac toted the fishing gear and picnic basket.

They didn't speak as they hiked. Ali drew a deep breath of air redolent with the fragrance of the forest—the clean, crisp scent of evergreen paired with the darker aroma of damp earth and decay. An occasional gust of breeze whispered through the leaves and needles of the trees, but for the most part, the woods remained quiet but for the soft crunch of twigs and sticks and dead leaves beneath their feet. In spots, sunlight dappled the forest floor. In the shadows, monster-sized toadstools made her think of leprechauns and pixies—until a two-foot-long brown snake slithering by wiped all thought of anything cute from her mind. Ali let out a little squeal, then stepped closer to Mac.

"You doing all right, honey?" he asked.

"I'm fine," she said, keeping her gaze on the forest floor. "How much farther, do you think?"

He stopped and took her hand. "I do believe we're there."

Ali halted, looked up, and said, "Oh, wow."

The high meadow was about the size of their neighborhood park in Denver and was awash in a sea of wildflowers, primarily yellows and pinks with a few blues and purples mixed in. At the far end a waterfall splashed down to a creek approximately six feet wide and lined with grasses and brush. The creek snaked its way through the center of the small clearing, then disappeared into the forest. It was a small, beautiful oasis.

"Definitely worth the hike," Mac said. "You want to pick a spot for the picnic blanket?"

He stepped aside and she led the way, spreading their forest-green blanket atop a patch of white columbines and clover a few feet from the water. Ali considered searching for a shamrock. *Maybe later.*

Following a brief debate, they decided to fish for a while before they ate. Mac, her hero, baited her hook with a nightcrawler rather than the salmon eggs she ordinarily used since she didn't do worms, and then he walked upstream with his fly rod. Ali found a spot where she could sit on a boulder and dip her hook into a crystal-clear pool. She watched the water gurgle and bubble and froth its way downstream and drew a parallel to her marriage.

Like this idyllic mountain stream, her marriage had frothed and bubbled along year after year, enduring periods of white water and enjoying slower-paced moments of peace and beauty. But over time, things changed. The bedrock of her marriage eroded, not by any cataclysmic event, but by the constant wear and tear of life.

Before yesterday, she would have said that all they had left was sand. Quicksand, even. But Mac's trip to Eternity Springs had given her second thoughts about her second thoughts. Maybe portions of their marriage bedrock had eroded, but not all of it. Sure, they had a few sandy spots, but they also had their share of granite.

Because first and foremost, she and Mac still loved each other. Maybe they'd allowed the detritus of life to hide it, but now Ali knew it was still there—solid and steadfast and strong.

Her gaze fell to her left hand and the ring she'd worn for half her life. Mac had chosen quality over carats in choosing the stone, and he'd presented his reasons for doing so with as much care and attention to detail as he'd used when he'd argued his very first case in court. He need not have bothered. Ali had loved the ring from the moment he offered it to her. For years after he'd started making money, he'd tried to replace it with something flashier. She'd refused to allow it. He'd given her the very best he could give. What could be better than that?

She wiggled her fingers. Sunlight glinted off the stone. Solid, steadfast, and strong. Just a little dimmed and dingy. Just in need of a good cleaning and polishing. Maybe that was the purpose of this time apart, maybe these last few months had been a dust rag for her marriage.

You've mixed up your metaphors, Alison.

"Actually, I've mixed up my life."

She focused on a leaf as it swirled and turned on the water, dancing it's way downstream. What was she doing in Eternity Springs? After this trip, Mac would expect her to come home. She knew that as sure as the creek was cold.

A part of her wanted nothing more than to do just that. She wanted to go to sleep with him beside her in their bed each night and wake up snuggled against him every morning. She wanted to bake him pies and argue politics and battle over control of the television remote. She wanted to kiss him good-bye when he left for work in the morning and revisit his reaction to her garter belt collection at night.

So do it. The work on the restaurant was almost done. She could get serious about hiring a cook instead of piddling along at it like she'd done so far. She could do most of that from Denver. She should just do it. She could go home with Mac tomorrow. Monday he would go off to work and she would . . . what?

I can volunteer, join a quilt group, go to lunch with

friends. If she went home, all would be right with her father's world once again. He'd surely want to resume their weekly lunches. She'd once again be a lady who lunches.

Oh, joy.

"Yes, joy," she softly declared, wanting to mean it. She'd be with Mac again. The man whom she'd vowed to love and cherish in good times and in bad, in sickness and in health—a vow she'd allowed to get lost in the malaise of her middle age. Well, shame on her. He'd made the first step, and now it was up to her to take the next one—all the way back to Denver—where she would be happy if it killed her.

She'd go back to her therapist. If things got shaky, she'd insist on marriage counseling. Her dad had been right about that. She should have suggested counseling again rather than running off to the mountains. Who knows, he might have agreed. Stranger things had happened. A NASA rocket scientist was living with Bear in the mountains.

I've been so happy in the mountains.

She could be, she *would* be happy in the city again. Mac would be happy to have her home. Her father would be pleased. The kids would be thrilled.

Everyone would be happy. Everyone would be satisfied.

She blinked away the tears that stung her eyes and told herself to grow up. This was her choice. It was the right choice. She could find ways to occupy herself in the city again. She could get another job if that was what she decided she wanted. She could make a new set of friends, interesting people like Sage and

Sarah and Celeste. She could even join another quilting bee if she wanted to continue learning that skill.

Frankly, at this point in her life, she could do almost anything she wanted. She had money. She had time. The world was her oyster. She could do whatever caught her fancy.

As long as she did it in Denver.

Because her husband was a federal judge. A federal judgeship was a lifetime appointment. He'd be working in Denver forever—unless political winds blew his way, and then they'd go to Washington, D.C., the pinnacle, the culmination of his dreams.

But what about your dream?

Mac was her dream.

Oh, yeah? Well, you're his dream, too, but he doesn't have to give up one for the other, does he?

That was okay. It was just the way it was. She'd known that when she married him and made those vows. It was wrong of her to have buyer's remorse at this late date.

Besides, she wasn't feeling buyer's remorse. She loved Mac. She wanted to be with him. Just because she'd found happiness here in Eternity Springs didn't mean that she couldn't find happiness again back in Denver. She'd been happy in Denver for a lot of years. Just because her kids were grown and gone and her social life no longer revolved around their activities didn't mean she couldn't invite one of the other school moms to join a quilting bee with her. Just because Mac's move onto the bench complicated her relationships at the family firm didn't mean she couldn't continue to attend yoga classes with the trio of female attorneys she'd made friends with years ago. They simply had to try to get past the awkwardness. They could do that. They were all bright women. Ali could have friends in Denver. Could have a life in Denver that was just as enriching and fulfilling as the one she'd begun to build in Eternity Springs.

If she said it often enough, maybe she'd begin to believe it.

How long she sat staring unseeingly at the water lost in thought she didn't know, but it wasn't until Mac reached out and took hold of her fishing pole that she jerked back to attention.

"Honey," he said, "here's a fishing tip. You'll catch more fish if you remove the ones you've already caught off the hook."

"Oh." She watched him pull a twelve-inch trout out of the stream. "I got distracted. How did you do?"

"I caught dinner. Made me hungry for lunch." He removed the trout from its hook, added the fish to his stringer, then returned it to the water and washed his hands. "Are you ready to eat?"

"Sure," she said, shrugging off her melancholy and smiling. Moments later, she reached into the picnic basket and set out the bounty they'd purchased at the Trading Post while Mac pulled the cork on a bottle of wine.

While they ate, they spoke of inconsequential things, and Ali thought they both made an effort to avoid subjects that could introduce controversy into the conversation. Gradually, helped by wine, a sweet summer peach, and a silly story Mac told about one of their neighbors, Ali relaxed and pushed the last lingering worries from her mind.

So relaxed was she that she had only a mild grip on her wineglass as she brought it to her mouth for a sip when a noise—a loud animal noise—sounded from right behind her. She startled, spilling half a glass of wine down the front of her shirt.

"Yeeek," she squealed, whirling around. "Was that a . . . moo?"

Mac's gaze was locked on her chest. "Uh-huh."

"From a cow?"

"That's a steer, Alison."

"What's a steer doing here?" She grabbed paper napkins from the picnic basket and wiped at the stain on her shirt. "An elk, okay. A mountain lion, fine. Shoot, even a bear makes sense. But a cow?"

"A steer." Amusement shimmered in his voice. "Ranches usually do have cattle, honey."

"I thought we'd crossed into national forest. I saw a sign."

"Hmm. You are right about that. I guess this steer can't read."

"Very funny, Timberlake. This is the first time I've worn this shirt and I've spilled wine on it. It's probably ruined."

"Take it off and rinse it in the creek before the stain sets." When she paused and looked worriedly around, he added, "No one will see you but the steer, and not only is it impossible for him to tattle on you, he doesn't have the equipment needed to take advantage of the situation. I, on the other hand . . ." He waggled his eyebrows wolfishly.

Ali frowned at him.

The amusement in his eyes transformed to heat. "Take off your shirt, Ali-cat."

A ribbon of heat fluttered through her. "I guess I do need to soak the stain."

"You certainly do."

After glancing around the meadow one more time, she reached down to pull the shirt up and off, then hesitated. "If I do, will you give me your shirt to wear on the way back to town?"

"I certainly will."

He sucked in an audible breath when she revealed the sexy red bra. When she knelt beside the creek and leaned over to rinse the shirt, he shifted to get a better view. Ali tended to the shirt, honestly fretful over the stain.

When she'd done her best with the shirt, she stretched it out to dry atop the boulder where she'd fished. When she turned around, Mac sat stretched out on their blanket, propped up on his elbows. He said, "I want to make love to you, Ali. Here. Now."

She licked her lips. It had been a long time since they'd last made love outdoors. This wasn't like Mac at all. He'd always put the kibosh on similar risky behavior when she'd proposed it. She pointed across the creek. "That is a national park. What if a park ranger comes along? It wouldn't look good for a federal judge to get arrested for public indecency."

"I'm of a mood to live on the wild side for a bit."

Just wait until he got a look at her panties—such as they were.

And yet it didn't feel right. She didn't feel right. She hadn't quite shaken her brooding mood.

Nevertheless, she made an effort to do just that by

reminding herself how much she'd missed him, how much she'd wanted his attention, how much she loved him. This was an off-the-charts romantic moment. What sort of fool would she be if she didn't take advantage of it?

Determined now, Ali threw herself into the effort. She toed off her shoes and socks, then turned around, facing away from him. Releasing the button on her jeans, she tugged down the zipper and slowly, sinuously, slid them down over her hips and off.

"Holy mother of God," Mac prayed.

She glanced back at him over her shoulder. "Like what you see?"

He scrambled to his feet, grabbed a corner of the blanket, and yanked it out from beneath the picnic basket. He carried it around behind the boulder, where tall grasses and a leafy bush provided additional shelter from any potential prying eyes, spread it on the ground, then returned to where Ali stood. As he lifted her into his arms, he said, "You take my breath away, Alison. You always have."

He laid her down onto the blanket and made sweet, almost reverent love to her.

Throughout the process, Ali tried to lose herself as she had before. She desperately sought that closeness, that sense of being one with him. She yearned for the connection they had reestablished during the night and earlier this morning, and while he gave her physical gratification, emotional satisfaction remained out of reach. She tried hard to pretend otherwise, but she simply couldn't shake the effects of her decision.

Mac, always perceptive, noticed. He rolled off her and lay beside her. They didn't touch. They didn't speak. Ali thought that if she stretched out her foot, she might find frost on their picnic blanket.

That's when she knew she couldn't do it. Sure, he'd made the first move by coming to her, but nothing really had changed. The problems that had driven her to the mountains still existed. Pretending otherwise, trying to wish it otherwise, didn't change a thing.

Their blissful idyll of peace and togetherness was over.

TEN

As Mac reached for his boxers, he felt old and tired and worn. Not because of the sex. The sex itself left his body energized. What dragged him down were the thoughts running through his mind. So much for his hope that his wife had returned to her senses. Been here, done this before with Alison.

Welcome back to reality.

Welcome back to misery.

Welcome back to his frostbitten marriage.

He couldn't reach her. She'd gone off into that world of hers where he couldn't follow. No matter how much he tried, no matter how hard he reached for her, she shut him out. They were right back where they'd started.

Mac wanted to drop back his head and howl his frustration toward the heavens. Instead, he pulled on his jeans, reached for his socks, and took a few moments to consider his options. He could pretend he hadn't noticed. He'd had more sex in the past twenty-four hours than he'd had all year, and the prospect of giving it up again was nothing to take lightly.

But the cost of such action was high. In those last few months when he'd continued to try with Ali, sex had given him relief but no pleasure. If that was all he was going to get out of the effort, his hand would do the job well enough with much less fuss.

His other option was to call her on it. Maybe if he did it in a nice, gentle manner, she wouldn't get defensive the way she had the last time he'd attempted to broach the subject. Maybe if he'd confronted the elephant in their bed the first time he'd sensed it, the animal wouldn't have grown so big so fast, and they might have avoided the trouble that eventually sent her running for the mountains.

The trick would be finding that nice, gentle manner within himself and maintaining it. He wasn't feeling very nice or gentle at the moment.

He shoved his foot into first one boot, then the other. One thing he did know with complete certainty was that he didn't want history to repeat. If they were ever going to fix whatever was wrong with their marriage, it had to be now. *So hold on to your cool, Timberlake. Keep your eye on the goal here. You want Ali back home where she belongs and for life to be normal again. The way to make that happen is to lock away your emotions for the time being and use your brain.*

Mac blew out a heavy breath, yanked on his shoelaces, tied the bows, and then rolled to his feet and turned to face his wife.

Ali had dressed in her underwear, then pulled on the wet shirt. Seeing her in the dripping shirt made him see red that had nothing to do with wine stains and everything to do with the sense that happiness was slipping beyond his grasp. "I told you I'd give you my shirt, Alison."

"I'm fine."

She said it all perky and sweet with a smile that didn't reach her eyes. That only stoked his anger more. Mac shoved his hands in his back pockets and dropped his chin to his chest. A litany of curses ran through his mind and his temper threatened to erupt, but he determinedly reined it in. Finally he judged himself to be in control enough to say, "Okay, I think it's better we have this talk now instead of later. In fact, I think we'd be better off today if we'd had it a long time ago. I need to understand what is going on here, Alison."

"What do you mean?"

"I couldn't reach you just now. This morning I could. Yesterday, too." Frustration thickened his voice as he finished, "But not now. I need to know why."

For a moment she looked like she might try to deny it, but he folded his arms and leaned against the boulder nearby, signaling that he was settling in for the duration.

Ali sighed and began to pace. "I'm sorry. It's my fault. I'd decided—"

She abruptly shut her mouth. When she didn't elaborate, he prodded, "Decided what?"

She halted, shoved her fingers through her hair, then plucked the wet shirt away from her skin and flapped the hem, attempting to dry it. "I'd decided we need to talk about our marriage, too."

And that was such a turnoff to her? Mac clamped his mouth tight to avoid the question that would certainly make her defensive. "Okay, good. Where do you want to start?"

"I don't know. It's almost overwhelming to think

about. I know we need to talk, but I'm worried about what we will say. What if we hurt each other and end up making things worse?"

"We're living apart, Ali. How can that be any worse?" When she looked at him then with tears in her eyes, he spoke from the depths of his soul. "Come home, Ali. Please, come home to me."

"I want you to love me."

He waited a beat as frustration flared inside him, fierce and hot. She wanted him to love her? What sort of nonsense was that? "Alison, I *do* love you. You should know that. Haven't I proved it? I came to you, didn't I? I swallowed my pride and I came to you because I love you. I believe that in your heart of hearts, you still love me. Because we have that going for us, I think we should be able to overcome everything else, don't you?"

She closed her eyes and rubbed them with her fingertips. "I hope so. Oh, Mac, I really hope so."

"Okay, then. Let's face our problems head-on and maybe we'll be able to do something about them. Talk to me, Ali."

"About sex?"

"Yes. I admit that's an important subject to me."

"To me, too." She licked her lips, then said, "I guess it's as good a place to start as any."

When she fell silent again, he thought it might help to give her a place to start, so he repeated his question. "I need to know why you made love with me in the shower this morning and had sex with me a few minutes ago."

The distinction was subtle but vitally important. Ali understood his point, because she whirled around and said, "Don't you see? That's the problem. We weren't making love this morning. We were having vacation sex. We've *always* been good at vacation sex, at shower sex and picnic sex and in-front-of-the-fireplace sex. It's sex with no worries, no distractions, and no reality. Well, it was lovely and fun and it made us both feel better for a while, but it wasn't real."

"It felt real to me." Knowing it wouldn't help, he bit back the additional words he was tempted to say. *More real than what just took place on that blanket.*

She appeared to wilt before his eyes. "I'm sorry, Mac."

"Don't tell me you're sorry. Tell my *why*. *Why* did you shut me out today? Why did you shut me out a year ago?"

At first he thought she wasn't going to answer him, but after a long moment, she said, "I think . . . I'm afraid."

"Of me?"

"Of being empty."

"Of being empty? What does that mean?"

Ali wrapped her arms around herself and resumed pacing, her words tripping over themselves and making little sense. "It's because we're like a creek and our bedrock eroded and we're quicksand."

"Oh, for God's sake. Let go of dramatic metaphor for just this one conversation, would you, please? Focus. You need to focus. You're not making sense. This is important."

"I know it's important," she fired back, temper snapping in her eyes. "You don't get it. This isn't a dramatic metaphor. It's my life! It's your life. It's our children's lives. Do you think I'm not cognizant of the effects my actions have had on you and on our children?"

Despite his best intentions, Mac's temper stirred. "I don't know, Alison. I don't know what is going on in your head."

"Guilt." She threw out her arms. "That's what's going on in my head. I feel guilty for leaving you. Guilty for what that has done to our children. Guilty for needing more when you've all given me so much. I'm being selfish and I hate that, but I can't help it, either. It's like these feelings have been fermenting inside me for years."

"So what do you want? What more do you need?"

"I need a life, Mac."

"You haven't had a life with me?"

"Of course I've had a life with you. A life as Mrs. Mackenzie Timberlake. I've had a life as my father's daughter and as Stephen, Chase, and Caitlin's mom. I've had a life as a volunteer and fund-raiser and team mom and the dog walker and the keeper of the Kleenex. When I say I need a life, I'm talking about Alison Timberlake. Me. That's what I've found in Eternity Springs—a life for Ali Timberlake. A life for me."

The drama queen was back. Mac literally bit his tongue to keep from firing off one of the smart-ass remarks that came to mind. Unfortunately, he was unable to hold back a bit of a sneer as he said, "I didn't realize you were so unhappy with the life I've helped provide."

She waved her hand. "It's not that at all. I was happy to be your wife and happy to be the kids' mother. For many, many years that filled me up. But the kids grew up and you achieved your dream. I think it made me regret never reaching for my own. I'm in my forties, and what do I have? So much is over. It's too late for Ali's dreams."

That one stumped Mac. What dream had she abandoned? "Have you had dreams you haven't shared, Ali?"

She shot him a chastising look. "Culinary school in Europe. I wanted a restaurant of my own. Don't you remember?"

"I remember the argument you had with your father about spending the summer after your sophomore year in Italy. I thought that was . . ." He snapped his mouth shut, but she finished the sentence for him.

"A silly, childish dream?"

A rich girl's tantrum. "I never thought it was that important to you."

"After I realized I was pregnant, I didn't allow it to be important. But I never forgot. It wasn't drama. It was real. It was my dream!"

At that, Mac knew a slither of guilt of his own. "So, what's the deal? You want to go to Rome now?" Then before she could answer, he added, "If that's what you wanted, then why didn't you go there instead of coming up here?"

She laughed without amusement. "Right. Like you and the kids would have let me get away with that."

Mac slipped his hands into his pockets. How had he missed this? She really did want something more. It wasn't drama. It wasn't a tantrum. It was a dream she'd lost.

A dream he had taken from her.

Ali bent and plucked a bright yellow wildflower from the ground. She twirled its stem between her thumb and index finger and said, "I don't regret our life, Mac. You need to know that. What I miss is having something that is mine. Something I've earned, something I've built. I want something that I've accomplished on my own, and it's not going to cooking school in Rome or Paris or Timbuktu. Frankly, I've learned a lot over the past twenty years. I've learned a lot the past few months as I've worked to get the Bristlecone reopened. If I wanted to open my own restaurant, I could do it and probably be successful at it."

"I'm sure you could. You're an excellent cook."

She closed her eyes and massaged her temples with her fingertips. "I know this whole thing sounds like one great big pity party, and frankly, it embarrasses me. I don't regret the choices I made. I'm proud of the job I've done as a mother. I think that until recently I've been a good wife to you. So my kids grew up and left home about the same time you got the judgeship you've worked for all your life. I wouldn't have it any other way. Really."

"Except now you are empty."

Mac watched her set her mouth into a grim line and knew he should have kept the guilt-fed bitterness out of his tone.

"No. I'm actually doing just fine. I love my job, and I've made wonderful new friends."

"Like the sheriff?"

She folded her arms. "Is that why you came to Eternity Springs? Do you think there's something going on with me and Zach?"

He looked down at the ground, then back up at her. "I came here because I wanted you. I was desperate for you, Alison. Desperate enough to risk . . ."

"Risk what?"

He pursed his lips, then decided the time had come to face that particular elephant. "The deep freeze. I hate it when you do that to me, Ali. It makes me so damn lonely."

She closed her eyes. "I'm sorry."

"It wasn't vacation sex, Ali. We made love. Yesterday and this morning, for the first time in months and months, we made love. I want that back in our lives."

"Me too, Mac. I want that, too."

"Then come back to Denver with me today. We can put this whole ugliness behind us."

"What about my job? Do you think I'm so irresponsible that I'd walk out on my job and other commitments in Eternity Springs at the drop of a hat?"

"Why not? Didn't you walk out on our marriage at the offer of an omelet?"

She flinched as if he'd struck her. "See? This is why I don't like to talk about our problems. We invariably end up saying hurtful things."

"Maybe so, but failing to talk about our problems didn't exactly work, did it?" Mac rubbed the back of his neck. "Look, Ali. I'm thinking we might be better off if we did this with a referee. Sometime last winter you brought up the idea of seeing a marriage counselor, and I vetoed it. I realize now that I probably made a big mistake there."

She blinked, her surprise evident. "You'll agree to counseling?"

He hated the idea. Anytime she'd even hinted at

marriage counseling in the past, he'd shot the idea down. The last thing he wanted was to have a stranger snooping around his psyche. He knew that if a psychologist took to probing around in his head, they might just uncover things he wanted to stay buried. They might find truths that had the power to destroy his marriage for good.

However, if he chose the right therapist and set some ground rules going in, he was confident that he could control the situation. Right now their marriage needed more help than he knew how to give it. "Yes, I'll agree to counseling."

It was a huge concession from him, and when Ali heard it, her smile bloomed slowly and tremulously. "Oh, Mac. That's huge. I never thought you'd make that concession, and it makes all the difference in the world."

"It does?"

"Yes. Mac, I don't feel right about abandoning Celeste before Bristlecone reopens. I think I could fix it to where I work part-time in Denver and part-time in Eternity Springs, at least until the restaurant is up and running smoothly."

That wasn't what he wanted, but it was better than nothing. "So you'll do it? You'll come home?"

"Yes." She took two steps toward him, about to fling herself into his arms, when the sound of a motorcycle's engine grabbed both his attention and hers. They turned toward the noise and spied Celeste Blessing racing toward them on the path from the road through the forest. She drove to within a few feet of them, then braked the bike. Removing her helmet, she said, "Ali, I'm so glad I found you. Rose called.

You'll never believe who wants to talk to us about the Bristlecone. Lorraine Perry!"

"Lorraine Perry?" Ali repeated. "You're kidding me."

"No. She apparently stayed at Angel's Rest last week incognito and peeked in while Zach was installing the curtain rods for you. She wants to meet with the two of us right away."

"Who is Lorraine Perry?" Mac asked. And why was the sheriff installing Ali's curtain rods?

"She's a famous chef," Ali explained. "She has a television show and is a best-selling cookbook author." To Celeste, she said, "What's her interest in the Bristlecone?"

"They haven't given me all the details, but what they have said leads me to think it could be big for Eternity Springs. Huge." Celeste smiled apologetically at Mac. "I'm so sorry to break up your afternoon, but I really need to borrow your wife for a few days."

"Days?" Ali repeated. "Not hours?"

"The meeting will be in Los Angeles. Tonight."

Mac exclaimed, "Tonight?"

Ali said, "Los Angeles!"

"Yes. Luckily, Jack Davenport is up at his mountain estate today and he said he'd fly us to Gunnison in his helicopter if we can get there in . . ." She checked her watch. "Forty minutes. He's leaving to catch his own flight home, so he can't wait any longer."

Mac shook his head. "You can't get anywhere from here in forty minutes."

"She can if I take her on the Gold Wing and we go

straight to Eagle's Way. Once we get to California, we can stop and buy clothes and whatever else we need."

Mac didn't like this plan at all. The situation was spinning out of control. He and Ali had been in the midst of a significant discussion that would have far-reaching consequences for their marriage, and now she was just going to dash away on a motorcycle? Wearing a wet shirt? "Do you even have an extra helmet?" he demanded of Celeste.

"Bear loaned me one of his."

Great. Just great. "Just who is this Davenport person, anyway?"

"He owns an estate on Murphy's Mountain—actually, I think he owns the whole mountain."

Mac didn't care what was in the guy's bank account. "Is he a licensed helicopter pilot? Do you know what sort of training he has? I don't like the idea of you just winging away with some rich frat-boy type who flies his own birds on the weekends for just enough hours to keep his license."

Ali gave him an entreating look as Celeste explained. "Jack was a pilot in the Marines, and he's still connected with the government in some way. You need not worry about her safety with him."

"He's not a sheriff somewhere, is he?" Mac asked, a definite grumble in his voice.

Celeste asked innocently, "Do you have an issue with sheriffs, Mac?"

He shook his head and waved the question away. "I just want to take care of my wife."

Ali placed her hand against his chest. "I appreciate that, Mac. I do. You've been taking care of me in one way or another since the day we met. Don't you think it's time I learned to take care of myself?"

"Don't be ridiculous. You're one of the most capable people I know." When she smiled, he realized he'd made her point for her.

"I'm sorry to run out on you. This isn't how I wanted our picnic to end." She rose up on her tiptoes and pressed a kiss to his cheek. "I'll call you when I get to Los Angeles."

Mac watched as his wife climbed on the back of a motorcycle, donned a hot pink helmet, and put her arms at the waist of a spry senior citizen who gunned the engine and darn near popped a wheelie as she drove away.

Mac watched until the dust from their passing settled and the sound of the motorcycle faded on the breeze. Then he picked up his fishing pole and turned toward the creek. The isolation that he'd enjoyed so much an hour ago now pressed down upon him with the weight of Murphy Mountain.

He should have brought the dog.

ELEVEN

Mid-August

A hot summer day had cooled into a pleasantly warm evening as Chase Timberlake pulled into the driveway to his childhood home. He'd completed his internship the previous week and had made a mad dash to the mountains, trying to cram a summer's worth of fishing and fun into a couple of weeks. He braked to a stop, shifted into park, then looked at his passenger, Lori Reese. "Here we are. Casa Timberlake."

Today's visit was a command performance because his brother was visiting from California and his parents had announced a family barbecue. Chase was glad to sacrifice a day of vacation to family bonding. He loved his brother and he was anxious to see him. It was too bad that Caitlin hadn't been able to make it due to some summertime sorority commitment.

"You are so lucky, Chase," Lori said, admiration warming her tone as she studied the house. "When my mom and I came here for Nic Callahan's baby shower, I told her this house makes me think of *My Three Sons* and *Leave It to Beaver.*"

Chase shot her a curious look. "*Leave It to Beaver*?"

"My mom bought the DVDs. She's a fan of old-time TV."

"Ah. Parents can be very strange."

"Ya think?" Lori clapped a hand against her chest. "One time for the Halloween party at school she borrowed one of my grandmother's dresses and pearls and handed out popcorn balls as June Cleaver."

Chase imagined it and grinned. "Your mom is much hotter than June Cleaver."

Lori sighed. "She is, isn't she? I keep hoping one of the newcomers to town will notice and do something about it."

Chase opened his mouth, then shut it abruptly.

"What?" Lori prodded.

"Guys notice your mom. That's not the problem. Your mom is the problem. I watched her give men the cold shoulder for two summers."

"I know." Lori sighed heavily. "I worry about her. She works so hard between the store and her baking. Nana's Alzheimer's is progressing and it's getting harder all the time for my mom to take care of her. I'd feel much better about going back to school if only Mom had a man around to help."

Chase understood her concern. He felt that way every time he thought about his mother in Eternity Springs without his dad. Supposedly Mom lived at home again and commuted to Eternity Springs for a night or two each week. Both she and his dad had told him that they had reconciled and were in the process of working out their problems. That might be so, but he knew his parents, and he didn't see how this commuting thing was gonna last.

Chase and Lori exited the truck and made their way to the Timberlake front door. Chase used his key, opened the door, and called out, "Dad? Mom? We're here. Stephen?"

No one responded.

"Bet they're in the backyard." He led the way through the house, and as they passed a wall filled with framed candid photographs, Lori paused. "Oh, wow. I didn't see these the last time I was here. Aren't you guys too cute? This must be your brother and your sister."

"Stephen and Caitlin. I'm the well-behaved child."

She gave him a sidelong look and drawled, "As evidenced by the photo of you jumping off the mailbox wearing a Batman cape and the one of you perched on the roof of the house with . . . Is that a backpack?"

"I was a World War II pilot. It was my parachute. Stephen, the tattletale, took the picture because he wanted proof to rat me out. My dad about walloped the life out of me when he found out about it."

"I guess that's one good thing about growing up without a dad. I didn't have to worry about dad wallops. Mom swats were bad enough." Grinning, Lori continued her perusal of the wall. She gestured toward one of Stephen in his high school baseball uniform. "Your brother is hot."

Chase scowled at her. "If you say so. Personally, I think he's too pretty for a guy."

Humor flittered at her lips. "You look like your dad."

Mollified, Chase dipped his head in acknowledgment. "For an old guy, he is a stud. Don't you think?"

"Fishing, Timberlake?" Chase flashed her a grin, and Lori rolled her eyes, then studied a recent photo of Chase's sister. "Caitlin is a doll. I see both of your parents in her."

"She's the favorite. They try to deny it, but Stephen and I know. It's really a pain because she's our favorite, too. She has the best heart of anyone I've ever met."

Sobering a bit, he added, "This situation with our folks has hit her harder than she lets on. A lot harder than my parents have realized. I think that's part of the reason Caitlin has gone gaga over Mr. Frat Daddy. She and Mom have always been so close. I'm surprised Mom has missed seeing it so completely."

"Maybe this is the summer for change," Lori replied. "A friend told me that sometimes when mothers and daughters are especially close, they do some really weird things as they go through the whole separating thing when the daughter grows up."

"I don't think my mom left my dad because she and Caitlin fought about Caitlin cutting her hair," Chase replied, his tone dry.

"Your mom and sister had that argument, too?"

Chase gave her a droll look, then said, "Come on. Let's find my folks."

Mac Timberlake was in the backyard pool playing Frisbee with his dog. Lori and Chase watched for a few minutes through the kitchen window before making their presence known. The dog stood at the end of the diving board, and when Mac threw the Frisbee, he'd leap, catch the disk, then swim to the steps where

Mac waited. Gus dropped the Frisbee, bounded out of the pool, shook to send the droplets flying, then raced for the diving board to do it all over again.

"I still can't believe my dad got another dog," Chase said.

When Mac Timberlake climbed out of the pool and reached for the beach towel draped across a nearby lounge chair, Lori let out a little sigh of appreciation. "You are right. He is a stud."

"That's sorta creepy, Lori."

"Hey, you brought it up." A teasing light entered her eyes as she added, "I wouldn't mind being Miss May if I could find a Mr. December like your dad. Just saying."

"Hey, you have Mr. June right here. What's wrong with me?"

"You live in Colorado and I go to school in Texas, for one thing. Another, we're too young." She slipped her arm through his. "Do me a favor, Chase. If you're not married in eight years, look me up."

"Eight years, huh?"

Lori shrugged and grinned. Chase opened the door and called a hello to his father. Mac pulled on a shirt, then approached them. The two men shook hands and Mac exchanged greetings with Lori. Chase asked, "Where is everyone?"

"Stephen made a run to the store. Mom isn't home yet."

"Oh. What's for supper, Dad?"

Mac gave Lori a rueful look, then said, "Some things never change. I'm grilling tonight. Steaks. That okay with you?"

"Rib eyes?"

"Strip."

"Awesome."

"It'll be a little while, though. I thought we'd wait on your mother. Her plane is running late, but she should be here by eight."

Lori asked, "Did she say how the meeting went with the chef?"

"No," Mac responded. "She didn't say much about it at all."

At that point, Stephen arrived home with a six-pack of beer and one of Diet Coke. Chase introduced his brother to Lori, and the conversation turned to their respective educational pursuits for a time. Then Chase asked Lori if she wanted to swim, and soon a water gun fight had commenced between Chase, in the pool, and Stephen, who had access to the water hose. Much laughter and frivolity followed, and even Mac got in on the act.

After Mac set aside his water pistol, Chase saw him watching the clock and knew he was thinking about his mom. Lori picked up on it, too, because she swam over to Chase and said, "I hope you know how lucky you are to have such a great family."

"I do. Nothing wrong with your family, though. I love your mom."

"I'll trade you," Lori cracked as she hooked her elbows over the edge of the pool for support and allowed her feet to drift up in front of her. "Just kidding. I know she's great. I worry about her, though, because she's so alone."

"I don't know, Lori. From what I've seen, she has lots of friends."

"Friends, yes. But she needs someone in her life like

your dad, and she won't let it happen." She sighed heavily while making little flutter kicks with her feet. "One of the reasons I want to find my father so much is because I've spent my entire life watching Mom turn away opportunities for love. Celeste told me that she thinks Mom needs to make peace with her past before looking toward her future."

"That sounds like Celeste," Chase observed.

"Well, I need to find Cam Murphy fast, because Mom is running out of future. In just a handful of years, she'll be staring down the face of forty."

His gaze on his father, Chase said, "You're right. It's best she get settled soon. People do some crazy things in their forties."

The phone on the wall of the backyard kitchen rang, and Mac answered it. When he hung up a few moments later he relayed the news that Ali's plane had landed and she was leaving the airport. As he fired up the grill, Lori asked, "What can we do to help, Mr. Timberlake?"

"I have it handled, thank you."

"He's the backyard barbecue king," Stephen explained. "He likes things done exactly his way. Don't even get me started about how precisely you have to fold the aluminum foil around the potatoes."

Mac chucked a rubber ball at his son on his way into the house to wash and precisely foil his potatoes for baking. When he came back outside fifteen minutes later, Chase noticed that he'd showered, shaved, and changed his clothes.

Stephen noted the spruce-up, too, because just as Chase caught the drift of cologne on the air, his brother quietly said, "Go, Mom."

* * *

Ali had a bit of a lead foot as she sped down the highway toward home. Exiting the freeway and making her way into the neighborhood, she made a conscious effort to slow down. She was anxious to be home, anxious to be with her husband and her children, regretting that Caitlin wouldn't be there with them.

Mainly, though, Ali was tired. All this traveling was wearing her down. She'd made three trips to California in the past three weeks.

Although things were better between her and Mac, their relationship still had a way to go to be considered healed. They'd managed to fit in only a single visit to the marriage counselor. Ali couldn't complain about it since the fault was more hers than Mac's. Her schedule had been ridiculously busy since the first trip to Los Angeles and the subsequent negotiations with Lorraine Perry's people on the phone, on site at the Bristlecone in Eternity Springs, and at their offices in L.A.

That didn't mean she hadn't done a lot of soul-searching about her marriage on her own, because she had. She'd concluded that the primary problem was that she and Mac wanted—and needed—two different things. Whether he admitted it or not, Mac wanted life to return to the way it used to be with a stay-at-home wife available for whatever he wanted or needed, whenever he wanted or needed it. Ali, on the other hand, wanted both her days and her nights to be fulfilling and satisfying. Mac did a fine job with the nights—a superior job, in fact—but the fact was that her old life in Denver didn't do it for her day-wise.

She pulled into the circular drive in front of her home, smiling at the extra cars in the drive that signaled her boys' presence. Her step was light as she entered the house. "Hello?"

When no one answered, she deduced that she'd find them outside. Mac had told her he intended to grill steaks for their supper. She dropped her bag at the foot of the stairs, then walked into the kitchen toward the backdoor, pausing when she caught sight of her husband, her sons, and Sarah's daughter throwing a Frisbee for Mac's dog. "Eternity Springs meets Cherry Creek," she murmured as she opened the backdoor. "My own slice of heaven."

"Hey, Mom," Stephen called as he lifted the lid of the charcoal grill and turned the potatoes. Seeing her eldest offspring at the grill, Ali wondered if Mac had taken the huge step of turning over grilling duties to his son.

Mac was a backyard barbecue purist who believed that only sissies cooked with gas—real men used charcoal. Twenty years' worth of steak, hamburger, chicken, and brisket had made his heavy, cast-iron and aluminum grill a prized family heirloom, so much so that his loving sons were already trying to lay claim to it "after the old man kicks the bucket." Up until now, Mac had turned over the spatula to no other man. Had things around the Timberlake house changed more than she'd realized?

Mac saw her, smiled, then sauntered over and gave her a quick kiss—on the mouth, not on the cheek. The tension humming inside Ali evaporated. He hadn't been happy about this trip. He'd had a day off from court, and he'd wanted to spend it with her. "Welcome home."

"Thanks."

To Stephen, he said, "Go get the steaks out of the fridge, would you?"

"Sure, Dad."

As Stephen strode passed his dad, Mac held his hand out and wiggled his fingers, silently asking for the spatula. Her son handed it over with a heavy sigh. Ali kicked off her shoes and grinned. What was that old saying? The more things change, the more they stay the same?

After Stephen wrapped her in a bear hug on his way into the house, Ali exchanged hugs and kisses with both Lori and Chase, then nodded when Mac gestured toward the pitcher of iced tea sitting on the backyard kitchen's bar. She slid onto a barstool while Mac filled a glass with ice from the backyard kitchen ice maker. "So, tell me about your trip," he said.

Ali gave him a cat-and-cream smile. "I have a preliminary contract from the TV people in my briefcase. I need one of my favorite lawyers to give it a once-over and advise me on areas to negotiate."

Mac's brows winged up. "Well, well. Aren't you something? Congratulations."

"Thank you." Ali dipped her head.

"Have your dad look at your contracts. He's a master." Mac studied her for a long moment, then slid a glass of tea toward her and asked, "So, what's wrong?"

"You know me too well."

Ali explained her unease about the TV chef's proposed investment in the Bristlecone and, as a result, Eternity Springs. "I'm probably being stupid about this, but the more I learn about what Chef Perry wants, the more uneasy I am about the idea of Hollywood coming to Eternity Springs."

"What is it that bothers you?"

"I don't know." Ali shrugged. "Yes, I do. I love a good meal as much as the next person, and Lorraine Perry's recipes are divine. But her menu is going to be expensive, well beyond the reach of most of Eternity's citizens. That's not what our town needs. We need a nice restaurant that serves excellent food at modest prices. That's not Lorraine Perry's Colorado cuisine, as shown on the Food Network on Tuesdays at eight!"

Mac looked up from the grill. "Have you talked to Celeste about it?"

"No. She is so excited. I swear I never expected Celeste to be someone who is blinded by celebrity. That's half the reason why I agreed to attend a meeting on Monday at Angel's Rest between Celeste and the chef's agent. Someone needs to hold Celeste's hand to prevent her from signing something she shouldn't. I'm afraid we don't have all the facts."

"Monday? Couldn't one of your friends do that?"

Though his tone remained casual, Ali read disapproval into the comment. Feathers ruffled, she stiffened. "I want to oversee this. It's *my* project."

Mac took a moment to reply. "Sorry. I didn't mean that as criticism."

She grimaced, knowing she'd overreacted, but also aware that her husband wasn't happy that her work required so much of her time. Both she and Mac had learned to step carefully in the minefield their marriage strayed into upon occasion.

Mac tried again. "What sort of menu does Lorraine Perry envision for the Bristlecone?"

She recognized the peace offering. "She's calling it 'upscale mountain cuisine.' Game meat, trout. What that town needs is a good Italian restaurant, not mountain cuisine."

Tired of fretting about the new Bristlecone, Ali changed the subject by asking Mac about his work and schedule for the next few weeks. He mentioned the upcoming Big Brothers/Big Sisters luncheon, then asked, "You shouldn't have a conflict with that, right?"

Ali mentally reviewed her date book and inwardly winced. She did have a meeting scheduled with one of the investors. This was the first Ali had heard about the charity luncheon, but she decided that this wasn't the time or the place to mention the conflict, so she only smiled and said, "That luncheon is always entertaining."

Luckily, Mac didn't appear to notice that she failed to directly answer his question, and Stephen took a seat beside her. Talk turned to his upcoming year at Stanford. A short time later, Chase and Lori joined them and the conversation broadened to include CU and Texas A&M. It was an enjoyable evening with good food and interesting conversation, and when Ali went upstairs with Mac, she was feeling warm, mellow, and happy.

In their bedroom, Mac walked to the window and in the process of closing the blinds, looked out toward the pool and observed, "I like Lori. I hope to hell he's responsible and careful with her."

Careful? What does he . . . oh. Sex. He was thinking about teenage sex and a teenage pregnancy. "Lori is a strong young woman who knows what she wants—and what she doesn't want. They're more friends than a romantic couple these days. She won't let Chase interrupt her dreams."

Mac opened his mouth, then shut it again without speaking. Ali realized that once again they'd brushed the boundary of another mine field. Biting back a groan, she turned toward the master bathroom. "I think I'll take a quick shower."

"Okay."

In the bathroom, she brushed her teeth and removed her makeup before stripping off her clothes and stepping into the shower. The hot water felt good as it washed the travel weariness away, and she lingered longer than she'd intended.

She'd just shut her eyes and lifted her face into the spray when she heard the shower door open. She turned her head and smiled as Mac stepped inside. "Well, hello there, handsome."

"I got impatient."

"Sorry. I guess I'm in the mood to move slow tonight."

"Oh?" He reached for the bath gel. "I can do slow."

He could. He did. Spectacularly. So spectacularly, in fact, that Ali found herself thanking his foresight in adding that second water heater when the kids were entering their teens. Though they'd showered together on his visit to Eternity Springs, they hadn't showered together at home in quite some time, and they hadn't needed the second water heater in far too long. By the time he switched off the now-chilly water, stepped out of the shower, and grabbed a towel to dry her, Ali was so relaxed that she sort of billowed her way to the bed and crawled beneath the sheets.

They smelled like Mac, and Ali smiled. It was great to be home. As Mac switched off the lamp, she murmured, "Home is where the heart is."

TWELVE

❧

Loud barking woke Mac the next morning. He pried open one eye and checked the bedside clock. 8:07 a.m. He'd slept in. He'd have to hit the gym at lunchtime.

Arf arf arf arf arf.

He glanced toward Ali, saw she remained fast asleep, and rolled out of bed to tend to Gus. His hand was on the doorknob before he remembered that they had guests. Mac paused long enough to pull on shorts and a T-shirt before stumbling downstairs.

He ambled into the kitchen, then stopped abruptly. "Caitlin?"

"Hi, Daddy!" She set the coffee scoop on the counter and flew into his arms. For that short moment, all was right with the world. After hugging her tight, he held her away from him and looked down into her beautiful face. Blond with moss-green eyes, a button nose, and a bee-stung mouth, she looked more like a woman than a girl. Mac took a moment to mourn before saying, "What a great surprise, kitten. I thought you had something important going on this weekend. Does your mother know you were coming home?"

"Everything's fine, my event got cancelled, and no,

I didn't tell Mom, either. I wanted to surprise you both." Nodding her head toward the window, she added, "I brought my guy with me, Daddy. I thought it was time for you to meet him."

Oh, hell. She brought the boyfriend. Mac's stomach sank even as he turned to look outside.

The young man was tall and lean and blond, dressed in khaki shorts and a long-sleeved sport shirt—a *pink* shirt—with Sperrys on his feet and a ball cap with sunglasses propped above the bill on his head. A picture-perfect frat daddy. Mac despised him on sight.

"Oh, okay. Tell you what. Let me run upstairs and wake your mom. You know she'll want her hair fixed and her makeup on when she meets your new, um, friend."

"Sure. Tell her not to hurry. We'll be out by the pool drinking our coffee and playing with the dog."

Mac climbed the stairs two at a time, then entered his bedroom and shook Ali's bare shoulder. "Wake up, honey. I have news."

As his wife stirred, he walked over to the window and peeped through the blinds. Ali sat up and said, "I think I could sleep for a week. What time is it?"

"Trouble time," he muttered. "Your daughter is home."

That brought her awake. "She is?"

He watched the boyfriend smile and wave toward the kitchen window. "She brought the boyfriend home."

Ali's eyes widened. "Patrick?"

"Is that his name?"

"Patrick Talley."

"What do you know about him?"

She joined him at the window and peeked outside. "He's pre-law at Vandy. From upstate New York. Hasn't she told you about him?"

"Yeah, but I was busy and distracted, and she went on and on until I quit listening."

"Caitlin says he's brilliant."

"What does she know?" he muttered. "What do you know about his family?"

Ali shrugged and headed for the bathroom. "I don't think his family is close. Cait mentioned his mother was a single mom. I think he's a scholarship student."

"Oh." *Like me. This just keeps getting better and better.*

"Cait says he's a very hard worker, and the profs all like him."

"In other words, he's a suck-up."

She shook her head at him. "Now, Mac. Don't be such a stereotypical dad. Cait is a smart, savvy young woman. She won't fall for a loser."

Mac muttered beneath his breath, "Don't be so sure."

Ali rushed to get dressed, and a short eight minutes later, they exited the house together. After Ali called Caitlin's name, mom and daughter squealed and ran into each other's arms. Mac sipped his coffee and told himself to be nice. When Caitlin stepped away from her mother, she motioned to the boy. "Mom, Dad, I'd like you to meet Patrick Talley. Patrick, my parents."

The boy shook Ali's hand, and then Mac's. He had a firm handshake, but Mac wouldn't have expected any less. "I'm so pleased to meet you, Mrs. Timber-lake, Judge Timberlake."

"Welcome to our home, Patrick," Ali told him, gracious as always.

They all made small, get-to-know-you talk for a few minutes. The Talley kid was polite, friendly, and respectful, and Mac saw that Ali was impressed. He'd thought she had better sense than that. The longer the conversation continued, the more suspicious Mac grew. Patrick Talley had ambitions with a capital *A*.

The boy had done his homework where the Timberlake family business was concerned. He knew Mac's clerkships out of school, knew about the Denver firm. He mentioned details about the Sandberg case that only someone closely following would know.

Mac didn't like this situation at all. If the little bastard thought he could use Mac's little girl, he had another thing coming.

He was glad when his sons and Lori joined them and the topic of conversation shifted away from the legal profession. Ali suggested a big breakfast, and Mac said he'd help. When Patrick offered his assistance, too, Mac was quick to insist that he stay outside and visit with the other young people.

In the kitchen, he rummaged in the fridge, then asked, "Bacon or sausage?"

"Bacon. French toast or pancakes?"

"Pancakes. Scrambled eggs? Not for you, of course," he hastened to add.

Ali smiled. "Absolutely."

Mac waited until she had mixed the pancake batter to ask, "So, what's the deal with this character?"

She glanced at him. "What do you mean?"

"Isn't he just a little too . . . nice?"

"Mac." Ali's look chastised him.

"It's true. He's smarmy."

"He's polite. He's clean-cut."

"He's wearing a pink shirt!"

Ali rolled her eyes. "He's on the honor roll."

"Yeah, well." He spread strips of bacon in the frying pan. "Those are the ones you have to watch out for."

"You are being a cliché, Mac."

He grumbled beneath his breath as he grabbed the egg carton from the fridge and began cracking eggs into a bowl. "I'm a father and a judge. I have good instincts about people."

She refrained from commenting as she poured pancake batter onto the heated electric griddle.

"I do," he insisted. "Look, have I ever reacted so strongly to one of her boyfriends before? No, I haven't."

"That's because she's never been this serious about a boy before. They didn't threaten you."

"Threaten me?" He almost crushed an egg in his fist. "What do you mean by that?"

Ali took a sip of her coffee, then faced him. "You've been the most important man in Caitlin's world since the day she was born. The idea that another man will usurp that place in her life is threatening."

"That's not . . . okay, maybe that's a little of it." He added milk to the bowl and whisked the eggs. "There's just something about him that bothers me. He knows too much about us."

"That's because he's interested in Caitlin. He wants to know about her life, and that includes her family."

Mac scowled. "Just how serious do you think she is about this pretty boy? Do you think they're, um . . ."

"Sleeping together?"

"No." He grimaced. "Don't say that. I don't want to think about that." Then, because this was in fact the heart of the matter, he met his wife's gaze and said, "I don't want her to lose her dreams, Ali."

Ali's eyes warmed with emotion. Was it sympathy he saw? Appreciation? Whatever it was, Mac could tell that he'd scored a point. She set down her spatula and faced him.

"Your daughter is an intelligent, responsible young woman with goals and a very strong sense of self. She and I have had that talk. We've had it a number of times, starting when she had her first period and as recently as three weeks ago. It's only natural you worry about her—about all the kids—and unplanned pregnancies, but I don't think you should invest too much effort in it. It wouldn't be the end of the world if it happened, although I'm way too young to be a grandmother."

"Wait a minute. Isn't an unplanned pregnancy at the root of our troubles?"

She shook her head. "Nope. Not the pregnancy itself. I've always said that I wouldn't trade Stephen for anything, and that still holds true. I've thought about this a lot in recent weeks, Mac. Where I made my mistake was in losing my identity to the family."

He frowned at that. "You regret being a stay-at-home mom?"

"No, not at all. What I regret is totally ignoring the

reality that someday my kids would grow up. If I'd planned ahead, I wouldn't have been rudderless the last year or two. Mac, you'd better turn the bacon."

He returned his attention to the skillet, and Ali brought the conversation back to Caitlin. "I know it's early yet, and I think there's a good possibility that Patrick might be the one. You do realize that he's the reason she didn't come home this summer. It wasn't us or any job."

"Yeah, I figured that out a few weeks ago."

"You need to prepare yourself for the possibility that he might be a permanent part of our lives, Mac."

"I don't like him."

"Learn to like him. Have some faith in her choice."

"I don't trust him."

"Why?" Ali frowned with exasperation. "This isn't like you. You usually give people a fair shot. Why rag on Patrick so much? Frankly, your daughter appears to have chosen a man a lot like her father. Weren't you a scholarship student? Didn't you work hard, study hard, and earn your grades?"

"I didn't wear pink shirts and Sperrys," he grumbled, unable to think of a point he could use to explain his suspicions. He could only imagine how Ali would react if he said Patrick Talley reminded him way too much of himself at that age. She hadn't known the truth then. She still didn't know it today. "It's an instinctive reaction. There's just something fishy about him. For Caitie's sake, keep an eye on him, would you, please?"

"Hmm." She moved cooked pancakes onto a warming plate, then added more batter to the griddle.

"I'll admit you do have good instincts. Okay, I'll pay closer attention."

"Thanks. Maybe I'm wrong, but . . ." Mac shrugged. He knew he wasn't wrong.

As the day moved forward, Mac decided that paying closer attention wasn't enough, and he watched for an opportunity to act. Chase, Lori, and Stephen had tickets to a Rockies game and after they left, Mac decided to take Gus for a walk. He invited the others to accompany him. Ali and Caitlin declined since they were busy tearing through closets and jewelry boxes in order to put together an outfit for some big dance Caitlin had on the docket for the fall. As Mac had expected, Patrick took him up on the invitation. Mac couldn't find the dog leash fast enough.

They talked about dogs as an icebreaker, but by the time they'd reached the park a quarter mile from the house, the conversation had turned to law schools. Patrick asked a question about Stephen's choices after graduation, which presented Mac the opportunity he'd waited for. "He'd like to come to Denver and work for his grandfather's firm, but that's not a possibility."

"Oh? Why not?" The kid's inquisitive smile reminded Mac of Eddie Haskell on *Leave It to Beaver*. Smarmy son of a gun.

"I'm not a believer in working family connections. That leads to too much inbreeding in a firm. I've told Stephen not to expect me or his grandfather to smooth his way securing clerkships, and that he will not be offered a spot at his grandfather's firm."

"Wow. I don't mean to sound critical, but isn't that kind of cold?"

"Not at all. I've been down that particular road. My father-in-law and I both thought he was doing me a favor when he helped me out with contacts and positions. In hindsight, I know such assistance hinders a young lawyer more than it helps. I want the best for those in my family. I want them to be the best. The way that happens is through experience. Stephen is going to have to compete with his peers from the very beginning. No special favors in this family."

"I see." The kid kept his smile in place, but it didn't seem quite as ingratiating as before.

Having planted the seed, Mac decided to let it grow. "So, are you a sports fan? How about the Vanderbilt baseball team? The Commodores were strong competitors in the SEC this year."

"Yeah, they were."

Talk remained on college sports after that, and Mac's steps were a little lighter on the way back home.

Ten days after the kids' visit to Denver, with meetings surrounding the sale of the Bristlecone popping up almost daily, work kept Ali in Eternity Springs more often than she had anticipated or Mac liked. Her misgivings about the sale had continued to grow until she'd decided to broach the subject with Celeste. It wasn't too late to revert to the original plan. The television chef's list of changes to the Bristlecone had yet to be begun. Celeste could call off the sale, Ali could turn her attention to hiring a manager, and the Bristlecone could be open within weeks. Celeste had listened, smiled, patted her knee, and said, "Not to worry, dear. I have a feeling all will work out exactly as it's meant to work out."

Mac was acting cranky, too, which didn't help Ali's mood at all. Yes, she was busy. But how many times over the years had she been patient and understanding during a particularly busy trial? Couldn't he return the favor?

When a knock sounded on her office door, she glanced up from the computer screen. Sage Rafferty stood in the doorway. "Hey, Ali. Are you planning to go to quilt group tonight?"

"Yes."

Sage held up a canvas tote bag. "My husband has talked me into skipping out this week, so would you deliver my squares for me? Colt is craving Italian food and he wants to drive to Gunnison tonight."

"I'll be happy to take your squares . . . although you know you'll catch grief from the group."

"I know, but he looked at me with puppy-dog eyes and I couldn't resist. Unless . . ." With a hopeful note in her voice, she asked, "Do you have any lasagna leftovers in your fridge? That's what he really wants. Your lasagna."

Flattered, Ali shook her head. "Sorry. I haven't cooked up here in weeks."

Ali thought of the conversation later as she made her way to the workroom at Angel's Rest where the Patchwork Angels met. Their Hopes and Wishes wedding gown quilt was nearly finished, and Ali thought it the most beautiful quilt she'd ever seen. Celeste intended to use it in the Timberline suite at Angel's Rest, and Ali couldn't wait to see it on the bed. Seeing strips of her own wedding gown in the quilt top gave her a warm sense of satisfaction. Despite Mac's cranky attitude of late, Ali was happier than she'd been in months, and she did have hope that her marriage would survive these trying times.

At three o'clock her phone rang, and Ali recognized the Los Angeles number on the caller ID. She groaned aloud, then drew a deep, calming breath, crossed her fingers, and answered the call. "Hello?"

"Alison Timberlake, please."

It was the same voice who had answered the call she'd placed earlier in the week. Bracing herself, she said, "This is she."

"Hello, Mrs. Timberlake. This is Paul Harrington's assistant. He asked me to let you know that he's unable to get away a day early after all. If you still want the meeting, we'll need to leave it for tomorrow as scheduled."

Well, shoot. Afraid this might be the case, Ali had made her decision beforehand. "That's fine. I appreciate your letting me know. I absolutely do want to keep the meeting, and I'll plan on meeting him tomorrow morning at ten at the Bristlecone, just like we'd planned."

"Excellent. I will let him know. Good-bye."

Ali disconnected the call, closed her eyes, and sighed. She wouldn't make it home for the Big Brothers/ Big Sisters event tomorrow. Mac wasn't going to like that.

That evening she climbed the stairs to the workroom carrying four dozen assorted chocolate candies, knowing LaNelle would scold her for bringing a potential mess into the workroom, but also aware that sometimes a girl simply needed her chocolate.

When she arrived, Rose, Celeste, and Sarah were

already there. Ali took one look at an obviously stressed Sarah and asked, "Is it your mother or Lori?"

"Mom. She had a little bit of a spell while at the store and ended up lost in the library."

"Someone is staying with her tonight, I trust?" Celeste asked.

"Yes. Linda Townsend. Could we not talk about it, please? I really need to kick back and relax."

Ali handed Sarah a box of chocolates. "Here, have two. You need them."

The evening sped by in pleasant company, but by nine o'clock Ali knew she'd better get back to the carriage house and call home. All in all, she'd rather invite the black bear that had wandered onto her porch yesterday in for tea than make this particular phone call to her husband.

Driving home from work, Mac was not a happy man. Today had been a real bear.

It wasn't enough that he couldn't enter or leave the courthouse without some idiot snapping his photograph, or that the prosecution team should be fired for stupidity and the defense team jailed for bad acting. Oh, no. He also got to deal with the Hollyweird people. What had Louise been thinking, giving his phone number to Court freaking TV? So what if his "leading-man good looks" appealed to the favored advertising demographic? Louise should have known that he had no desire to be "Judge Mac," especially since he already had his fill of those types due to the grief they were causing Ali. But no, even his silver-haired secretary had fallen for this celebrity nonsense. It was pitiful.

Dangerous, too, as he'd discovered during the lunch break.

Two or three times a week, Mac walked to the deli a couple blocks away from the courthouse and grabbed a sandwich. Today, right after he'd placed his order for a turkey sandwich, a man showed up brandishing a gun.

At first, Mac had thought he'd stumbled into a robbery, but when the nut job starting shouting about earned-run averages, he'd realized that the word *fan* truly was short for *fanatic*. The fellow actually got a shot off before the deli owner pulled a baseball bat, appropriately enough, from behind the counter and felled the attacker with a swing for the bleachers.

The only saving grace in the entire situation was the fact that the paparazzi weren't on hand to photograph the whole thing live, and the one cell phone video that popped up on YouTube didn't include Mac in any of the shots. Still, it made for a long, crappy afternoon.

Arriving home to an empty house didn't improve his mood any, either. "Ali should be here," he told Gus as he let the dog inside. "Any day a man gets shot at while at work, his wife should be around to kiss him when he gets home."

This was where she belonged, not up in Eternity Springs. He needed her. He wanted her. She should be here.

He hit the button on the answering machine as he flipped through the mail. Fifteen messages from friends. He'd already talked to the kids, calling them as soon as he'd realized the event was going public. Perversely, he hadn't phoned Ali. He told himself he didn't want to interrupt her workday, but in a moment of self-honesty, he admitted that he waited for her to hear the news and call and fawn over him.

One of the messages on the machine was from her, though it wasn't fawning. All she said was that she was on her way to quilt group but would call when it was over. Obviously she hadn't watched the news today or talked to the kids.

Hungry because he never did get his turkey sandwich but too tired to cook, he ordered a pizza, then opened a beer and sat down in front of the television, remote in hand, watching an ESPN Classic college football broadcast of the 1993 Sugar Bowl. After this trial, baseball might be ruined for him forever.

The phone rang shortly after the pizza came while Mac shared the crust of his first piece with Gus. Expecting it to be Ali, Mac didn't check caller ID before answering. "Hello."

"Hello, Mackenzie," said the familiar, smoky voice.

Mom. He closed his eyes. He should have expected this when he'd answered her letter. He should have known that she wouldn't settle for a long-distance form of communication. "How did you get this number?"

"The Internet is a grand invention."

"I'm not listed."

"No, but it's amazing how much one can learn with a birth date and social security number."

Mac closed his eyes and rubbed his forehead. "What do you want, Brenda?"

The pout in her voice hummed along the phone wires. "What happened to Mom?"

That's the question I've always asked.

He waited her out and she finally said, "Okay, if you're going to be that way . . . I'm in a bit of a bind."

Surprise, surprise.

"I'm afraid I've lost my job—the poor dear passed on last week—and the rent's due."

It was on the tip of his tongue to ask if she'd helped the "poor dear" along on her way, but he kept his mouth shut.

"I was hoping you could spare a little cash."

Of course. What else? He was surprised it had taken this long for her to ask.

Before answering her letter, Mac had considered the probability that this request would be forthcoming, and he'd prepared a response. Although he'd expected to do it by letter or maybe email, not the phone. "Brenda, where are you?"

"Oklahoma. Tulsa, Oklahoma."

Oklahoma was too close. He grabbed a pen and a piece of paper from the end table. "I will pay your rent this month. Give me the name of the place."

"You can just send it to me."

"Yes, I could, but I won't. Name and address of the landlord?"

Following a pause, she said, "Well, aren't you just a little pain in the ass."

"I'm willing to help you, Brenda, to a point. However, I won't be lied to. If you want my help, you need to be honest with me."

She waited a moment, and he imagined the wheels

spinning in her head. Mac put the chances of truth coming out of her mouth at less than fifty-fifty. "All right," his mother said, sighing heavily. "I didn't want you to learn this. It's embarrassing. I'm with a man and he's abusive. Not physically, so the cops can't do anything, but mentally. I want to get away from him, and I've been squirreling money away so that I can leave."

Mac knew then that he'd been a fool. One thing about his mother, she'd always been smart. She could figure the angle on any situation and make it work for herself. Obviously he had to rethink his position on what sort of help he was willing to give her. He had to figure out the point in his own mind where soothing his conscience became extortion. "Listen, Brenda. I'm in the middle of something here. Call me this time tomorrow and I'll have something for you."

He disconnected the call without allowing her the opportunity to argue, then shoved himself off the sofa and began to pace his office. Anger and annoyance churned through him. He didn't need this. Not today. Not any day. He'd kept this life separate from that life for a quarter of a century. When he first started dating Ali, he'd told her his mother was dead! Imagine how she'd react if Brenda showed up on the doorstep now. Ali didn't abide lies, and if she were to discover one this big, at this particular point in their lives . . .

It wouldn't be good. It would damage the marriage.

Yet if she were here right now—where she should be—he just might confess all. He could almost see himself laying it all out, telling her the truth about his childhood, his teenage years. Admitting what he'd done at his mother's behest.

Hell, if Alison were home right now, he might even admit what he'd done to her, back when he'd still been his mother's son.

Right at this moment, the idea of doing that didn't sound so bad. Maybe that's what he should do. Just get everything out in the open and see if they could survive it.

"Doesn't matter, though, does it?" he muttered aloud. "She's not here. She's not home. I get shot at today, my serpent of a mother slithers out of the past, and my wife is up in Eternity Springs playing Mountain Susie Quiltmaker."

Gus whimpered his support as Mac stared at the phone, willing it to ring. Although nothing stopped him from picking up the phone and calling her, that wasn't what he wanted. He wanted her to call him, to fawn and fuss. He wanted Ali to be his wife and mother him. She mothered everyone else in the world. It was his turn.

But the phone didn't ring. Gus began to whine. Mac was seconds away from throwing something or kicking something when he decided to go for a swim. It took him forty minutes in the pool to work off his temper and the stress of the day.

When he returned to the house, it took exactly eight seconds for it to come roaring back.

The message light blinked on the phone. He punched it and heard his wife's voice. "Hi, Mac. Sorry I missed you. It's been a really busy day, a tough day, and I'm whipped and on my way to bed. I, um, need to let you know that I have a meeting with a

California money guy in the morning that I'd hoped to move up but couldn't, so I won't make it to the Big Brothers/Big Sisters event. I'm really sorry, but this meeting is really important for Celeste and the sale of the Bristlecone, and I know you'll understand. Again, sorry I missed you. I'll see you tomorrow evening. Love you. G'night."

She had a hard day? Mac stood in his office, breathing hard, eyeing the answering machine like it was something dirty. He could call her back and have this out now, over the phone. After a moment of deliberation, he decided against it. This was a conversation they needed to have in person.

Instead, he unplugged the answering machine, picked it up off the desk and tucked it beneath his arm, then carried it out to the trash can behind the garage. He yanked off the lid, threw the machine inside the empty metal can, then slammed the lid back on. It clanged satisfactorily, and Mac went back inside the house and went to bed.

He let the dog sleep at the foot of the mattress.

THIRTEEN

Ali first heard the news about yesterday's shooting when Gabe Callahan stopped her as she walked to her car following the stupid meeting with the egotistical Californian and observed, "After that excitement yesterday, I bet your husband avoids deli lunches for a while."

Ali smiled up at him. "What excitement yesterday?"

Callahan's eyes widened, then narrowed. "Let me guess. You didn't watch the news last night or this morning?"

"No, I didn't," she said warily.

He briefly summarized the incident, then added, "I guess Judge Timberlake took it all in stride if he didn't mention it to you."

Ali recalled the chaos of her day yesterday. "Mac and I played phone tag." She swallowed hard. "I haven't spoken to him."

Later, she didn't recall what she'd said to Gabe as she hurried to the carriage house and her phone. She dialed Mac's cell. The call went straight to voice mail.

Next she called his office. Mac was in court, but Louise caught her up on the frightening events.

"Please ask him to call me as soon as he's able," Ali requested. "I just learned about the shooting, and I'm desperate to talk to him. I'll be on my cell. I'm leaving Eternity Springs now."

"Of course."

As the minutes and then hours passed, her cell phone remained stubbornly silent. She told herself not to be surprised that Mac didn't call during the morning hours, but when time for the Big Brothers/Big Sisters luncheon came and went without a return call, her stomach sank. She knew her husband. He was angry.

The last two hours of her trip home passed in alternating bouts of guilt and defensiveness. When the guilt controlled her, she imagined how he'd reacted during and after the attack. Mac would have been stoic, reassuring to everyone around him, outwardly calm, cool, and collected. But in his heart, he would have wanted her to fuss over him.

In more than twenty years of marriage and forty years of daughterhood, she'd learned that no matter a man's age, his inner boy never entirely disappeared. The inner boy never outgrew his need for being mothered.

Since Mac hadn't returned her call, Ali knew his inner boy was probably pouting.

That thought jolted her into a defensive state of mind. If the man had wanted her to fuss, he should have let her know that something fuss-about-able had occurred. How unfair of him to assume she remained tethered to news outlets while she was working! Would it have hurt him to meet her halfway? Why couldn't he have called and said, "Hello, honey. An insane man took a potshot at me today"? Was doing so asking too much? Really?

And why hadn't the children called? Not one of them? That made no sense whatsoever—unless he'd told them not to bother her. Had it been some sort of stupid test?

The jerk. Mac Timberlake needed to grow up. He shouldn't expect her to read his mind any more than he should expect her to tune into the news 24/7. All he needed to do was to place a call and tell her something had happened, and she'd have cancelled the meeting and hit the road within minutes. She might put her job for Celeste ahead of Big Brothers/Big Sisters, but her family always came first. Mac should know that.

He knew that until you left him to live in Eternity Springs.

At that, Ali shifted back into guilt mode and continued her drive. Approaching Denver, she placed another call to Mac's office. Reaching Louise, she said, "It's Ali again. Is he still in court?"

After a moment's pause, Louise said, "Let me see if he is available."

Well. Ali's mouth tightened into a grim smile. That told her he wasn't in court and that he darn well could have returned her phone calls but had chosen not to do so. Steaming, she briefly considered hanging up, but decided against replying to childishness with childishness. No matter the provocation.

Louise came back on the line and said, "Ali, he asked me to tell you he's in a meeting and will see you at home this evening."

Fine. Just fine. She forced a cheery note into her voice and said, "Thanks, Louise. You have a nice afternoon."

Upon reaching home, she greeted the dog, gave him extra treats from the dog treat jar, then went upstairs to her bedroom, where she took a shower, fixed her hair, and reapplied her makeup. Like any woman going into battle, Ali wanted to look her best.

When Mac saw Ali's car in the garage, he pursed his lips and blew a slow, silent whistle of relief. He hadn't really expected her to run back to the mountains just because he didn't return her phone calls, but Ali had surprised him more than once this past year or so. He was glad to find her home. The time had come for them to hash a few things out.

Unfortunately, he wasn't in any better mood for this today than he'd been yesterday. Nobody had taken a shot at him today—not physically, anyway—but prosecutors on a tax case had annoyed him by asking for a continuance when they should have known better, and then the clerk had thrown the high-heat fastball directly at Mac's head by assigning him the Hutchinson trial, a *Denver Post* reporter's wrongful-termination case that was bound to be yet another high-profile circus. It was exactly the kind of case Mac didn't want and didn't think he should have. He had expected that he and his colleagues would share the wealth regarding high-profile cases. His docket was as full as those of the other judges. Why did he get all the fun?

As Mac whipped the Porsche into the driveway and

parked behind Ali's car, he lectured himself to accept this as part and parcel of the job—a job he'd wanted since childhood. He'd set his sights on a judgeship and he'd worked hard and he'd earned it.

In his mind's eye, a memory rose of Ali lecturing a crestfallen high school freshman who had learned that the varsity tennis team slot he'd won meant he no longer had time for guitar lessons. "The lesson here, Stephen, is to be careful what you wish for."

He switched off the engine and sat for a moment, his eyes closed, wondering why he was so unhappy. Was it the job? Was it Ali? Was it their marriage or the fact that she acted like a part-time wife?

Mac let out a sigh and grumbled, "All of the above."

He opened the door and exited the car, pocketing his keys. Then he walked to the kitchen door and stepped inside hoping to detect the unmistakable aroma of Ali's homemade red sauce, which would mean that she'd felt compelled to concoct a peace offering. Instead, all he smelled was pine-scented cleaner.

When Ali felt guilty, she cooked. When she was ticked off, she cleaned.

"Great," he muttered. "Just great."

He hung up his jacket and yanked the knot from his tie, then carried his briefcase toward his office. Down the hallway from it, he heard Ali say, "You're a doll, Zach. Thank you so much. I'll see you tomorrow."

The sheriff again. It was one too many annoyances on top of a day, a week, overflowing with them. His mouth set in a tight frown, Mac stepped into his office and saw that the contents of his bookshelves were scattered around the room. Ali stood on top of a step-stool dressed in running shorts and a scoop-necked hot-pink T-shirt. She held a dust rag in her right hand while with her left she lowered her cell phone from her ear. With the usual spot for his briefcase now occupied with books, he set the case down on the wood floor. Hard.

She looked around. "Oh, Mac, I didn't hear you come in."

"You were on the phone," he replied.

She slipped her cell phone in her pocket. "I have a few last things to coordinate for the reception for Sage tomorrow."

Oh, yeah. One of her friends—the artist—had been invited to speak at the Denver Art Museum, and a bunch of people from Eternity Springs planned to attend. Ali had offered to host a reception for her afterward. He'd forgotten all about it.

He waited, expecting her to descend the stool and cross the room to greet him with a kiss like she'd been doing each evening since their reconciliation. Instead, she wiped a bookshelf with her dust rag and remained perched on her step stool.

Mac was annoyed. He recognized that his behavior was childish, but recognizing it didn't seem to change anything, and that simply annoyed him even more. He scowled at the mess in his office. "Why didn't you have the service do all this?"

She visibly bristled, lifting her chin and squaring her shoulders. He noted that her makeup was perfect.

"We're having guests in tomorrow," she said. "I wanted it done right."

We *aren't having guests*. She's *having guests*. Those people were part of her life, not their life together.

The tension in the room was palpable, and as his own temper built, Mac decided a swim was in order before he opened his mouth and said something he shouldn't. "I need a swim," he stated flatly, then turned and left before she could say anything more.

He took the stairs two at a time, changed clothes quickly, and dove into the pool a few minutes later. He swam hard, taking out his anger and frustration on the water until his sixth lap, when something hit the water in the shallow end in front of him. Mac halted in midstroke and pulled up, his feet finding the bottom of the pool. He blinked the water from his eyes, thinking he must be imagining things. "Ali?"

She'd jumped into the pool. Wearing her clothes. When he said her name, she drew back her arm and sent a big splash of water flying at his face. "Damn you, Mac Timberlake. You should have called me. Why didn't you call me? Some maniac takes a shot at you and you let me hear about it from somebody else!"

Mac's chin fell until another splash of water had him snapping his mouth shut.

"Why, Mac?" She beat the water again. "Why didn't you call me?"

As he shut his eyes against the wash of water, his temper and frustration swelled to a breaking point. He would never, ever hit his wife, but here she was in his pool, interrupting his swim, splashing water at his face. She'd chosen this battlefield, and it was one that allowed him to slip free of the tight tethers of control.

So he splashed her back. "Because I wanted you to call me, Alison. I wanted you to care. I wanted you to be here where I needed you, when I needed you!"

"You should have called me!" She splashed the water with both hands.

"You should have been here!" he fired back, moving toward her.

She swiped her hand across her face, wiping water from her eyes. "I'm sorry that I wasn't here when you needed me, Mac. I called the moment I heard and you didn't answer. You wouldn't call me back. Since when does a federal judge act like an eight-year-old boy?"

"An eight-year-old? Really?" He smiled then, showing her lots of teeth, and he wondered if she just might hear the theme song to the movie *Jaws* in the background. "Okay."

He let his knees go soft, dropped beneath the surface, grabbed for her legs and tugged her beneath the surface. When she bobbed up, he put his hands on her shoulders and shoved her underwater once more. Then he stepped back, folded his arms, and waited.

She launched herself at him like a rocket. Mac fell back a step as she wriggled and wrestled and grappled and grasped. The woman was slippery as a fish and hissing like a kitten. Holding her was heavenly.

Mac wrapped her in his embrace and held her tight. "Ah, Ali. Don't." Then he spoke the two most powerful words in any language. "I'm sorry."

She melted against him and began to cry. Mac kissed away her tears, whispered for her to hush, told her that he loved her, that he was sorry he'd hurt her, that he was sorry for being an ass. Ali responded by saying that she was sorry, too, that she wished she'd been here for him, that hearing about the shooting had frightened her to death. She gave him the attention he'd craved yesterday, and her sobs soothed his soul. Admitting that made him feel like a world-class ass. Or an eight-year-old.

Wanting to rid himself of the eight-year-old boy inside him, he gave himself over to the forty-four-year-old man and turned his attention to making love to his wet and oh-so-sexy wife. He always enjoyed makeup sex. And pool sex . . . well, it had been way too long.

At first when she wriggled away from him, he thought she was playing. Then he tuned into what she was saying. "No. I'm not doing this. Not now, like this. I'm not ready for makeup sex because I'm not ready to make up. I'm sorry I hurt you, but Mac, I'm so mad at you!"

Disappointment morphed into confusion. "Me! How is this my fault? I'm the one who was shot at."

"That's right. You were. And somehow the problem became my fault. Because I have a job and jobs are your territory, aren't they?"

"What does that mean?" And where had the "I'm sorry" disappeared to?

"It means every decision in our family, in our marriage, has revolved around your career. Where we're going to live, who our friends are, even what schools the kids attended. Now that I've found something worthwhile and fulfilling, you can't stand it."

"That's bull. Helping Celeste sell that restaurant to

outsiders who think reality TV is real life isn't something you find fulfilling. You don't like what's happening with the restaurant. You don't like those Hollywood people any more than I do. You should have cancelled that meeting and come to the luncheon with me."

"Well, you should have called me yesterday. It was ridiculous for you to assume I'd see the news, and selfish and childish for you to wait for me to call you, and just plain mean to ignore me when I did call. Bet you thought I'd be wallowing in guilt because I wasn't there to comfort and mother you. Bet you thought you'd find me in the kitchen cooking marinara, didn't you? Because once again, like always, everything is always about you. My wishes and desires are inconsequential compared to yours. You don't take me seriously, Mackenzie Timberlake. You never have. And another thing. Did you tell the kids not to bother me with the news?" She must have read the guilt on his face because her eyes glittered with triumph. "I knew it."

"Fine." Mac folded his arms across his chest. "I should have called. My bad. But don't try to lay all the blame on me. How many counseling sessions have we had? Hmm? That would be one, wouldn't it? And whose schedule is the reason for that?"

Now she was the one with guilt on her face. "Once I get past the sale—"

"Then something will come up with the Patchwork Angels."

Her chin came up. "Or, maybe the Sandberg trial or even a new case."

Like the Hutchinson circus. Mac closed his eyes, feeling weary to the depths of his soul.

"Enough of this," Ali said, her voice tight. "I don't have time for this. I have a million things to do. It'll have to keep for another time."

She partially swam, partially walked to the steps and climbed out of the pool. She grabbed a towel and as she headed for the house, an irrational anger rose inside Mac. His voice scathing, he called out, "So what, now we have to fight on your timetable, too?"

She paused, glanced over her shoulder, and offered him a silent, withering look.

The silence between them continued the rest of the night. When time came to go to bed, Mac seriously considered the couch in his office, then decided against it, partially because he knew it would hurt her, but mainly because the symbolism of it depressed him. They'd come further than that, hadn't they?

Apparently not. He went to bed in the master bedroom, and he lay there for a full hour before falling asleep.

Alison never joined him.

After a fitful night's sleep on the bed in Caitlin's room, Ali rose early to complete preparations in time for the afternoon party. When she came downstairs, Mac was in his office slipping papers into his briefcase. Uncertain of his mood—or her own, for that matter—she tentatively said, "Good morning."

He shot her an angry look but didn't speak. He simply nodded shortly and abruptly.

Ali felt the urge to stick her tongue out at him. Instead she went to the kitchen and poured herself a cup of coffee. A few minutes later, he walked through the kitchen on his way to the garage. He didn't veer to kiss her good-bye, and the arrow scored a hit against her heart.

With his hand on the doorknob, he paused. He must have had second thoughts, because he cleared his throat, then said, "This party is an afternoon event, correct? Would you want to go out to dinner tonight?"

Ali shut her eyes and fought a wave of frustration. He was trying, but why was he so bad at it? "Mac, it's less than two weeks until they film the first show at the Bristlecone. I am drowning in work. I know we discussed the fact that I needed to be in Eternity Springs during this time. I have a breakfast meeting myself tomorrow morning. I'm driving back after the party."

He stiffened. "Of course."

"Mac, can we talk about—"

"I don't have time," he said, cutting her off. He opened the door saying, "I have a full day scheduled. You'll probably be gone before I get home. Gus will be fine in his crate during your event, but be sure to put him in the backyard before you leave. Drive safely."

With that, he stepped outside and shut the door behind him, just shy of a slam. Ali decided to give herself five minutes to fret and fume and fight back tears, but after that she needed to get to work. She still had a lot to do before her guests arrived.

She did a fair job of putting the whole mess out of

her mind until midmorning, when the doorbell rang and she spied Celeste Blessing's warm and friendly face through the peephole. Opening the door, Ali said, "Hi, Celeste. Please come in. I'm so glad you're here."

"As a co-hostess and your friend, I came early to help with preparations. Your other co-hostesses should be along shortly, too."

At that, tears pooled in Ali's eyes. "Party prep is under control. I'm afraid it's my marriage that needs help."

Celeste clicked her tongue. "Oh, dear. Why don't you pour us both a glass of iced tea and tell me all about it?"

Ali did just that, pouring out her troubles and speaking from the heart. Celeste reached across the table and patted her hand. "Honey, if you need to leave the job, I'll manage without you. In fact, I might just give in and sell the place to Lorraine, like she wants."

"No." Ali shook her head forcefully. "Don't do that. We've worked too hard on the rental agreement. I want to see this through. I honor my commitments. Besides, I really don't think I'm the problem here. Part of the problem, sure, but not all of it. Something's going on with him that I simply can't put my finger on. I don't know. Maybe it's his turn to have a midlife crisis."

The ring of the doorbell signaled the arrival of her guests. As Ali rose to answer the door, Celeste gave her arm a comforting squeeze. "Don't give up on him, dear. Don't give up on yourself."

"I won't."

Smiling thoughtfully, Celeste added, "It's a shame that Eternity Springs isn't three hours closer to Denver. I think that your Mac could do with a little dose of heaven, too."

FOURTEEN

Unhappy with the way he'd left things with Ali that morning, Mac cut his day short and arrived home before the party had ended. The weather was gorgeous, thus cooperating for an outdoor event and as Mac exited his car and approached the house, he heard the sound of laughter coming from the backyard. He was smiling as he stepped inside. Then he spied his wife and his smile faded.

He retreated upstairs to change.

Moments later, Ali followed him up. She entered their bedroom, shut the door behind her, then leaned against it. "I'm surprised to see you home this early."

He unbuttoned his shirt. "I hoped to catch you before you left. I didn't like leaving things the way we did this morning."

"Me either." She took a step toward him, then stopped. "Mac, I'll find a way to get back to town for a counseling session next week if we can get an appointment."

He smiled sadly. "Next week is tough. The Sandberg trial will probably go to the jury."

"Oh."

Now Mac took a tentative step toward her. She looked as miserable as he felt. "Ali, it's okay. We can wait until after you're done with the Bristlecone. I know it's important to you to finish what you start."

"It is." She smiled tremulously and took another step toward him.

Mac returned her smile and opened his arms. She ran to him and he wrapped his arms around her, holding her tight. "I love you, Alison. That much I'm certain of."

She lifted a teary-eyed, searching gaze his way. "What is it, Mac? What's wrong?"

What wasn't wrong? He didn't enjoy his job. He was being stalked by his larcenous mother. His wife was headed for the mountains, and his new dog had fleas. He closed his eyes and shook his head. "I don't know. Life just isn't very much fun these days."

Later, after the shower was done and his wife and her guests had departed, Mac had to get out of the house. He walked to the laundry room and reached for the dog leash hanging from a hook. Seeing what was happening, Gus leapt in the air, chased his tail, and dashed for the backdoor. "Wait for me, speed demon."

He snapped the leash to Gus's collar, then opened the kitchen door. The phone rang at that moment, distracting Mac. Gus took advantage, yanked the leash out of Mac's hand, and dashed away. "Gus! Get back here."

Ignoring the phone, Mac chased his dog. Loping around the side of the house, he was shocked to see Gus flop down at the base of his front porch steps, where a woman he recognized as Ali's employer reached out a hand and began scratching him behind the ears. "Um, Ms. Blessing?"

"Call me Celeste, dear."

She smiled up at him, and Mac reacted in a way that was downright strange. The tension inside him just sort of . . . melted. He returned her smile. "Did you miss your ride?"

"No, dear. My car is parked down the block. I waited because I wanted to speak with you."

Gus plopped his head onto her lap and whimpered. Mac shook his head at his dog, then asked, "What about?"

"Oh, various things. Would you mind if I accompanied you and Gus on your walk?"

All Mac truly wanted at that moment was to be alone, but he didn't have it in him to be rude to an elderly woman—even if he did nurse a resentment toward her for giving Ali the job that kept her away from him.

"We'd be glad to have you join us," he lied.

They walked down the drive and onto the sidewalk, Gus leading the way. Mac anticipated taking a slower pace than normal in order to accommodate Celeste. Instead, he worked to keep up.

Celeste Blessing was full of surprises. He didn't quite know what to make of her. She was elderly, but far from old. She was kind and gentle and compassionate, but she wasn't a dotty grandmother type. What sort of widow drove a motorcycle, made friends with everyone she met, and took on a dying town as her pet project? She was definitely a puzzle.

And what did she want with him?

"This is a lovely neighborhood," she said. "Ali tells me you've been happy here and that it was a fine place to raise a family."

"Yes." He glanced up the street and pictured his boys riding bikes, Caitlin on a scooter. He remembered games of tag with a dozen neighbor kids. "It's been a good home for us."

"Do you resent that Ali wants something different now?"

Mac was taken aback. "That's a personal question, ma'am."

"True. I don't shy away from them, nor should you shy away from the answers." They paused while Gus hiked a leg to water a fire hydrant. When they resumed walking, Celeste continued with tidbits of information about Ali's ideas and her successes, her skills and her talents.

"Your wife has excellent instincts," she added, waving gaily to a curly-haired toddler throwing a ball with her father in the yard across the street. "I wanted to reopen the Bristlecone as soon as I purchased it, but she convinced me to take the opportunity to do some remodeling. Then the lightning strike turned a little remodeling into a major remodel, and I don't know what I'd have done without her. Your wife really put her own special mark on the restaurant."

After that she talked about Ali's work ethic, her friendliness, and her compassion until finally, Mac felt compelled to respond. "I know she's a wonderful woman, Celeste. You don't need to sell me on her."

"Don't I?" She gave him a sidelong, knowing look. "I've been speaking for, what, ten minutes? How much of what I told you did you already know? Ninety percent? Seventy-five? Fifty?"

He frowned. "I might not know she vetoed using

yellow in any of the Bristlecone's furnishings, but I do know her character."

"That's a good point. The bedrock of one's character doesn't change." They'd reached the corner and turned toward the park at the end of the block. Celeste continued, "However, Mac, dreams, wishes, and desires are something different. Some change over time. Others stay consistent throughout life. Tell me, dear, what do you know of Ali's dreams, wishes, and desires today?"

He opened his mouth, then hesitated. What did he know of Ali's wishes and desires? He knew she wished Celeste wasn't renting the restaurant to people from Hollywood. As far as dreams and desires went . . . He stood tall and said, "She still desires me."

"I should hope so. You're a stud."

Mac tripped over his own foot, and her laughter rang out on the air like church bells. She slipped her arm through his, then asked, "Am I going too fast for you?"

"Something like that."

"It's a habit of mine. I like to live life to the fullest. That's important, don't you think?"

"Probably. Yeah." Some strange urge of honesty caused him to add, "I don't do a very good job of it."

"And why is that, Judge Timberlake?"

He mentally pulled back, shaking his head. "I'm afraid that answering that question would take deeper thought than I am capable of on this pretty afternoon."

"Chicken." She chuckled and gave his arm a

squeeze. "You should think about it, Mac. Alison has."

"Are you still talking about those wishes and dreams?"

"I am. May I tell you what I see when I look at your wife?"

Hadn't she been doing that already? "Sure."

She paused beside a flowering shrub and gestured toward a yellow butterfly flittering around the pink blooms. "I like to think that Alison is a butterfly going through metamorphosis. These months in Eternity Springs have been her chrysalis. She's been growing her wings and developing her color. Now she's a butterfly almost ready to emerge."

"I don't care for the metaphor, Celeste," he replied as the butterfly flew away. "See?"

"Don't be silly. She's not flying away from you. Besides, aren't you in the metamorphosis process yourself?"

"Excuse me?"

"You're just a little bit behind your wife. That's often the case in nature, you know. Females take the lead."

Mac scowled. "Are you calling me a butterfly?"

"I'm calling you a caterpillar. It's time for your metamorphosis, Mac. It's time for you to pursue your wishes, dreams, and desires."

"I've been pursuing my dreams since I was nine years old." He stepped away from Celeste Blessing and tugged the leash to draw Gus away from a dirt pile he was sniffing.

"That's the problem, don't you see? You've been

focused on the first half of your life, but now it's time to explore what you want in the second half."

Mac turned his head and stared at her.

"Never thought of it that way, have you?" A wayward Frisbee came flying toward them over someone's back fence. Celeste caught it and sent it sailing back in a smooth, practiced movement. "Wishes and dreams and desires need not be static, Mackenzie. Don't you think life is more interesting, more exciting, if they change and adapt and grow according to the man you are today? Not the boy you were when you were nine?"

He opened his mouth to argue with her, but found he didn't have any words to say. Her questions unsettled him. They challenged him. They made him think.

"There's my Land Rover," Celeste said, gesturing toward the SUV parked parallel to the curb beside the neighborhood dog park. "I need to get on the road. It's quite a drive back. Isn't it handy that we walked this way? Ali asked her guests to park away from the house so as not to spoil the surprise for Sage. It was a lovely afternoon. Thank you for sharing your home with us, Mac."

Distracted by his thoughts, Mac murmured absently, "You're welcome."

Celeste removed a set of car keys from her handbag, thumbed her key fob to disengage the locks, then opened the driver's-side door. She spent a moment petting and cooing at Gus, then reached into her handbag once again. "Speaking of wishes and dreams, I have something to show you."

She removed a white envelope and handed it over, saying, "I thought of you when I saw this."

"What is it?"

"Let's just call it a possibility. Somebody's dream changed, and they not only recognized it, they embraced the new. Now it's up to you to decide where your dreams and wishes for the second half of life lie." She climbed into her Land Rover, shut her door, started the engine, then rolled down the window. "Thanks for the walk, Mac, and for the hospitality. Know that you are welcome at my place anytime."

Still staring at the envelope, he said, "Um, thanks. You drive carefully."

She put the SUV in gear, then finger-waved and pulled away from the curb. Mac stood dumbly for a long minute watching Celeste Blessing drive away. What an unusual woman. What a scary woman.

Gus let out a yelp and strained at the leash. Mac allowed him to pull him toward the dog park gate.

It wasn't until later when, freed from his leash, Gus put his nose to the ground and went on a sniff mission that Mac turned his attention to the envelope. Why did his instincts tell him to beware the contents?

Mac leaned against the spreading branches of an oak tree, blew out a heavy breath, and removed the folded sheet of paper from the envelope. The letter read:

Dear Celeste,
The rain forest is amazing. We are living among monkeys and macaws and sloths and boa constrictors, to name just a few. As much as I love Colorado, this land and its inhabitants speak to me in a way I never expected. We are happy here. Life

has taken us in a new and exciting direction. We
have decided to make this place our home.

As a result, we wish to put our Colorado prop-
erty on the market, and we'd like to take you up on
your offer to oversee the arrangements should we
make this decision. Will you please put the matter
into motion? Heartache Falls is a good place filled
with positive energy. It brought both Patricia and
myself great happiness. It is our hope that you find
new owners who will experience similar joy from
life lived in a Rocky Mountain yurt.

God's peace,
Bear and Patricia

Judge Mackenzie Timberlake folded the page and
returned it to the envelope, then stuffed the letter in
his pocket. He whistled for his dog and wondered
why in the world Celeste Blessing had given him the
letter. What nonsense was she thinking?

Needing a distraction, Mac called Gus and insti-
gated a game of fetch with a stick. They played until
Mac's arm grew tired and a new scent caught Gus's
attention. Mac let him explore for another few minutes, then called, "Come on, boy. Time to go home."

Mac got more of a distraction than he bargained
for upon arriving home to find Caitlin sitting on the
front steps, crying. Seeing his daughter, Mac dropped
the dog leash and ran toward her. "Honey? What is
it? What's wrong, kitten?"

She looked up, tears flowing from eyes a mirror
image of her mother's. "Daddy! Oh, Daddy. Patrick
broke up with me!"

Mac sat beside his daughter, took her in his arms,

and held her while she sobbed. As his shirt grew wet with tears, he silently acknowledged a few undeniable truths. He was filled with relief that the frat daddy was out of his daughter's life. Second, he acknowledged once again how profoundly his selfish decisions had affected Ali's life. Finally, he understood that as Caitlin's father, he had a good shoulder for her to cry on, but beyond that, he didn't know how to help her. She needed her mother. *He* needed her mother. Ali ought to be here.

Or we need to be with her.

Two weeks later

On the second anniversary of the opening of Angel's Rest, Hollywood was due to set up shop in Eternity Springs. Ali's alarm woke her at seven-thirty that morning. Glumly she stared at the clock and sighed. Today was a big day for Celeste, a big day for Eternity Springs. She wished she could be more positive about it. What she wanted to do was to bury her head beneath her pillow and pretend this day had not arrived.

The television program concept proposed during negotiations by Lorraine Perry and embraced by Celeste was to show the progression of a little mountain mom-and-pop restaurant to a five-star success that would attract celebrities from all over the world. Lorraine Perry's combination reality and cooking show would take Eternity Springs another big step along the road to revitalizing the town's economy. The locals would reap the benefit of visitors with deep pockets. Times wouldn't be so hard. Maybe the whole TV

thing wouldn't change the town as much as Ali
feared. After all, Celeste had proven time and again
that she had good instincts, had she not? Ali should
put aside her doubts and trust in the "angel" of
Angel's Rest.

With that she rolled out of bed, showered, and
dressed. She wanted to make one last sweep of the
Bristlecone while it was still hers—so to speak. The
final addendums to the lease agreement were to be
signed today.

Her keys hung in their usual spot on a hook beside
the door. She eyed her cell phone, connected to its
charger, and wondered if her day wouldn't go more
smoothly if she left it behind. Caitlin's post-breakup
call volume was down to less than a dozen times a
day again, but her life could be a roller coaster and
today, especially, Ali didn't want to get drawn into
drama. Not having a phone might also help her avoid
her personal obsession of late: checking every five
minutes to see if Mac had called or emailed or sent
her a text message.

Something weird was going on with Mac. He
should be happy because the Sandberg trial had
ended and the paparazzi no longer stalked him. She
couldn't put her finger on what it was, but something
wasn't right. She'd mentioned it to her father last
night when they talked, but he seemed to think it was
nothing more than that Mac had already turned his
attention to his next case. Ali wasn't so certain.

She and her husband played phone tag more often
than not. When they did speak, Mac seemed both dis-
tant and preoccupied, though he didn't come across
as angry or cold. With her own hands full between

long-distance hand-holding for Caitlin and preparing for today, Ali had found little time to worry about it. But as the days passed and the situation continued, she'd begun to fret. He had said he would try to make it today, but they hadn't connected in a couple of days, so she didn't know whether or not to expect him.

She decided to bring her phone with her, but she'd leave it upstairs in the Bristlecone office.

Outside she noted that the streets were already bustling—another sign that the Bristlecone deal was good business for Eternity Springs. This was the tail end of the tourist season, after leaf peepers had taken the place of families on summer vacations, but in another week or two, the autumn colors—and the tourists—would be gone. For the last two years, visitors to Angel's Rest had filled the economic gap for the locals. Now, as the television show began filming, a whole new type of visitor was arriving.

She arrived at the Bristlecone to find a car parked in front of it—in a no-parking zone. Couldn't they read a sign? As she unlocked the door, two men climbed out and one of them asked, "Mrs. Timberlake?"

"Yes."

"My name is Bob Dickerson. I work with Ms. Perry. I know we're early, but would it be all right with you if my set director and I looked around for a few minutes?"

"Come on in, gentlemen."

Twenty minutes later, she showed them out the door with a smile. She twisted the lock behind them, counted a slow ten, then kicked the door hard. "New paint? New curtains? New tables? Excuse me? What have I been doing for the past few months?"

Wasting her time, apparently. Chef Lorraine had decided the decor simply wouldn't do for her "mountain cuisine." They were going to begin gutting the restaurant as soon as the papers were signed. Ali was furious, and if she was honest, she had to acknowledge that her feelings were hurt. The remodeled Bristlecone was her baby, and now her baby wasn't pretty enough? Really?

She wanted to talk to Mac, to complain about the celebrity chef and confess her concerns about the effect on the town, and to cry on his shoulder over the destruction of all her recent efforts. She hurried to her office, found her phone, and turned it on. First she tried their house, but he didn't answer. Next she called his cell. The call went straight to voice mail. She glanced at the clock. Finally she dialed the office. Louise didn't answer, but when Ali asked to speak to Mac, the stranger manning the phone said, "Judge Timberlake has taken a leave of absence, may I refer you to someone else's office?"

A leave of absence?

After a moment's pause, the voice said, "Hello?"

Flustered, Ali hung up without saying good-bye. She tried both the home phone and Mac's cell phone again, then dialed each of her children. Neither boy answered, but she did connect with Caitlin. "Honey, have you spoken to your father lately?"

"Yes, just this morning. What's wrong, Mom?"

"What did he say to you about his work?"

"That he was glad the Sandberg case was over, and that the trial had almost ruined baseball for him."

"He didn't say anything about a leave of absence?"

"Leave of absence from what?"

"His job. I called the office and they said he's taken a leave of absence."

"You're kidding me! That's his dream job."

"I know. It doesn't make sense. I also think he's dodging my calls on purpose." Hearing a knock on the Bristlecone's front door, she glanced at her wristwatch. "I've got to go. Things are starting to pop around here. Listen, Cait, see what you can find out and let me know. And, if you do talk to your father, tell him he'd better call me and do it fast."

"I will. Good luck today, Mom. I hope everything goes great."

They ended the call, and Ali nibbled worriedly at her lower lip as she stuck her phone in her pocket and headed back downstairs to admit mayhem into her carefully constructed world.

In short order, that's exactly what occurred. First the crew descended with their cameras and cords and lighting. Then Celeste arrived, a vision in green and gold, happy and bright as summer sunshine. Ali's father showed up next, dapper in his Savile Row suit, serving as Celeste's attorney. Ali shook her head. Her dad in a reality TV show? How crazy was this?

By the time the great chef herself swept into the Bristlecone with an entourage of eight, the street outside was filled with curious sightseers. Ali hung back, not bothered one bit by the fact that the office was too small and crowded for her to witness the contract signing. But once that happened, her job was officially finished and she was out of here. No way would she hang around and watch them begin taking apart what she'd worked so hard to put together. What a waste.

While she waited, she wandered back to the kitchen where she poured herself a glass of iced tea. She stood in the doorway, sipping her drink and observing the little mountain restaurant she'd put together well enough to catch a Hollywood chef's interest, but apparently not well enough to pass muster with her.

"I should have tried to talk her into going Italian after all." Then she could have designed this space the way she'd *really* wanted it, and with any luck, Lorraine Perry would have walked right on by her restaurant during her summertime visit to Eternity Springs.

Applause broke out in the office, signaling that the morning's business was done. Ali lifted her tea glass in a sad salute, then exited out the back. She'd catch up with Celeste and her father at the celebration at Angel's Rest.

A small crowd remained gathered outside the Bristlecone, but people were beginning to congregate on the healing center's grounds for the birthday barbecue. Ali used the opportunity to attempt to reach Mac. Again he didn't answer. For the next hour and a half, she tried his phone every fifteen minutes or so. Nada. What was going on with him?

A call to the neighbor's house informed her that Mac had packed up and left and taken the dog with him. That made her want to drop everything and head for Denver, and she might have done just that had she known where to look for the man.

She told herself that Mac wasn't one of her children. He was an adult. He could take care of himself.

Next time she saw him, he'd be taking care of the black eye she was going to give him for worrying her to death.

By one o'clock, four different people had come up to Ali to ask her why those Hollywood people were undoing all the improvements she'd made to the Bristlecone. By one-thirty, she had upset her father by snapping at him for waxing on about lovely Lorraine's smile. When two o'clock finally rolled around, after she'd stood on the Angel's Creek footbridge and watched the television people carry armload after armload of her carefully chosen items out of the restaurant to be thrown carelessly into the bed of a pickup truck, Ali was ready to forgo the iced tea and head straight for the bourbon.

To top it off, despite having left fully a dozen messages, she'd yet to hear a word from Leave-of-Absence Mac.

At two-thirty, Celeste stood on the front porch of the old Cavanaugh Mansion and rang the big brass bell, inviting her guests to gather around.

"Welcome friends, neighbors, special guests, and"— she winked at Lori Reese who was on a visit home from college—"coeds. God has blessed us once again with a spectacular day, has he not?"

She paused while the crowd burst into applause. Once it died down, she continued. "It's been another exciting year for Eternity Springs as we've further developed our Angel Plan. I want to thank you all for you support and enthusiasm. Please, let us once again give ourselves a round of applause."

The crowd cheered, and as Celeste continued to

recap the strides forward the town had made during the past year, Ali found herself surrounded by a group of dear friends: Sarah and Lori Reese, Rose Anderson, Sage and Colt Rafferty, and Nic and Gabe Callahan and their darling twin daughters. She smiled warmly at them all and was pleased when Sage linked her arm through hers. Ali had found friendship and acceptance in Eternity Springs, but that wasn't all. Here in this little Rocky Mountain town, Ali Timberlake had found herself.

"Now, my fellow Eternity Springsians," Celeste continued with a twinkle in her eyes. "I have a special announcement. As most of you know, today we have VIP visitors in town, Chef Lorraine Perry and the crew of the brand-new reality TV show, *Reality Bites*. Our own Ali Timberlake has worked frightfully hard, first preparing the Bristlecone for reopening, and then, when we were offered the opportunity from our friends to the west, negotiating our lease agreement. She's done a spectacular job for me and for all of us in Eternity Springs. Please join me in giving Ali a big round of applause."

Embarrassed, Ali waved her thanks. Her father made eye contact with her and winked, and she felt a little rush of pride. It was nice that he had been here to witness the public kudos. *Mac, where are you?*

"Now, without further ado, I am going to announce the name of the winner of our contest to name the Angel's Rest mascot." She held up a little stuffed poodle with wings that she'd asked Sage to design. "I must say this was a difficult decision. You all submitted some fun and creative names, but one name in particular called to my heart. Now, I promised a spectacular prize for the winner of this contest, so before I announce the winner, I should announce just what that prize is. I've asked Jeffrey Colmes to assist."

The young member of the school band offered up a drumroll. Celeste allowed seconds to pass and anticipation to build before she declared, "The winning prize is an all-expenses-paid two-week trip for two to . . . Australia!"

The crowd cheered. Ali's brows arched. Last she'd heard, the prize had been a trip to Hawaii.

"Australia!" Sage exclaimed. She glanced at Ali. "Why Australia?"

"I haven't a clue. It's news to me."

Sarah sighed dreamily. "I've always wanted to go to Australia. Ever since I was a kid. Cam and I used to—"

Realizing what she'd said, she snapped her mouth shut.

Celeste nodded to Jeffrey for another drumroll, then said, "Eternity Springs, I introduce you to Serenity!"

In on the surprise, Ali continued to watch Sarah, who simply stared at Celeste, a quizzical look on her face. Lori, having made a visit home for the weekend, stood next to her mother, her arm linked with her grandmother's. Watching Sarah, Lori gave an exaggerated roll of her eyes. Finally it registered. Sarah stiffened. Blinked. Her chin dropped, and she started to stammer. "I think . . . oh, my. It's me. That was mine. Serenity. That was my idea! I think I won the contest." She reached over and clutched Ali's sleeve. "Did I win the contest?"

Ali let her smile free as she met Celeste's gaze. From the podium, Celeste announced, "I want to thank Sarah Reese for suggesting the perfect name! Congratulations, Sarah. You and the person of your choice—in other words, Lori—are going to Australia!"

Sarah let out a high-pitched squeal matched only by her daughter's. She and Lori flew into each other's arms, then jumped up and down, giggling and squealing some more. Nic Callahan approached them, saying, "Sarah! Australia? That's been your dream trip since we were kids!"

"I know. Can you believe it? I can't believe it. Why, I've never been outside the United States. I'll have to get a passport. Oh, wow." Sarah's big violet eyes shimmered with excitement. "Australia. Lori, can you believe this?"

"It's awesome. And who knows, Mom? Maybe you'll meet the man of your dreams on the trip of your dreams."

"Ooh, yeah. A tall, broad, handsome Aussie." Sage gave an exaggerated shiver. "One who knows just how to say g'day."

Nic rolled her tongue around her cheek, then added, "And goodnight."

As Mac Timberlake watched his wife cheer and hug his son's sometime girlfriend, he decided to reassess his plans. He'd come here today intending to tell Ali about the leave of absence, but seeing her with her friends, observing what she'd accomplished with that café, and listening to the accolades from the townspeople gave him pause. This was an Ali Timberlake he'd never seen before. He wanted—he needed—to think about it.

So while Eternity Springs continued the anniversary celebration for Angel's Rest, he slipped away to reevaluate his plans. Twenty minutes later he arrived back at Bear's yurt. Gus, who had taken to mountain life with alacrity, met him with barks of joy.

After the walk he'd taken with Celeste on the day of Sage Rafferty's museum lecture, Mac had reflected on their conversation at length. As the Sandberg trial drew to a close, he'd taken the first step toward reexamining his dreams, wishes, and desires by requesting a formal leave of absence. Then he'd contacted Celeste and made a confidential agreement to lease Bear's mountain property for a month, paying a premium for the opportunity to buy the Heartache Falls acres at the end of the lease period if he so chose. Each time he'd talked to Ali, he'd tried to tell her about his big decisions, but he'd never managed to force the words past his lips. He finally realized that he didn't want to tell her about it until he actually went through with it.

Now, when the time had arrived to come clean with his wife, he still had second thoughts. Why? Glancing down at Gus, he asked, "Am I worried she will read something into it that I'm not ready to commit to?"

Maybe.

"Am I worried she'll influence me? That I'll make decisions based on what she wants instead of what I want?"

Gus yipped. Mac shrugged. Perhaps.

He hadn't figured out just what he wanted yet, had he? Not for this—how had Celeste put it?—this second half of life.

He reached down and scratched the dog behind his ears. "Based on her latest cell phone message, she's already torqued at me. What would it hurt to take a few more days, try to get beyond that caterpillar stage Celeste talked about?"

Mac decided to go for it. That evening he composed an email to his wife and children. After hitting the send button, he stepped outside and listened, half expecting to hear Ali's shriek of fury all the way from town. When all he heard was the whisper of the wind through the evergreens, he grinned at his foolishness, went back inside, and turned off all his electronics. Celeste knew where he was. If anyone in his family had an emergency, she'd know how to contact him.

For the next little while, Mac intended to see about shedding his caterpillar skin.

Days passed in a solitude that he found he particularly enjoyed in the wake of the circus of the Sandberg trial. The crisp mountain air cleared his mind, and the beauty of the mountains in autumn soothed his soul. He hiked, he fished, he photographed. Most important of all, he thought. He invested a significant amount of time engaged in self-analysis as he took Celeste Blessing's advice to heart. It was his time of metamorphosis, of transformation.

He tried to figure out what he wanted to be when he grew up.

After two weeks of self-imposed isolation, disguised beneath a ball cap, sunglasses, and a beard, he ventured into town, introducing himself as Steve while volunteering no surname, he made the round of businesses in town and slowly got to know the citizens. He quickly discovered that his wife was accepted, admired, and respected by the people of Eternity Springs.

He also learned that the people of Eternity Springs liked to gossip. In Ali's case, much speculation centered upon why she hadn't returned to Denver now that her work at the Bristlecone was done. Comments she'd made since the Angel's Rest anniversary party had left some wondering. A conversation he'd overheard between two women in the paper goods aisle at the Trading Post had given him warning.

"That was some hissy fit Ali Timberlake pitched last night at quilt group."

"Don't you know it! She has a mad on at that man of hers like nobody's business. I wouldn't want to be Mac Timberlake the next time she sets eyes on him."

The words rang in Mac's thoughts the rest of the evening and haunted him while he slept. He awoke the next morning to a dusting of snow on the ground and a sense of certainty settling into his bones. Glancing down at his canine companion, he said, "Gus, how about we go for a walk?"

He hiked the boundary of Bear's property and ended up at Heartache Falls. By now, sunshine had melted most of the snow. A crisp but gentle breeze swept down from the mountain and whooshed through a stand of aspen, causing brittle autumn leaves clinging to branches to quake. Mac smelled pine on the air, and he lifted his gaze toward the tallest peak in sight and focused on the clouds gathering there. He couldn't deny that winter was bearing down upon them. Nevertheless, here in this high mountain valley where sunlight sparkled off the clear water pooled behind beaver dams and his dog's happy barks rose like music in the air, Mac felt as though springtime had arrived.

Celeste Blessing was one intelligent woman.

At her suggestion during this time of self-exile, he had redefined his dreams, his wishes, his desires. Mac Timberlake, husband, father, and forty-four-year-old federal judge, knew what he wanted from the second half of his life.

How in the world would he break the news to Ali?

FIFTEEN

With a satisfied sigh, Ali closed the novel she'd just finished. She was a sucker for happy endings. She normally shied away from thrillers for that exact reason. She liked going into a book knowing that favored characters would not die in the end. But this time, with her husband off who knew where, she'd been in the mood for murder.

Go figure.

She glanced at the clock and winced. Shoot, she'd dawdled too long over the book. She was meeting her friends at Sarah's tonight for a girls' night out and she was already five minutes late. She'd better get a move on.

Ali changed clothes, dragged a brush through her hair, then took a minute to check her email. Nothing from Mac, again. She hadn't heard word one from him since that short, exceedingly frustrating email he'd sent a little over two weeks ago where he'd stated he was sorry to have missed her earlier, that he had some decisions to make, and he needed some time to himself to make them. He'd assured her that he loved her, told her not to worry, and asked for her patience.

She'd made a valiant effort, but her patience had

worn as thin as the ice this morning on Angel Creek. If he didn't contact her soon, she swore, she'd hire a private detective to track him down.

Ten minutes later she knocked on the door at the Reese house. Inside, she found Celeste, Sage, and Nic seated around the kitchen table. "Sorry I'm late, everyone. I was reading and lost track of the time. I've learned that I don't read as fast when I mentally rename every murder victim in the book Mac."

"Yeowz," Sarah said, wincing. She shared a look with the other women that struck Ali as curious, but before she could comment on it, LaNelle Harrison entered the kitchen with Sarah's mother, Ellen. While Sarah set the table with the chef salad she'd prepared for the pair earlier, Ellen entertained them all with a silly story about Nic and Sarah as children.

Ellen Reese was as sweet as could be, and Ali knew from how townspeople spoke of her that she'd always been that way. Scuttlebutt said that before her illness, Ellen had been Eternity Springs's go-to person whenever a good deed needed doing. People spoke of her kindness, her devotion to her family, and her faith, which she still exhibited despite middle-stage Alzheimer's disease. The entire town doted on Ellen, which made caring for her easier for Sarah with Lori away at college. Faced with placing her mother in a facility two hours away or accepting offers of help, Sarah had chosen to bend her pride. Everyone benefitted from the arrangement, because in Eternity Springs, the citizens appreciated the opportunity to be good friends and neighbors.

"You girls enjoy yourselves and don't fret about us," LaNelle said, shooing them out the door. "Don't hurry back, either. Ellen and I are going to watch a movie after dinner, and I don't want you interrupting the ending."

"Yes, ma'am," Sarah said, and shut the door behind her.

"What are we doing for our girls' night out?" Ali asked as Nic led them north on Aspen.

"We thought we'd start by going out to dinner," Sage told her. "After that, we'll play it by ear."

"Out to dinner?" Ali asked. "Tell me we're not going to the Bristlecone."

"No," Sage said. "We're smarter than that." After a moment's pause, she added, "I think."

Since neither the Mocha Moose nor the Blue Spruce opened for supper this time of year, Ali figured that meant they'd be eating in the Angel's Rest restaurant. The only food the other choice, the Red Fox Pub, served was peanuts and pretzels. "Are you thinking Mexican food in Gunnison, maybe?"

"No, dear," Celeste said. "You've been so consumed with your pique with your husband that you've missed the big news. A new restaurant has opened in Eternity Springs—the New Place."

"Oh? You're kidding. That is big news. Where is it? Who's the owner? What type of cuisine do they serve?" After a moment's pause, she added, "That's a weird name for a restaurant."

Sarah's smile was bright. "It's in that building that's been between the fire station and the auto center on First Street, the one that's been empty forever. Someone from out of town owns it, and I think the menu is considered eclectic."

Ali couldn't help feeling a little twinge of envy. She

missed the work that had filled her days during the Bristlecone project. As they walked, she relaxed and began to enjoy herself as Nic regaled them with the latest antics of her twins, which caused Sage to groan, "Thank goodness I'm doing this babysitting thing one kid at a time."

Next, the talk turned toward Sage's annual art exhibit in Fort Worth. When they drew close to First Street, Ali sniffed the air. "I smell steak."

"Yum. I understand that steak is one of the mainstays of the new menu. Apparently the restaurant only offers entrees cooked on a barbecue grill. Guy who runs it says it's the only way he knows how to cook."

Ali shot her a baffled look. "If he can't cook, then why is he running a restaurant?"

"That's an interesting question," Celeste observed. "You'll have to ask him."

Ali sniffed the air again. The aroma did smell tantalizing.

"What about your desserts, Sarah? Will you be supplying them to the New Place?"

"Yes, eventually. I hope. I think the new guy still has some issues to iron out."

They arrived at the New Place, and at the door, Ali's friends hesitated and met one another's gaze. Celeste reached over and patted Ali's arm. Sarah grasped the door handle saying, "Well, I don't know about you girls, but I'm hungry."

They filed inside and Ali glanced at the service area, noted the apron-wearing man standing in the doorway to the kitchen, then froze. She blinked once, then twice. Was she dreaming?

Underneath the ball cap and shaggy hair, behind the beard that camouflaged a square jaw, she recognized those brown eyes. Why was her husband standing at the back of the building? Why was he holding a meat fork?

"Mackenzie Stephen Timberlake? What in heaven's name are you doing?"

Though he pasted on a brazen smile, he failed to hide a flicker of uncertainty. "Getting ready to cook you a rib eye, sweetheart. Your favorite. Medium well, just like you like it."

Ali's stare trailed around the room. It was as if she'd entered an alternate universe. Mac in a beard? With shaggy hair? In Eternity Springs? She felt the weight of her friends' gazes, sensed them lining up beside her, behind her. *They have my back.*

No, she realized. They'd known he was here. They'd led her here tonight. They'd known he was here and they hadn't said a word. She snapped her head around and glared at the quartet of traitors. To a one, they smiled back at her.

Fine. She'd deal with them later. Mac came first.

But how to deal with him? How to react? While she considered her options, Mac continued, "Welcome to the New Place, ladies. I have your table all ready. A table for five, correct?"

Ali hesitated. She could demand her friends leave, then re-create one of the murders she'd just read about in her novel. She could turn around and walk out and wait until he came after her. She could yell at him like a fishwife in front of her friends—in front of the entire town, for that matter.

Or she could let this play out, see what scenario he

had cooked up. At least she'd get a steak out of the deal.

She nodded regally, and Mac looked just a little relieved as he led them to the only table in the otherwise empty room. Taking her seat, Ali spread her napkin in her lap, then leveled an accusing gaze on each of her friends in turn. Mac handed them a handwritten menu that offered the choice of steak or grilled chicken with a green salad and baked potato, or hamburgers or hot dogs with tater tots. "Tater tots?" Sage questioned, amusement in her tone.

Ali wrinkled her nose. Tater tots were one of Mac's favorite junk foods.

Mac cleared his throat. "I'll be back in a few minutes to take your orders."

When he'd retreated to the "kitchen," which was actually a barbecue grill set out on the back stoop, Ali folded her arms, pursed her lips, and gave her friends a schoolteacher stare. "Well?"

Sage and Nic shared an uneasy glance. Celeste gave Ali one of her beatific smiles. Sarah shrugged and said, "He wanted it to be a surprise. He was so cute about it. We didn't want to spoil it for him, or for you."

"He bought the building," Sage added.

Nic smiled encouragingly. "He said it's always been your dream to have a restaurant. Your own Italian restaurant."

"I'm not sure, but I think he might have bought Bear's land, too," Sarah said. "Something I heard at the bank today makes me think that."

Ali slumped back against her chair. "I don't believe this."

Sarah met Celeste's gaze. "I told you she'd be stupid about this."

"Stupid?" Ali repeated.

"Yeah. Stupid. Your husband just made a grand romantic gesture for you." Sarah made a sweeping wave toward the room. "Do you know how lucky you are to have a man who would go to such lengths for you?"

With that, Ali's temper flared. "I understand that point, Sarah. What you don't understand is that while my husband's grand romantic gesture is in some ways quite lovely, it is also one more instance in a long line of instances where he has failed to respect me."

She smoothed her napkin on her lap. "See, he decided all on his own to walk away from the job he'd worked all his adult life to earn. It's his job, his life, so okay. Only he didn't let it stop there."

The words poured out of her despite her efforts to stop them, and she knew without turning to see that he had walked into the room and was listening. "Next he made the momentous decision not only to buy personal property, but business property, too. Again, he did this all on his own without including me in the process. It's the same thing he's been doing all his life. Taking charge. Taking over."

She felt shaky, as if she were coming down with the flu. Something certainly wasn't right with her, because she didn't do this—she didn't air dirty marital laundry in front of others. Not only did it belittle her and Mac, it surely made her friends feel uncomfortable.

What is wrong with me?

Maybe it was the realization that after everything

she and Mac had gone through this past year, in the end, nothing had really changed in their marriage. He still captained the boat; it was his hand firmly on the tiller.

And have I figured out that I'd rather be along for the ride than sailing my ship alone?

Her stomach sank. Was that it? Was she willing to settle, after all?

Ali was confused. She needed to think. Now, however, wasn't the time. Mac *had* gone to a lot of trouble. He *was* trying. She couldn't throw that in his face.

Therefore, once again, just like a million other times in her marriage, Ali swallowed her feelings and buried her emotions. "I'm sorry. I shouldn't have spouted off like that." Then, pasting on a crooked grin, she glanced up at her husband. "I think we're ready to order."

After a moment's hesitation, he warily observed, "Okay."

Sage made a stab at slicing through the tension by saying, "Tater tots, Mac? Really?"

He shrugged and offered a bashful grin. "I don't know anything about menu planning."

"You don't know anything about running a restaurant," Ali said.

"I know that," he replied, watching her closely. "I certainly need some help."

"I might be able to pitch in," she told him. "Another time, though. Not tonight. This is girls' night out."

He visibly relaxed just a little at that. "In that case, I'd better get to work."

"I guess you'd better. Do you have a wine list?"

He named her favorite cabernet, and she nodded. "That will be fine."

Following that shaky start, she and her friends actually had a lovely meal. Mac did know how to grill a steak, and once everyone realized they weren't about to become part of an ugly marital spat, they relaxed, too. Conversation, laughter, and general good times flowed. Eventually Nic broke the dinner party up by saying, "I need to get home before I fall asleep right here."

"Well, sorry you find us so boring," Sarah fired back in mock offense.

"True." Nic glanced at her watch, then wryly added, "The nighttime schedule of twins has nothing to do with it."

As her friends stood to leave, Celeste called out, "Mac, may I have the check?"

He came out of the kitchen and shook his head. "Tonight's meal was on the house, ladies."

Sage snickered and looked at Ali. "He needs *a lot* of help running a restaurant."

"I won't argue that."

At that point, everyone looked expectantly at Ali, and she realized they were waiting to see if she intended to stay to talk with Mac or leave with the girls. Part of her wanted to leave, but what good would that accomplish? "It's been fun, ladies. I'll see you all tomorrow."

After thanking Mac, her friends departed. Ali followed them to the door, then flipped the lock. The last thing she wanted now was to be interrupted by a curious citizen investigating why lights were on in an empty building.

Mac poured himself a scotch, leaned back against the bar, and said, "Well, then. Something tells me that this surprise ranks right up there with the electric broom I bought you for our second anniversary."

Mac alternated between feeling bad and feeling put out. His big surprise hadn't thrilled her like he'd expected, but for crying out loud, what was wrong with giving her something he knew without a doubt that she wanted very much?

After more than two decades of marriage, he knew this woman inside and out. So why did he so often miss the mark about pleasing her? Why couldn't he make his wife happy?

"I'm sorry for the flash of temper," Ali said quietly. "I shouldn't have embarrassed us both in front of my friends."

He accepted the apology with a shrug. "So how badly did I screw up? Are you going to call it quits again?"

"No, I'm not going to call it quits again," she parroted, a snippy note in her tone. "That said, I have to ask. What in the world were you thinking, Mac? You are a federal court judge! You can't walk away from that to run a restaurant."

Working to maintain his patience, he spoke in a conciliatory tone. "Actually, I don't want to run a restaurant. That's your dream."

She dropped her chin to her chest and linked her fingers behind her head. Knowing Ali, he sensed that she was counting to ten. Quietly she asked, "How do you know that, Mac? You didn't ask me."

"You brought it up last summer," he shot back. "That's how I know. More than twenty years later and you still mention it—that's real."

Now she dropped her hands to her sides and walked toward him, stopping at the table closest to the bar, her hand grasping the back of a chair. "Let's shift the focus for a minute. I think this might go better if I understand why you took a leave of absence from the federal bench."

Mac stared down at his scotch on the rocks and rotated the glass, swishing the amber liquor over and around the ice. Maybe she had a point. "I have a laundry list of individual reasons, but they basically all add up to the fact that I was miserable." He glanced up. "I didn't like the job, Alison. It wasn't what I'd always expected it to be."

"It was the Sandberg case," she replied, shaking her head. "And the Desai case before that. You didn't feel that way until the high-profile trials took over your life."

"That's what I told myself, too, until I spent some time thinking it through. That's what I've been doing these last few weeks. I came up here where it is quiet and peaceful, and I examined every aspect of my life with the goal of assessing where I am now and how I want to go forward. It's something your friend Celeste suggested to me."

Surprise lit her eyes. "Celeste?"

"Yep.

Now she arched her brows in disbelief. "She told you to quit your job?"

"No." A smile played on Mac's lips. "She introduced the concept of the second half of life. It helped me realize that just because I wanted something when I was young didn't mean I still had to want it today."

"Well, as your wife of twenty-four years," Ali said, tugging a chair out from beneath the table and taking a seat, "I have to say I find that less than reassuring."

"Stop it." Mac circled the end of the bar and joined Ali at the table. "I'm not talking about you and you know it. I'm talking about the bench. I don't want it."

For a long moment, she stared at him. "I'm sorry, but this just blows me away. Your goal of becoming a judge is . . . who you are. It's what you worked to achieve for as long as I've known you. Every important decision of your life has been made to further that goal. And now that you have it, you're ready to throw it away?"

He sipped his drink. "Sad, isn't it, that I was so wrong about myself?"

"I don't get it." She drummed her fingers against the tabletop. "At risk of being as rude to you as you were to me last spring, maybe this is some sort of midlife crisis, a hormonal thing. Something you'll get past with a little distance."

For a long moment he simply looked at her. Then he observed, "Wow, if this is how it felt, it's a wonder you didn't throw something at me that day."

She shook her head. "I'm sorry, but this is simply wrong. You can't do this. Not when it's your life's goal." She rose from her seat and began pacing the room, staring blindly into space. "This is my fault. If I'd gone straight home and stayed there after your first trip to Eternity, we wouldn't be having this discussion."

"Now, Ali."

"Don't 'now, Ali' me." She rounded on him. "I hate it when you placate and patronize and . . . and . . . pat me on the head. Can you deny it? Had I gone home with you, would we be having this conversation?"

"Maybe not, but—"

"No buts, Mac. Don't you see the problem here? Because I'm still involved in Eternity Springs, you jump off and make this decision precipitously. Then time will pass and your storm of weirdness will end and you will realize you made a huge, horrible mistake."

"Storm of weirdness?"

"And whose fault will it be?" she continued as if he hadn't spoken. "It'll be my fault. Mine. You'll resent me. Maybe you won't mean to do it, but it'll happen anyway. We'll be worse off than ever."

She walked over to him, and her eyes looked a little wild as she clutched his arm. "Tell me it's still a leave of absence. Tell me you haven't actually resigned!"

"No, Ali, I haven't resigned." He tried to pull her down into his lap, but she drew away. "Nevertheless, I have made my decision."

"See? That's another thing." She held up her index finger. She didn't quite shake it at him, but she did use it to punctuate her sentences. "You've made *your* decision. Let's get back to that part of this issue."

Grim, Mac swallowed the words *Let's not* and washed them down with another sip of scotch.

"I hate the way people have come to use *disrespect*

as a verb," Ali said, "but I'm going to use it that way now. You disrespect me, Mac Timberlake. You disrespect me every time you make a decision that affects my life without including me in the process. I'm tired of it." She put her hands on her hips. "How dare you buy a building in Eternity Springs without consulting me beforehand! And the Heartache Falls property? Good heavens, Mac. You must have drained our savings completely."

"I financed most of it," he snapped back as he shot to his feet. Her charge touched a nerve. He was willing to take only so much grief. "And I wanted it to be a surprise. A gift for you. Actually, a really great gift. You loved that acreage. Don't pretend otherwise. I'm not going to ask your permission to give you a gift. It isn't like the old days when your family money propped us up. I bought it with *my* money and *my* credit."

"Okay, fine. Just what am I supposed to do with this gift? Live in a yurt?"

"Actually, the yurt is pretty great, too. Very comfortable. Can't beat the scenery. But no one is saying we have to live there. There's a spot near the falls that is perfect for a house."

"Oh? So now you've picked out the site for my next home? Gee, do you see a pattern here?"

"Wait a minute, Alison. I don't get it. I don't get you. You want to live in Eternity Springs, and you want to work in Eternity Springs. But when I provide you the perfect opportunity to do so, you pitch a hissy fit. What is it you want?"

"I want to be your partner!"

"You *are* my partner. You're my wife."

"Yes, and this isn't the 1950s anymore. You don't get to make all the decisions for me."

"I *don't* do that."

"You've *always* done that. I've just let you get away with it. My bad."

He raked his fingers through his hair in frustration. "You have to be the most frustrating, infuriating female ever born. Explain to me, would you please, why after all these years I still find you so utterly and completely fascinating?"

She stopped, stared at him, and he watched her anger deflate. "No fair."

"Sorry," he said with a shrug, even though he wasn't sorry at all. He took a step toward her. "I love you, Alison Michelle Timberlake."

Now she pouted. At least pouting kept her mouth shut.

"I'm sorry that my effort to surprise you shocked you instead. I hear what you are saying about partnership, and I promise to consider that from here on out."

She sighed. "What about the leave of absence? Will you cancel it and return to work?"

He sighed right back at her and moved closer still. "You need to believe me, Ali. I'm certain about this."

"Well, I'm not." She wrinkled her nose. "Promise me you won't make this leave of absence permanent without talking to me about it ahead of time."

"I promise." He took her in his arms. She remained stiff until he buried his face against her neck and kissed her. As she began to relax, he murmured against her ear. "I don't want to be a judge anymore. I want to practice law."

"In Eternity Springs? You'd have one client a quarter."

"That'll give me more time to help you run the New Place—or whatever you decide to name it. It needs a better name, don't you think?"

Ali shut her eyes and shook her head. "Mac, that's crazy. Just flat out crazy."

"Why?"

"I don't know anything about running a restaurant."

"Sure you do. You raised three children, two of them boys. Tell me our house wasn't like a restaurant back when you had kids who needed feeding between football practice and car wash fund-raisers and band concerts and soccer practice and—"

"Okay, okay. Enough." She rested her head against his chest and closed her eyes. "I need to think about this."

"Isn't it lucky, then, that I have access to the perfect place to think? There's this spot near Heartache Falls where you can spread out a blanket."

"I said think, Timberlake, not have sex."

"That isn't what I was thinking," he protested. When she gave him a look filled with disbelief, he added, "There's a nice big bed inside a comfy warm yurt for that. It's too cold for that this time of year. I'd shrivel up and be of absolutely no use to you."

"Hmm." Ali pulled out of his arms. "Is the cold really that much of a detriment to your, um, capabilities? I seem to recall one Groundhog Day in college . . ."

His mouth twitched with a grin. "Oh, yeah. Unfortunately, I'm not twenty years old any longer."

"In that case . . ." Her hand drifted down and cupped him. "We'd better not take any chances."

Recalling that she'd locked the front door, Mac eyed a rectangular tabletop. "I have an apron that would fit you."

"An apron?"

"Yeah. An apron. And nothing else."

SIXTEEN

October

Chase Timberlake slipped his key into his parents' front door, then glanced over his shoulder. "Don't worry about the cooler, Granddad. I'll come back and get it."

"Oh, just hush. The day I'm too old and decrepit to carry a cooler full of beer to a football game is the day I turn in my man badge."

"You brought me beer?" Chase asked as they went inside.

"Root beer. I have a nice German pilsner for myself."

"Gee, thanks, Granddad. I'll be sure to remember that next time you don't get the game because you have the wrong satellite provider."

"I didn't realize you were the gatekeeper to your mother's house." Charles Cavanaugh set the cooler on the theater room floor, reached into his pocket, and pulled out a ring of keys. Choosing one that matched the key Chase held, he observed, "I guess your mother gave me this just to placate me?"

Chase grinned. "It's not the key I control, Granddad. It's the surround-sound remote. I programmed it myself. I don't think Dad has figured out how to use it yet."

"Smart aleck," Charles said. "However, since you're so smart, get to work. I don't want to miss the kickoff. I have the feeling that the Buffaloes are gonna kick those Longhorns' butts all the way from Austin to the Gulf of Mexico."

"From your mouth to God's ear," Chase said. "The 'Horns are the luckiest team in college football."

"Their luck ends today. I can feel it."

As Chase and his grandfather settled in to watch the game, Chase couldn't help thinking about Lori, since she was at Texas A&M and the Aggies and the Longhorns were big rivals. Chase and Lori stayed in touch on Facebook and from all appearances, her undergrad years were going well. He was glad. Lori was a special girl, real special. He was a long way from wanting to settle down, but if he'd been older—if she'd been older—she was the kind of woman who would make a man a good wife. She sorta reminded him of his mom.

Lori did have her goals, though. She wanted to be a vet more than anything. He hoped she didn't let some Texas farm boy change that for her. *Like Dad changed Mom's dream of going to cooking school in Europe.*

His parents had never admitted it, but Chase and his sibs had long ago realized that Mom had been knocked up with Stephen when they got married. He'd sometimes wondered if his parents would have ended up together had the pregnancy not occurred.

They seemed so different. When he was growing up, his mom had been laid back and easygoing. Dad was the definition of driven. That's what made this mountain man fantasy of his beyond weird. When the game went to a commercial break, he asked, "What do you think is going to happen with my dad, Granddad?"

"Are you referring to his Grizzly Adams impersonation?"

"Who?"

Charles shook his head. "It was a television show long before your time."

"Whatever. Do you think he'll resign from the bench? Mom says no, that this is a temporary brain cramp and that he'll be back to work just as soon as he's had time to forget about Desai and Sandberg."

Charles thought about it for a moment. "I tend to agree with your mother. She knows him better than anyone. That said, I've always thought there was something beyond ambition to your father's desire for the bench. That may be the missing puzzle piece here."

"Hmm." Chase didn't say any more because the game resumed and Colorado put together a great scoring drive on the nationally ranked Longhorns. Following the touchdown and after exchanging high fives with his granddad, he settled back into his seat fairly happy with his world. During halftime, however, when his mother wasn't around to serve homemade sandwiches and snacks like usual during family game-watching gatherings, his thoughts returned to his parents. "I do understand why they'd want to live in the mountains. I can't imagine living anywhere else. Ever since I was a kid, I've wanted to work in a field that would allow me to live in the mountains. It's weird, Granddad. I always felt like I was letting Dad down because I didn't want to be a lawyer like Stephen does. Now it's like Dad has come over to the dark side."

"Your father always understood that your dreams and desires went in a different direction than his. Who knows? Maybe you, rather than your brother, are the son who most takes after his father. It'll be interesting to watch and see what Mac decides."

"Or what Mom decides for him," Chase said with a rueful snort. "She's gone just as crazy as Dad. She might throw down an ultimatum. It's like they've got some weird role reversal thing going on."

"Alison reminds me more and more of her mother every day."

The resumption of football interrupted further observation about Chase's parents. To Chase's amazement, the Buffs did make a game of it, and they entered the fourth quarter down by a field goal. With less than a minute left in the game, the score tied, and the Buffs driving, Chase and his granddad were so intent on the game that they almost didn't hear the doorbell. When Chase did hear it, he ignored it.

"Go answer that," his grandfather said.

"Not now! Whoever it is can wait."

Just then, the Longhorns called a time-out, so Chase made a rush for the door. In a hurry, he didn't bother to check the peephole before yanking the door open. He didn't recognize the woman standing on his parents' front porch. "Can I help you?"

"I'm looking for Mackenzie Timberlake."

Hearing the crowd noise swell, Chase glanced back over his shoulder. "Come on in. Follow me."

He dashed back to the theater room, all but dismissing the visitor from his thoughts as he arrived just in time to see Colorado let fly a pass toward the end zone as time on the clock ran out. An orange jersey and a white jersey went up, and two pairs of hands reached for the ball. Someone caught it, but at first Chase couldn't tell who.

Then he saw the referee's hands signal a touchdown, and he shouted, "Woo-hoo!"

Charles Cavanaugh pushed to his feet and yelled, "Touchdown!"

"Game over! We did it, Granddad! We won!" Chase and his grandfather exchanged more high fives and hoots and cheers. Eventually both men noticed the woman who had joined them.

"May we help you?" Charles said.

"Oops." Chase winced. "Sorry, I forgot."

"That's okay," the woman said, a touch of the South in her voice. "I obviously came at an inopportune moment." Glancing at the television, she added, "I'm always glad to see the Longhorns get beat. I'm an Oklahoma fan myself."

"I'm really sorry I abandoned you, ma'am," Chase said. "You're looking for my father?"

"Mackenzie Timberlake is your father?"

"Yes, ma'am."

She smiled and met Charles's gaze. "And he called you Granddad. Isn't that handy!"

"Pardon me?" Charles asked, his tone suddenly suspicious.

The woman made a sweeping gesture toward Charles and Chase. "You're family."

Next she put her palm against her chest. "I'm family. I'm Mackenzie's aunt Sally. I need to speak with him about his mother."

Ali sat in a rocking chair in Nic Callahan's house, cuddling one of the sleeping twins against her breast. She, Sage, Sarah, and Celeste had volunteered to babysit for Nic and Gabe and their guests from Texas, Gabe's brother Luke and his wife and three children, so that the two couples could enjoy a meal at the Bristlecone. At this moment in time, after a relatively wild couple of hours, all five children were asleep, thank God.

"That's another problem with the new Bristlecone," she said. "It's not a family restaurant, and Eternity Springs is a family kind of place."

"Aren't you just Little Ali Sunshine tonight," Sage observed, snuggling Nic's other daughter in a second rocking chair.

"I'm sorry. I know I'm grumpy, but Mac is driving me crackers. He told me today that his leave of absence is over in less than two weeks, and nothing I say can convince him that resigning is the wrong thing to do."

Celeste looked up from the embroidery she was doing on a quilt square. "In that case, have you considered that perhaps it is not the wrong thing to do?"

Ali went quiet for a long minute, then said, "That's just about all I think about. My problem is that I know my husband very, very well. I know how hard he worked and all that he sacrificed to earn this job. He talks a good game when it comes to walking away from it, but I don't trust it. I learned the hard way that buried resentment is terribly destructive for a marriage."

"You think that's what would happen?" Sarah asked.

"Maybe not right away, but eventually, yes. If he does this, there's no going back when he changes his mind. Unfortunately, a federal judgeship isn't something a person can walk into and out of at will. So one day he'll wake up from this midlife crisis, look around, and blame me. We'll be worse off than before because he'll be the one stewing instead of me, and I can deal with it better."

Sarah, who was also working on a quilt square, accidentally jabbed her thumb with a needle and winced. "So what are you going to do? Tie him up and deliver him to the courthouse to resume his job?"

"I don't know what I'm going to do."

"I know what you should do," Celeste said. "You should have faith in your husband. Trust in him and in his love for you."

"I do," Ali protested. When Celeste looked over the top of her cheaters at her, she amended, "I try."

Celeste shook her head. "That lack of faith is what is holding you back from full happiness. You do realize that, don't you?"

"Can we change the subject, please?"

Sage grinned and let her off the hook. "Tell us what's happening at the New Place. I understand Mac has been a regular worker bee in the restaurant."

Ali rolled her eyes. "He's a wild man. He's remodeling the place top to bottom. When he's not working on the remodel, he's poring over house plan magazines and pestering Gabe for ideas. He wants to start building a house up near Heartache Falls next spring."

"Gee," Sage said, a gleam of amusement in her eyes. "I'm disappointed for you. I understand that life in a yurt can be very romantic. By the way, I've been meaning to ask—how did that harem costume you borrowed go over?"

"Harem costume?" Sarah and Celeste said simultaneously. Celeste added, "Well, she does live in a tent."

Sarah shot Sage a curious look and asked, "What were you doing with a harem costume?"

"That's another story for another time," Sage answered, smiling smugly. "On that note, if you guys think you have it handled here okay, I need to be going. I have a date tonight."

"Oh, yeah? Who with?" Ali asked.

"A paintbrush and canvas," Sage replied with a sigh. "My next show will be here before I know it."

Shortly after Sage departed, the Callahans returned, quietly raving about their meal, but wondering how long a menu that pricey would last in Eternity Springs. The babysitters donned their coats, hats, and gloves, then left the Callahan home.

Sarah needed to pick up her mom from her visit with Reverend Hart and his wife, so she headed in the opposite direction from Ali and Celeste. Fat snowflakes swirled around Ali and Celeste as they walked together toward Angel's Rest. "I wonder if the snow will stay around this time. We're getting to that part of the year."

"Not if the weather forecast is correct," Celeste said. "It's supposed to be lovely tomorrow—a good day for a bicycle ride."

"Not your motorcycle?"

"I like to diversify," the older woman replied with a grin. Slipping her arm through Ali's, she changed the subject. "I hope I didn't get too personal in front of the others, dear."

"Not at all. I'm grateful for your advice anytime, anyplace, Celeste. It hasn't missed my notice that you are one of the most intelligent, intuitive people I've ever met."

"In that case, I'd like to say one more thing. Don't let your past get in the way of your future."

"What does that mean?"

"You need to make a leap of faith, but something is holding you back. Be watchful. It is my belief that lasting happiness is within your and Mac's grasp if you—both of you—take advantage of the opportunity coming your way."

Ali gave her friend a hug. "You'd better be glad you're living now instead of the 1700s. They'd have burned you for a witch."

"Oh, darling. If you only knew."

At that point, Ali's cell phone began to ring.

"My wife is up to something," Mac muttered to Gus as they walked along the shoreline of Hummingbird Lake early Sunday afternoon. First she'd dragged him down the mountain for the early church service, then she declared her intention to christen the new appliances at the New Place and told him to make himself scarce for a while as she rustled up a special meal. "What do you think she has up her sleeve, boy?"

Gus was too busy tromping and sniffing his way through the brittle brown leaves beneath a cottonwood tree to respond with either a bark or a whine, which left Mac to decide the question for himself. "It's payback for my surprise dinner, and I'll bet it's the kids. I bet the kids are coming. She's probably concocted some sort of intervention scene. She's into those, you know."

He could picture it now. She'd tie him to a chair with a dinner napkin, then stuff his face with . . . hmm, what would she be cooking today? Italian? If she felt guilty about siccing the kids on him, then yeah. She'd stuff his face with spaghetti until his face turned green, then turn the kids loose on him. Stephen would display stoic disappointment. Chase would rant and rave. Caitlin would turn on her puppy-dog eyes and emote at him. Yeah, he'd bet his bottom dollar that Ali was bringing in the big guns.

"Well, Gus, I'm always happy to see the kids, but they're going to leave here considering this to be a wasted trip." Mac had complete confidence in his decision. Very little in his life had ever felt as right as did walking away from the bench.

"Hello, you two," called a voice to his right.

Mac turned his head to see Celeste pedaling toward him on a bicycle, and he grinned. That woman never failed to surprise him. "Good afternoon, Celeste."

She pulled up beside him and stopped. Unfastening the chin strap on her helmet, she removed the head protection and finger-combed her hair. "I am so glad to see you. I was hoping for the opportunity to speak with you before I make my trek up to Sinner's Prayer Pass."

"That's a tough ride."

"I'm a tough woman. Besides, I can't think of a more spiritual place to be on a gorgeous Sunday afternoon, can you?"

Mac thought of the building site up at Heartache Falls. "A person doesn't have to look hard to find a spiritual locale in Colorado. Especially not around Eternity Springs."

Celeste put her hand on Mac's shoulder. "Our town has worked its magic on you, hasn't it, young man?"

Young man? Mac's lips quirked at the thought. When he moved past his amusement at the older woman's phrasing, her question registered and words bubbled up from deep inside of him. "Ali's decision to come here has proven to be the best thing that could have happened to us both. I feel reborn, Celeste. My marriage is reborn."

He paused, surveyed the silhouette of Eternity Springs before him, and added, "This little burg is balm for wounded souls. You picked the right spot to build Angel's Rest, Celeste."

"Yes, the energy here is special." She gave his shoulder a friendly little pat, then added, "Speaking of special, I have something I'd like to give you."

She unzipped her fanny pack and withdrew a silver chain and pendant. "This is the official Angel's Rest blazon, awarded to those who have embraced healing's grace. Wear it next to your heart, Mac Timberlake. Carry the grace you found here with you upon whatever life path you travel. Call upon it when you require a reminder of the peace and joy you have found here in Eternity Springs."

That almost felt like a blessing, Mac thought as he accepted her gift. He'd never worn a necklace in his life, but since this place was all about newness, and the medal was rather cool—Sage's design, he'd bet—he slipped it over his head. Then he leaned over and kissed Celeste Blessing on the cheek. "I'm honored. Thank you, Celeste."

"You're very welcome," Celeste replied as she fastened her helmet's chin strap. "Now, don't forget, Mac. New lives face challenges, too."

Was that a hint? "Do you know what Ali is cooking up in her kitchen today?"

Celeste responded with only a wave as she pedaled away from him. Watching her go, Mac said, "Why do I have a feeling it's trouble?"

Ali pulled the lasagna from the oven and set it on the warming tray. Glancing at the clock, she noted that she was right on schedule. Good. She expected her guests to arrive any minute now.

She really hoped she was doing the right thing. This morning when she awoke, the prospect of surprise delighted her. Then about an hour ago, she started getting butterflies in her tummy. Now, with the family due to arrive at any moment, her butterflies had butterflies.

The cloud of foreboding hovering above her warned her that she'd screwed up. Royally.

What had she been thinking? She could count on one hand the times Mac had referred to his family without prodding from her in all the years they'd been married. She shouldn't have sprung this surprise on him, no matter what her father said or how much Mac's aunt begged. Mac had never been one to be overly enthused about surprises, anyway.

"What have I done?" she asked as she heard the restaurant's front door open. She shot a panicked glance at her cell phone, recognizing she'd waited too long. Sucking in a deep breath, she wiped her hands on a dishtowel, pasted on a smile, and exited the kitchen.

Ali's gaze skidded over her father and Chase before settling on the stranger. The woman didn't look a generation older than Mac, but then a good surgeon could be responsible for that. She was attractive—bleached blonde and fit. Ali could see something of Mac in her smile.

Ali extended her hand. "Hello, I'm Alison Timberlake."

"Sally Sutherland. It's lovely to meet you, Alison." She glanced around curiously. "And where is my dear nephew?"

"He'll be here shortly," Ali said, then turned to greet her father and son. "Can I get you something to drink while we wait?"

She expected Mac's aunt to ask for iced tea or water, and she was taken aback when the woman requested a martini. "I'm sorry. The restaurant has been in the midst of remodeling, and we haven't stocked the bar. I do have wine I intend to serve with dinner. Would you care for a glass of that?"

"Is it white zin? I can't stand anything else."

"Um, no, it's an Italian Chianti. It's one of Mac's favorites."

"In that case, I'll try it." She flashed a smile.

Ali's stomach churned. She served the wine, then asked Chase to assist her in the kitchen for a moment. Once they were alone, she asked, "So? What do you think?"

Her son grimaced. "I don't know, Mom. At first I thought she was cool. She acted friendly and seemed interested in Dad. But coming up here, she and Granddad rode together, so I had time alone to think." He rubbed the back of his neck and frowned. "There's something off about her. I can't tell what. What do you think this legacy for Dad from his mother is all about?"

"I don't know, honey. I just don't know."

She did know that she feared she'd made a very bad mistake. Yesterday when her father and Chase called, their enthusiasm about Sally Sutherland had been infectious. Mac's aunt had a legacy from his mother to deliver to Mac, and she wanted to surprise her nephew.

Ali had known better. After all, look at how she'd reacted to the surprise he'd concocted for her. Why had she gone along with it? Was she subconsciously trying to administer a little payback to her husband? If so, then she deserved whatever grief he sent her way.

The timer buzzed, and Ali removed bread from the

oven. "Tell you what, Chase—if you'll keep an eye on things here, I'm going to duck out the back and hunt down your father. I think he needs a heads-up before he walks into a situation he's not prepared to face."

Ali stepped toward the back door and had just reached for the knob when the door swung open. Mac stepped inside, sniffed the air, then said, "Red sauce. Okay, Alison, what did you do?"

SEVENTEEN

His wife looked more ill than guilty as she glanced worriedly over her shoulder. "She showed up yesterday at our house in Denver while Dad and Chase were there watching ball."

Mac's stomach dropped. He knew. In his heart of hearts, he knew. "She?"

"Your aunt."

He closed his eyes. *I don't have an aunt.*

It was her, of course. She was scamming them. That's what she did. She'd shown up at his house? She'd spent time with his son? With Charles? Deep within Mac, fury flared to life.

"Your aunt Sally. She wanted to surprise you, and Dad and Chase were charmed, and I went along with them, but now I realize that was disrespectful of me and I should have known better. But it's too late now because they're here."

Mac glanced from Ali to Chase. "Here?"

His son nodded and hooked his thumb toward the front of the restaurant. "Out there. She and Granddad are chatting. She's been real nice to him."

"I'll just bet she has," Mac muttered beneath his breath.

He'd been a fool. He should have expected this.

Women like her never disappeared, not when there was more trouble to be made. How dare she come to his house. How dare she approach his son. Mac stared at the doorway, feeling as if he stood at a precipice on Murphy Mountain and his next step would take him over the edge and send his life crashing down.

He wanted to walk out there and do violence. He wanted to turn his back and run away, to get as far from her as possible, as fast as possible. Hey, it had worked before.

Don't be stupid, Timberlake. You're not going to leave your family to her oh-so-tender mercies and you are not going to kill her—no matter how attractive the idea sounds at the moment.

He inhaled a deep breath and stepped into the dining room. He saw a table set for five. Charles Cavanaugh leaned back against the bar. Mac's mother stood in front of Charles, a glass of wine in her hand.

She looked . . . good. Older, yeah, but not old. She might have had some work done. Could have found a sugar daddy or two along the way. As Mac watched, she laughed up into Charles's face and casually touched him. Blatantly flirted with him.

Scammed him.

Every protective instinct Mac possessed went on high alert, and he marched forward saying, "This was a big mistake."

She didn't hesitate, but let fly a smile and extended her arms wide, rushing toward him. "Mackenzie! It's so wonderful to see you."

As a child, he'd have given anything to have her greet him in such a way. Now when she attempted to throw her arms around him, he grabbed her and held her firmly away. "What do you want?"

Her eyes narrowed, but her smile never faltered. Softly so that the others couldn't hear, she told him, "Get rid of them and I'll tell you."

Mac didn't—couldn't—look away from his mother, but he sensed Ali coming up beside him. "Mac?"

"What's going on here?" Charles asked, confusion and surprise evident in his tone.

Mac's mother lifted her chin. Her dark eyes challenged him. He was gripped by a maelstrom of emotion—fear, loathing, fury and the never-shed, never-outgrown hurt of a child abused by his parent. He cleared his throat. "Let's take a walk, shall we?"

She scowled. "It's cold outside. Can't they—"

He dropped her arms and headed for the front door, confident that she would follow. Lord knew she never missed an opportunity to follow a meal ticket.

This woman was his mother. She'd found him. She'd met his family. They'd ask questions and he'd have to give them answers. More lies? No. He couldn't do that. Not now. *Dear God, help me.*

Outside, clouds had begun to gather in the previously blue sky. Upon noting them, Mac spared a thought for Celeste, hoping she paid attention and wouldn't be caught on the road if snow began to fall. Shoving his hands in his pockets, he crossed Cottonwood to the asphalt path that ran alongside Angel Creek. He walked north toward the new footbridge spanning the creek. His mother walked beside him. "Don't go so fast. I'm in heels and I can't keep up."

"You'll catch up. You always do."

He crossed the bridge, then led the way to his destination, the garden Gabe Callahan had designed around the hot springs on the far end of the Angel's Rest property.

"Why are you taking me here?" his mother complained. "It stinks."

"Yeah, it surely does. It stinks to high heaven, and it's the most appropriate place I can think of to deal with you."

It was also an isolated spot away from the main area of hot springs pools; Mac expected they could stop there and not be interrupted. The last thing he wanted was an audience for this showdown.

Besides, if I decide to drown her, maybe nobody will see me do it.

Finally he stopped, folded his arms, and leaned back against the trunk of a huge cottonwood tree. "All right, Brenda. Let's hear it."

"Now, Mackenzie. Be nice." She took a seat on the park bench, then patted the space beside her. "Sit down, son."

"Give it up. Since you claimed to be my aunt rather than my mother, you obviously came with a plan. What is it?"

"I simply didn't want to push you into any corners. I didn't know what you'd told your family about our family, so I thought it best to keep things loose."

"Our family? We didn't have a family."

She clapped a hand against her chest. "Why, Mackenzie. I'm hurt."

I wish.

"I watched out for you back then and I'm watching out for you today. I told your boy and that darling

Charles that I had a legacy from your mother to share with you."

"I understand all about your legacies, Brenda. What do you want from me?"

"I want to be part of your life, your family. I want to be a grandmother to your children."

Mac almost laughed. Maybe Caitlin got a little bit of drama from his side of the family after all. "And I want to hit a golf ball like Phil Mickelson, too. Neither one of those things is going to happen."

"Why not?"

"Because I tend to slice my drives. So, Brenda, what do you really want?"

She crossed her legs and set her toes to tapping. "You've grown up to be a hard man."

"I learned early. Had to be hard to survive."

When she rolled her eyes in response, he flashed back to one time in some run-down hotel room in some run-down town when his mother was with one of her run-down lovers. The guy—some married insurance salesman, if he remembered correctly—had actually hit his knees while he begged Mac's mother not to leave him. She'd promised to stay, talked him into handing over all the cash in his wallet, then shut the door behind the sap. And rolled her eyes.

She was a real piece of work. For the first time in, well, maybe ever, he wondered what had happened to make Brenda Timberlake the woman she was. "Where are you from?"

"What?" The question obviously startled her.

"Where did you grow up? What town?"

"What does that have to do with anything?"

"Humor me. With the truth, please. I've become quite adept at spotting lies over the years."

She measured him with her glance and he could all but see the wheels turning in her mind. She would ask herself if this was part of the negotiation. "I was an Air Force brat. I grew up all over the place."

"Do I really have an aunt Sally?"

She shrugged. "At one time, yes. I really couldn't say now."

Now that he'd cracked this particular door open, Mac discovered he had dozens of questions, and he realized he must be more curious about his past than he'd allowed himself to admit. He asked her about her parents and learned that in addition to an aunt named Sally, he had an uncle Ben and an uncle Ray. Her family name was Hellman. "So is Timberlake something you pulled out of the air?"

Something flashed across her expression—a wash of pain, of grief. It was a look Mac had never associated with his mother prior to that moment.

"I married Joe Timberlake in Vegas," Brenda said. "He fell off a ladder three weeks before you were born and never woke up."

When Mac was little, she had told him that his father had been a carpenter named Joe. He'd been intrigued by the thought because the wheelchair-bound woman his mother had worked for in Tulsa, Leanna West, had read him Bible stories and she used to go on and on about how Jesus' father was named Joe and he was a carpenter, too. The storybook illustration of Jesus and Joseph in his workshop remained a vivid memory for Mac to this day. "You rarely talked about him."

She shrugged and looked away. "I'm getting cold. Can we cut to the chase here?"

"In a minute." This might be Mac's only chance to learn something about his family roots. Things he hadn't cared about all that much had become more important to him as he grew older, especially after he had children of his own. "Tell me about my father."

She closed her eyes. "You look just like him. Or how he would have looked had he lived longer. He liked to read spy novels and could sing . . . oh, my, how he could sing. I thought he could make it in Nashville if he ever tried. I met him on the base in Wichita Falls, Texas, three months before his discharge. My dad forbade me to see him, but . . ." She shrugged. "We married as soon as he separated from the service."

"How old were you when he died?"

She opened her mouth, then abruptly shut it. This time Mac was the one rolling his eyes. "I won't tell anyone how old you are."

"Fine. I was eighteen and pregnant, and he had no insurance. I did what I had to do to get by."

"What about your parents?"

"What about them?"

"They wouldn't help you?"

She shrugged. "Look, I'd made my choice. I didn't regret it, either. I loved your father."

He gave her a long, measuring look. "You kept me."

Again she shrugged. "Like I said, I was eighteen. I didn't know how hard it would be."

In that, Mac could relate to her. He'd been a little older than she and about to earn a college degree, but when Ali told him she was pregnant, he hadn't had a clue as to just what a big hill parenthood was to climb.

Mac realized he was starting to feel a little sorry for the woman. That wouldn't do. "What are you doing now? How do you make a living?"

She rose slowly to her feet. Her smile was as cold as her heart. "That's where you come in."

"Gee, Mom. You never fail to disappoint."

"I need a lawyer," she told him. "There's a good chance I'm going to be indicted on embezzlement charges."

"Embezzlement? You talked someone into trusting you with a checkbook? How much did you steal?"

"It's all a mistake."

I'll bet. "Are you currently on probation?"

"No. I've served my debts to society."

Plural noted, Mac thought.

"I also need living expenses. Unfortunately, I will most likely need to establish myself in a new career field, and in this economy that could be difficult."

"How much do you want?"

A shrewd light entered her eyes. "I've done some research. You've done very well for yourself, Mackenzie, and you are obviously a wealthy man. That said, I'm also not blind to the fact that you have no use for me. Since that's the case, I think we'd both be more comfortable if we just took care of this once and for all so that I don't have to continue to interfere in your life. I think one hundred thousand dollars should do it. And a lawyer, of course."

"Of course," Mac said wryly. "One who will

defend you against embezzlement and extortion charges."

"I'm a mother asking her son for help. That's not extortion."

"So I'm free to tell you no?"

"Of course." She glanced at her fingernails, then added, "Although I will insist on meeting my grand-children. What have you told them about me, Mackenzie? Do they even know I'm alive? I'm sure they'll want to hear stories about you when you were growing up. You had the hands of a Gypsy back in the day. Could pick a pocket slicker than snot. Of course, most of the people we were stealing from were old, deaf, and almost blind, but you were good, Mac."

"I was a child."

"Now, that's not entirely true. You were older when we ran that sting in Kansas after I got out of jail the first time."

"I wasn't part of that."

She arched a brow and smirked. "Really? Funny, that's not how I remember it. If you decline to help me, I'll be forced to find other ways to make a living. You're famous now. I don't doubt that the *National Enquirer* would buy a story about you."

Yep, she was definitely a piece of work.

Mac rubbed the back of his neck and evaluated his options. The first time he'd met Alison Cavanaugh, he'd claimed to be an orphan, and in all the years since, he'd never deviated from that story. He was ashamed of his youth, about who he'd been and what he'd done. He was ashamed to be this woman's son.

He was ashamed for having lied about it for so long to the most important person in his life.

And yet he *had* lied to Alison all this time. That wouldn't be something she would easily forgive or forget. The last thing he wanted at this particular time was to introduce another issue to fight about into their marriage.

Oh, hell. Mac's stomach took a nauseated roll, and he wished he had the power to pack another year or two onto Sandberg's sentence for opening this can of worms. "Brenda, whether I like it or not, you are my mother. I intend to respect that even if I don't respect you."

"You wound me."

If only. "Let me make certain I understand what we're talking about here. You want me to arrange legal representation and give you one hundred thousand dollars or you will introduce yourself to my family as my children's grandmother. Correct?"

"I want you to pay for the lawyer, too."

"Of course." Mac closed his eyes and tilted his head toward the heavens. *Yep, she's a real piece of work.* "All right, then. I think we're done here. I'm sure Ali is wondering what's happened to us."

"So you agree?"

His heart heavy, his conscience clear, Mac nodded once. He knew what he had to do. "Let's get this done, Aunt Sally. Once and for all, I need this behind me."

As Ali peeked through the front curtains of the New Place, she decided that they needed to be replaced sooner rather than later. She'd had no clue they were this dingy.

In fact, if Mac didn't show up soon, she just might take them down and start washing them herself in the kitchen sink.

Where had they gone? What were they discussing? Just how angry was her husband, really? Pretty darn angry, she thought.

"I think we should go ahead and eat, Mom," Chase said. "No telling how long he's going to be, and cold lasagna doesn't do it for me like hot lasagna."

"The boy is right," her father added. "Besides, my mouth has watered so much since I walked through the front door that I am about to expire from dehydration."

Ali frowned at her son and her father. "It would be rude to start without them."

"I'm sure Sally will understand. She's a lovely woman."

Ali eyed her father sharply. "Chase isn't so sure of that."

Chase swiped a black olive out of the salad bowl and earned a hand slap from his mother for the effort. "Mom's right. That lady was eyeing you like steak on the grill, Granddad."

Charles looked surprised, then he preened a bit. "You think I'm too old for a woman to find me interesting, young man?"

Chase flashed his father's grin. "Not at all. You are a silver fox. It's just that she strikes me as a wolf and you know what wolves can do to foxes."

"Ah, but foxes are sly, are they not?"

"You don't have to worry about Granddad," Ali said. "I've watched him avoid wolves pretty much all my life."

Charles smiled and said gently, "Come away from the window, Ali. Let's sit down to eat."

Ali knew she wouldn't be able to eat a thing, but the process of serving the meal did provide a welcome distraction. Nevertheless, she was unable to stop herself from reliving the moment she told Mac that his aunt had come to visit. He'd gone hard and cold as the granite cliffs on the north side of Murphy Mountain in February.

I really screwed this one up.

Ali joined her father and son at the table without filling a plate for herself. She did, however, pour a glass of wine before second-guessing herself. She should have gone straight for the vodka.

Her father sang her culinary praises and asked for a second helping of pasta. Chase plowed through three servings and half a dozen breadsticks. Watching his grandson, Charles shook his head. "Don't they feed you up in Boulder?"

"Not like this."

Ali sipped the spicy Chianti and waited, thoughts whirling through her mind as time crawled by. Finally the front door opened and Mac and his aunt stepped inside.

EIGHTEEN

Ali lowered her wineglass to the table and studied her husband. He didn't look like he wanted to murder her for springing this surprise. When he met her gaze and gave her an uncertain little smile, some of her inner tension dissipated. Most of it remained, however, due to the lines of tension bracketing his mouth. He wasn't furious, but he certainly wasn't happy, either. Aunt Sally, on the other hand, appeared downright smug.

Ali didn't like it. Or her, she decided.

Once the door closed behind Mac and his aunt, he looked at Sally, then at Chase, Charles, and finally Ali. "I want you all to know that this woman is not my aunt. Her name is Brenda Timberlake. She is my mother."

In the echo of that bombshell, Ali absorbed a variety of reactions. Her son's mouth gaped open. Her father's eyes narrowed. Mac stood straight as an aspen. Brenda Timberlake—his mother!—jerked her head around to look at Mac, fury filling her face.

Ali's own reaction was a combination of shock and anticipation. Mac had told her his mother was dead! Why had he lied? And kept lying? What was the big secret? She knew her husband well enough to realize that this story was just beginning.

"Um, Mackenzie?" Brenda asked. "What are you doing?"

"I'm telling my family the truth. Finally. It's long overdue." He stared straight at Ali, holding her gaze like a man facing a firing squad. "I was always too ashamed to tell you. I grew up panhandling. Picking pockets. And, to my dying shame, stealing from the elderly."

Ali's chin dropped. Mac? Her Mac? A thief? He had stolen from old people?

Even as Ali processed his words, Brenda warned, "You better stop right there, boyo."

He totally ignored her. "She came to Eternity Springs to extort money from me. If I didn't give her what she wanted, she threatened to sell her story to the tabloids and create a nifty little scandal that would hurt my family and my career. I refuse to bend to the threat of blackmail, so here we are. Now you know that my mother was . . . still is . . . a grifter."

Now he broke eye contact with Ali and glanced at his father-in-law and son. "Do you all have any questions? I'm prepared to answer them thoroughly and completely."

Ali watched her mother-in-law. Brenda looked furious and a little bit afraid and definitely shocked. Obviously she hadn't anticipated this sort of reaction from her son.

Seated at the table, Chase looked confused as he set down his fork. "You always told me that your parents were dead, Dad."

"I lied, son. I'm sorry. It was wrong of me, and I apologize to you, to all of you, for it."

"He always was a liar," Brenda snapped.

Ali's father took another bite of lasagna, chewed thoughtfully, then said to Mac, "Pickpocket and thief, hmm? You don't have a record, so I assume you were never caught?"

"No."

"I protected him," Brenda declared.

At that, Ali's maternal instincts rebelled, and she rose to her feet. "Oh, really? And exactly how did you manage that? Weren't you the one forcing him to pick pockets and steal?"

"You don't know that."

"I know Mac." Ali's gaze flicked toward her husband. "You told me you went into foster care when you were nine. Was that the truth?"

"Yes. That was the first time—an eighteen-month stint while she was in jail. The second time, let's see, she was picked up for nicking a checkbook when she was on parole. Or was that your third stint in the slammer?"

Brenda audibly sucked in a breath. "Do you know what you are doing? I wasn't kidding, Mackenzie. That baseball trial might be over, but your fifteen minutes aren't done yet. I'll ruin you professionally."

Ali literally hissed, and she thought fleetingly that if she looked down at her hands, she might see claws instead of fingernails.

Mac reached into his pocket and pulled out his cell phone. He tossed it to Brenda, saying, "Call them. I don't care."

"Mac!" Ali stepped toward him. It was one thing

to come clean with the family, but something else entirely to do it in the press. "She's right. You can't let the papers get hold of this. You're a federal judge!"

He took Ali's hand, brought it up to his lips for a kiss, then said, "She can't hurt me, Ali-cat. She doesn't have that power. You, on the other hand, could destroy me."

"I won't."

"I hope not, but I haven't told you everything yet. It's time I come clean with everything. You and I are starting a new life together. I refuse to repeat the mistakes of the old, and I refuse to bring old rotten baggage along with me. Can I tell you the rest of it? Would you listen to me?"

"Hey! You can't just ignore me. I'm your mother!"

"Unfortunately, that's true. I'd like nothing more than to tell you to take a hike. However, because you are, in fact, my mother, here is what I am prepared to do." He raked Brenda Timberlake with a cold, unfeeling gaze. "I will provide—and pay for—legal representation for you. Once your future is known, I will buy a house for you to live in. I'm thinking Florida would be a good spot. I will hold the deed, however. In addition, I will provide a monthly living allowance for one year, which should give you enough time to reestablish yourself."

"How much allowance?"

Mac considered the question, then looked at Ali. "How much do we give Caitlin?" She told him, and he nodded. "That sounds fair."

Brenda sputtered. "But . . . but . . ."

"I'd take it, Grandmaw," Chase drawled. "That's the best you're gonna do. Believe me. I know him."

She drew herself up, lifted her chin, and declared, "If you think you can buy my silence with that . . ."

"You misunderstand. I'm not buying your silence. You're free to sell whatever story you want wherever you want to sell it. That offer is what my conscience compels me to settle on you because, like it or not, you are my mother."

That shocked her into silence. Ali's dad took the opportunity to toss her the keys to her car, saying, "I think you should be going. You'll want to make it at least to Gunnison before it gets dark. I'll be riding back with Chase."

She caught the keys, stared at them with confusion, then lifted her gaze to Mac. "What is *wrong* with you?"

Mac went still for a long moment before he slowly shook his head. "Wow. Do you know what? I asked that exact question, in a similar tone, of my wife last spring." He stared down at Ali, his eyes warm and soft with love. "I didn't know it at the time, but it was the start of something new and wonderful for me."

Ali blinked, tears stinging her eyes. *Oh, Mac.*

He brought her hand back to his mouth for another kiss. "Maybe you'll be lucky and the same thing will happen for you. Good-bye, Mom. Leave a number where you can be reached, and I'll arrange for an attorney to call you on Monday."

She sputtered another moment until Ali's dad stepped forward. "I'll walk you out."

Brenda Timberlake snatched up her handbag, lifted her nose in the air, and sniffed loudly with disdain. "Fine. We'll talk next week."

When the door finally shut behind her, Chase observed, "I didn't think she'd ever leave."

Mac continued to hold Ali's gaze. "Chase, do me a favor. Get lost."

"Dad, I haven't had dessert yet."

"Your grandfather always likes to walk off his meal before he has his dessert. Go walk with him."

"Oh, all right."

When they were alone, Mac dropped her hand and stepped away from Ali. "Well, I don't know about you, but I'm just about cured of surprises forever."

Regret welled up inside of Ali. "I'm so sorry, Mac."

He shook his head. "No, don't be. This was actually a good thing." He explained how his mother had contacted him through his office during the summer, then added, "I knew she wouldn't disappear now that she'd found me. This confrontation was going to happen sometime, and honestly, I'm glad to get it behind me."

"Why did you never tell me about her, Mac?"

He shoved his hands in the pockets of his jeans and began to pace. "I didn't want you to know who I was. Ali, I did some awful things as a kid. Her favorite con was to hire out as a companion for elderly widows. We'd move in, and she'd turn on the charm and take fabulous care of them for a bit. My job was to look and act innocent whenever family members checked up on us, and win everyone's heart. After all, who would suspect that a young widow with a well-behaved young child would steal from an elderly woman? Then, once she won everyone's trust, she started her tricks. Most of the time she talked her marks into giving her money straight out. Other times, well, we'd take it. Once she stole an eighty-six-year-old woman's leather coat."

"That's horrible!"

His mouth twisted, and he shrugged. "That wasn't the worst thing she did, however. The lowest thing she did was to steal medicine. Pain meds."

Scandalized, Ali gasped. "You're kidding!"

"Nope. She had a nice little resale business going on."

"Oh, Mac, that's just horrible."

"Yep. That's who I was when we met, Ali. I was Brenda's son and I was dirty and ashamed. I couldn't let you see that. You were clean. Clean and bright and wonderful. I'd rather have died than let you know that I was nothing more than trash."

"Don't say that, Mac. It's not true. You were a child. It's your mother who was trash." She wrinkled her nose and added, "Is trash. But what if she talks to the tabloids?"

"It doesn't matter. Really." He met her gaze. "I don't want to return to the bench anyway. I don't think our friends and neighbors here will care that I was a childhood criminal, do you?"

Ali studied him. Really studied him. "You mean it, don't you? You truly mean it."

"I've been saying it for weeks now. You just haven't heard."

Slowly happiness bloomed inside Ali. He meant it. This wasn't just a hormone blast. He honestly wanted to walk away from his job.

So what did it mean? "We'll stay in Eternity Springs, then?"

"I'd like that, yes, but other options are certainly

open to discussion. I've learned my lesson, Alison. Your wishes and desires are just as important as mine."

Wow. Just wow. "We can build a house at Heartache Falls."

"I'd like Gabe Callahan to design the landscape. Have you seen the pool he did at Eagle's Way? It's fabulous."

Excitement sparked and began to burn. Ali gazed around the New Place and thought that the dream had never completely died, after all. Ali turned to hug her husband, but the expression on his face stopped her cold. His chin was set. His eyes were hard. "What's wrong?"

"I'm not done. I need to tell you something else." He sighed like a condemned prisoner, then added, "Something else to confess."

No. Oh, no. Not now. Not when true, happily-ever-after, life-can't-get-any-better-than-this joy is right within my grasp. "No, Mac. That's okay. Whatever it is, I don't want to know."

"I need to tell you."

She held up her hand, palm out. "I don't need to hear it! I don't care, Mac. I don't care if you have a gambling habit or a sister who's a porn star or a newly discovered predilection for cross-dressing, I don't need to know about it."

"Ali, I'm sorry. I'm so very, very sorry, but we need honesty between us. This lie, my guilt, is a cancer in our marriage and it needs to be cut out. I will spend the rest of my life trying to make it up to you if only you'll forgive me."

What lie could he have told that would make him

feel this miserable? *Oh, God.* Ali thought her heart might break in two. "Did you have an affair, Mac?"

He drew back, obviously offended. "No! That's not it at all."

"Fine, then forget it." She tried to walk away. He reached for her hand and stopped her.

"No. Ali, I need you to know . . ." He raked his fingers through his hair, filled his lungs with air, then exhaled in a rush. "I targeted you."

She frowned. *He targeted me?*

"Back when we were in college, I acted like Brenda's boy. From the moment I hit South Bend, I was on the hunt. I was looking for a girl just like you. After we met that first time? I did my research on you. I found out who your father was, and I figured out that being his son-in-law could help me in my career, so I set out to win you. I wasn't going to let you get away from me."

All right. Well, that's not so bad.

But it obviously wasn't all. The man looked miserable. He looked tortured. "For heaven's sake, Mackenzie. What did you do?"

"I got you pregnant, Alison."

"Um, yes, I know."

"I wanted you to get pregnant. I didn't want to risk losing you."

The confession hung on the air. Ali waited for more. More didn't come. "That's it? That's your big confession?"

Closing his eyes, he nodded.

She took a moment to absorb that, and then another minute to think it through. "Why me?"

"What do you mean?" Now he scowled at her. "I just told you."

"Not really. There were other girls at Notre Dame who had well-connected fathers. Lots of them. You were a jock. A big man on campus. You could have had any girl."

"I wanted you."

"Because of my dad?"

"Yeah."

Ali folded her arms. "What about Larisa Holcomb? She had a crush on you, and if I recall correctly, her father was a judge on the Illinois Supreme Court."

"So?"

"Or what about Theresa Williams? Her father was a partner in a San Francisco firm that's twice the size of Dad's firm. Then there was the girl from Georgia. What was her name—Pansy? No, Puffy. What sort of name was that, anyway? She totally had the hots for you."

"I didn't want her," Mac snapped. "I didn't want any of those girls. I wanted you."

"Why?"

He shot her a hot, frustrated glare. "Because I was in love with you!"

There. Was it that hard? Ali couldn't suppress a smile. "I see. So let me see if I have this straight. When you were eighteen, you started looking for a potential wife. You found someone you liked, someone who met your preconceived criteria, and you asked her on a date. Over time, you developed a relationship with this girl, and over the next two years, at a time mutually acceptable to you both, that relationship became a sexual one. As often happens in such circumstances, a child was conceived."

He closed his eyes and rubbed his temples. "Alison, I wasn't stupid. I knew it wasn't your safe time, and I didn't use the condom I had in my pocket. I wanted you to get pregnant. I was my mother's son and I wanted to tie you to me."

"Because you wanted my dad's support."

"Yes."

"And because you loved me."

"Yes."

"And because you wanted to build a life with me, make a home with me, have a family with me."

"Yes!"

"What about being my friend and my spouse and my lover for the rest of our lives? I'll bet you wanted that, too, didn't you? Why, Mackenzie Timberlake, that is *such* a horrible sin to confess! I'm appalled. Do you want me to call Reverend Hart so you can confess to him? I know neither one of you is Catholic, but maybe you'd feel better."

"Come on, Ali." Unwilling to quit, he folded his arms. "I seduced you."

"Come on yourself!" She braced her hands on her hips and advanced on him. "Has this really been eating away at you for all these years? For crying out loud, Mac. That's sad. And stupid. Sad and stupid.

"In that case, I have a question for you. One question." She held up her index finger. "At what time in our relationship did I give you control over my hormones?"

"Excuse me?"

"My memory might not be as sharp today as it was

when I was in college, but I do think I would remember if you had forced me. Mac, use your brain. I could have said no. I could have brought my own condom to the party. I certainly knew my own body's schedule, which meant I knew the risk I was taking that night."

"But—"

She cut him off. "But nothing! We are equally responsible for that pregnancy. Besides, did you ever stop to think that maybe I wanted to be tied to you, too? That maybe I wanted you more than I wanted Europe?"

He visibly swallowed. "What are you saying, Ali?"

"Mac, do you know what one of my going-away-to-college gifts from Daddy was? A hunting vest. A bright orange hunting vest!"

Stunned, he blinked. "I remember that. You had it hanging in your closet in the dorm. I thought that was strange." Then he shook his head. "But what about cooking school? Running a restaurant? That was your dream!"

"Maybe it was. Or maybe it was my backup plan."

At that, the man sank into a seat. He looked poleaxed. "Are you saying you got pregnant on purpose?"

Ali lifted her eyes toward heaven and sighed. "What I'm saying, Mac, is that I loved you then and I love you today and I expect I'll love you until the day I die. I feel terrible for you that your mother was such a poor excuse for a human being, and it's horrible that you felt like you had to keep her secret, and I understand what motivated your actions back when we first met. Meeting her explains a lot about you. For instance, now I see why you reacted so negatively to Caitlin's Patrick."

"He reminded me of me."

"And I could wish for nothing better for our daughter than that she find a man like her father to love."

Mac closed his eyes, and Ali thought she saw him shudder. She moved toward him and sat on his lap. His arms came around her reflexively. "I'm proud of you, Mac," she said softly. "And I'm proud for you."

He touched his forehead to hers. "Ali, from the very beginning, you've been the best mother I could have chosen for my children. I never had to worry that you would neglect them or cause them harm of any kind. I knew that I could trust you with their little hearts . . . and with my own."

His words had caused tears to swell in Ali's eyes and overflow. He reached up and wiped them off her cheek with the pad of his thumb. "Don't cry, Ali-cat. Please. It breaks my heart."

"These are happy tears."

"Yeah, well, they still make me feel like a jerk."

"You're not a jerk, Mac Timberlake. You are honorable and admirable. You are an excellent father for my children, and the perfect husband for me. I'm so happy we trapped each other into marriage."

"Me too." He leaned forward and kissed her, gently and ever so sweetly. "Alison Cavanaugh Timberlake, your ancestor might have found a fortune in silver in Eternity Springs, but I believe we have found something infinitely more valuable."

"You do?" She touched his cheek and smiled. "And what is that?"

"Ourselves. Our marriage. Our life together."

Ali's heart overflowed. "Our own little slice of heaven."

"Amen."

Their lips met, and as the kiss went from sweet to steamy, Mac skimmed his hand along the side of her breast and said, "I wish . . ."

"Me too." Ali smiled wistfully at her husband as the restaurant's front door opened. "Hey, Mom? Dad?" Chase called. "Granddad and I stopped to talk to Mrs. Blessing, and she told us about an old Model T Ford in her garage. We're gonna take it for a ride. We'll be back in about an hour. Okay? Bye."

Mac waited until the door shut, then said, "That's the great thing about Eternity Springs. Here, miracles happen."

EPILOGUE

"Another grand opening in Eternity Springs," Sage said to Sarah. "Four years ago, who would have believed it?"

Sarah pulled on her parka and zipped it up. "It gives a girl hope. Life around here seems to be filled with hope these days. Hope and happiness." Sarah gazed around the walls of Sage's gallery and added, "I see it in your paintings."

Sage glanced at the trio of paintings she'd hung the past week, patted her burgeoning belly, and smiled. "I never knew life could be so wonderful."

"I'm jealous."

"Hey, life is pretty wonderful for you, too. Lori is home for semester break and the two of you are knee-deep in Australia trip plans—though I think offering boomerangs for sale in the Trading Post is going a bit too far."

"It's just a beginning," Sarah said with a grin. "Speaking of beginnings, we'd better get going or Ali will start without us."

Sage frowned and glanced at the clock. "You go on. I'll wait for Colt. He's upstairs finishing up a bowl he made for Ali's place, and he's being picky about getting it just right. Tell her to start without us."

"Will do." Sarah opened the gallery door and stepped out into the bitter air. She drew a deep breath that seared her lungs with cold but only heightened her sense of anticipation. She sensed a weird hum of something in the air that made her think the year ahead would be filled with something new—something good, she hoped.

She chuckled aloud at her own imaginings. Was she always this giddy on New Year's or was it the effect of too much midnight champagne?

Either way, for the first time in a long time, she looked forward to the new year. And, more immediately, to a taste of Tuscany. She was hungry.

She turned at the sound of her name to see Sage and Colt walking fast toward her. Colt carried a box tied with what she guessed was a leftover Christmas bow. He must have finished his gift.

Sarah waited for the Raffertys to catch up. The friends were on their way to the grand opening of Ali's restaurant, formerly Mac's the New Place and now La Cucina Gialla, which translated to the Yellow Kitchen. The Italian restaurant featured recipes that Ali had learned from her father's housekeeper in addition to those she'd learned how to prepare during the two-week cooking school she'd attended after Thanksgiving while she and Mac were on their second honeymoon in Italy.

"Smell that?" Sage asked as she and her husband caught up to Sarah. "Isn't that the most divine aroma ever? I'll bet you a hundred bucks that Chef Hollywood's menu doesn't hold a candle to Ali's."

"I'm not taking that bet," Sarah replied. "Lori talked to Chase yesterday and he recommended the *peposo*. It's a beef stew of some sort."

"I'm all over that," Colt declared.

"Chase also said that his parents booked a trip to Paris in the springtime. Another cooking school."

Sage nodded. "Ali told me. She has this idea to change her menu after every trip in order to keep things interesting for the town's year-round residents. She's going to keep the name the Yellow Kitchen, but she'll change the language it's written in according to the cuisine."

"Always thinking, our Ali." At the corner of Second and Pinyon, Colt gestured up the street and waved. "There's Celeste. You ladies want to wait for her? Sage, you're not too cold, are you?"

"I'm fine."

Sarah stomped her feet, wishing she'd worn an extra pair of socks. "It is freezing. The temperature dipped below zero this morning."

Sage wrinkled her nose. "I know. That evil Nic Callahan called to chortle about it. She said she was in shorts."

"The witch," Sarah observed. The Callahans were spending New Year's with Gabe's family in Texas.

"Happy New Year, my dears," Celeste called out as she joined them. "Isn't it a lovely day?"

"It's ten degrees, Celeste," Sage protested.

"A gorgeous ten. Have you ever seen a more brilliant blue sky?"

As the quartet resumed walking, Sage glanced at the basket Celeste carried. "What's that?"

"A little restaurant-warming gift for Ali," Celeste replied. "You'll want to see this."

She rustled among the contents and removed a small shadow box. Inside it, hanging from a sunshine-yellow ribbon, was one of the Angel's Rest blazons that Sage had designed and Celeste gifted to those for whom Angel's Rest had worked its healing magic.

"That's so pretty," Sarah said.

Sage grinned. "I like how you've used it on a ribbon instead of a necklace. That's for Ali, I assume?"

"Yes."

Sarah stared at the angel's wing medal and knew a yearning so deep and so sharp that it bordered on painful. "It's beautiful, Celeste. I want one of those. Nic and Sage and Ali all have one. When do I get mine?"

Celeste halted in midstep. She turned to face the others and, her arm extended in presentation, turned in a slow circle. "Look around you, Sarah Reese. See the brilliant blue sky above and the snow-decked mountains around us. Smell the heavenly scents of pine and wood smoke and Italian spices on the air. Listen to the gentle winter wind. Can you hear it?"

Sarah saw and smelled and listened, and a lump formed in her throat. "It's Mac and Ali and their kids."

"Joyous laughter of a loving family at peace." Celeste smiled gently, winked at the Raffertys, then linked her arm with Sarah's. "You have lived in Eternity Springs all of your life, Sarah Reese. Whether you've been aware of it or not, that is a blessing that those around you envy."

"I know I'm lucky," Sarah said.

"Then give thanks for your blessings, my dear friend. Open your heart to all of life's possibilities. It's a new year. A new world. Rest assured that your turn is coming."

ACKNOWLEDGMENTS

New beginnings are exciting things. For this one, I'd especially like to thank my awesome, talented, oh-so-keen-eyed editor, Kate Collins, and my agents, Meg Ruley and Christina Hogrebe, for their support and guidance and belief in this series. You ladies rock. Special thanks to Lynn Andreozzi for the spectacular cover designs for the Eternity Springs series. I love this look! Also, tremendous thanks to my dear friends Scott and Christina Ham, who knew just the motivation to give me to find my way to Eternity Springs, and to Mary Dickerson for being my reader, my red-liner, and most important, my friend.

Read on for an excerpt from

LOVER'S LEAP

by

EMILY MARCH

ONE

❧

Near Cairns, Australia

"Mom! Hurry up," Lori Reese urged, sounding more like a six-year-old than a young woman in college. "We don't want to be late!"

At the sound of her daughter's voice, Sarah Reese rolled over in bed, buried her face in the thick, downy pillow, and contemplated how many banks she'd have to rob in order to afford a return trip to this resort. She and Lori were nearing the end of their two-week, all-expenses-paid Australian vacation, and the experience had given her a tantalizing taste of traveling in the lap of luxury.

"Ten more minutes," she mumbled into her pillow. This bed was heaven.

"It's already 6:15."

The bus to the marina didn't pick them up until 7:00 and getting ready would take fifteen minutes, tops. "Five more minutes."

Indulgent frustration laced Lori's voice. "When exactly did we switch roles? I think it must have been the first day of the trip when you spent half of that interminable plane ride flirting with the man across the aisle."

Sarah grinned, then lazily rolled her head and looked at her daughter. "I was just being friendly. He was the one doing all the flirting."

"Yeah, right." Lori's eyes gleamed with amusement as they made an exaggerated roll. "Okay, here's the deal. I'm going to head over to the lobby and get two cups of coffee. If you're not out of bed by the time I come back, I'll drink both of them."

Sarah scowled. "Obviously, I didn't spank you enough when you were little."

Laughing, Lori finger-waved good-bye, and a moment later, Sarah heard the door to their suite softly close. She gave a wistful sigh, rolled onto her back, and sat up.

Her reluctance to rise had more to do with the fact that today was the last day of their dream-of-a-lifetime vacation than with fatigue. They'd had an absolutely, positively wonderful trip, seeing enough of the country to give them a taste of it, but not so much that they'd felt rushed. They'd spent the past three nights here at this magnificent resort on the Coral Sea, and today, they would ice their vacation cake with a catamaran trip to the Great Barrier Reef.

Sarah lifted her arms above her head and stretched as she gazed out through glass-pane French doors, past the verandah with its private spa tub, and across the golden sand beach toward the turquoise sea. Crossing to the doors, she pushed them open and inhaled deeply the fresh morning air as she took a moment to count her blessings. This trip had been the grand prize in a contest sponsored by Angel's Rest, the healing center and spa owned by her friend Celeste Blessing in the little Colorado mountain town where they lived, Eternity Springs. At home, a foot of snow covered the ground, and the thermometer flirted daily with 0°. As the warm, seaside breeze softly stirred, Sarah murmured, "I still can't believe I'm here."

She'd dreamed of visiting Australia for a long time. Back in high school, she and Cam Murphy had spent hours stretched out on a quilt up at their favorite make-out spot, Lover's Leap, and planned how they would travel the world together. They'd talked of backpacking across Europe, exploring the pyramids of Egypt, and, most exciting of all, diving the Great Barrier Reef. Of course, life had taken a pair of unexpected turns their junior year, and youthful dreams had faded in the face of stark, cold reality.

She wished one of those realities would hurry back with the coffee.

Sarah turned away from the breathtaking view and headed into the bathroom. When she emerged showered and dressed ten minutes later, she spied Lori seated outside on the verandah. Two cups of coffee and two huge cinnamon rolls waited on the small round table in front of her.

"You are both wonderful and wicked, my child," Sarah told her, taking her seat. "I'll gain two pounds just looking at that roll."

"Nah, we have a strenuous day ahead of us. We need the calories. Besides, you need to check out the competition. You might want to tweak your recipe for the cinnamon rolls you make for the Mocha Moose."

Sarah sipped her coffee and lifted her brows in disdain. "My cinnamon roll recipe doesn't need to be tweaked, thank you very much."

"Okay, you're right." Lori licked sugar from her fingers. "It's impossible to improve on perfection."

At home, Sarah operated Eternity Springs's only grocery store, the Trading Post, established by her great-grandfather and run by family members ever since, but she supplemented her income by baking for a number of the businesses in town. She nodded her acceptance of her daughter's compliment, then tore off a piece of roll and popped it into her mouth. Cinnamon and sweetness exploded on her tongue. "Yum, this is good. Could use a tiny bit more vanilla, though, I think."

The two women shared a grin, then polished off their breakfast. Moments later, tote bags stuffed with necessities for a day on the water in hand, they exited their suite. Seeing that the shuttle bus to the marina had yet to arrive, Sarah lamented, "I could have had my ten minutes, after all."

"Oh, stop it. I'm too excited to listen to you whine. Aren't you excited?"

"Yes, I'm excited." Sarah threaded her arm through Lori's and squeezed. She was excited. The tour's itinerary sounded divine. First, the catamaran would take them to a cay famous for its protected, sandy lagoon, gorgeous beach, and migratory bird population. Sarah had never learned to dive, so she would snorkel while Lori, who'd earned her certification while away at college, would join other tour members in a drift dive along the reef. Following a gourmet lunch and some beach time, they would sail to the Outer Barrier Reef, where Lori would make a wall dive and Sarah could snorkel some more or just be lazy.

Imagine. Small-town girl Sarah Reese snorkeling at the Great Barrier Reef. Wow.

As a shuttle bus sporting the Adventures in Paradise Tours logo pulled into the resort's circular drive, Sarah couldn't help but think of Cam. She seldom allowed her mind to go down that rocky path, but today, as their daughter was about to fulfill one of those Lover's Leap dreams, she couldn't hold back the memories.

Cameron Murphy. From the time he was born, Eternity Springs had waited with baited breath for the Murphy bad blood to show itself. They didn't have to wait very long. Cam first ran afoul of the law when he spray-painted threats on the courthouse wall when he was nine, shortly after his father's manslaughter conviction. For the next few years, he'd been in trouble more often than he'd been out of it.

But my oh my, he'd done it for her—long before she even knew what "it" was. Tall, handsome, those mesmerizing eyes. As a young man he'd been as wild and beautiful as the cougars that prowled the surrounding forests. And just as dangerous.

Like the rest of Eternity Springs, Sarah's parents had recognized the threat in him, so when Cam first turned his smoldering intensity her way, she'd instinctively kept it a secret. The relationship that developed between them over the next year had remained a secret, too. To this day, most people in Eternity Springs believed the lie she'd told to protect her precious child's shoulders from bearing the weight of "Murphy bad blood."

Yet she had loved Cam Murphy with every fiber of her foolish, teenaged soul, and it had taken time for that love to die. Time and his rejection for the hope to die.

Time, his rejection, and the reality of a child dependent upon her for Sarah to finally grow up.

She gave her head a shake when the shuttle braked to a stop and the driver's door opened. A young man with sun-streaked hair and suntanned skin climbed from the bus. "G'day, ladies," he said in that wonderful Aussie drawl. "Reese, party of two for Adventures in Paradise Tours?"

"That's us," Lori confirmed.

"Great. M'name's Mike and I'm your transportation to the marina and the Freedom. Hop on in and I'll introduce you to our other guests."

The two physicians and their wives were from Minnesota, the men in their mid-forties, the women a decade younger, nearer to her age, Sarah guessed. The doctors were divers. One of the wives planned to snorkel, but the other confessed to a fear of sharks that kept her out of the ocean.

"I'm perfectly happy to sunbathe," she told Sarah. "Some friends of ours took this tour a year ago and said the scenery of the cay alone is worth the price of the ticket."

The other wife leaned toward Sarah and lowered her voice. "She also said the captain and crew weren't half bad to look at, either."

Lori must have overheard that exchange, because she glanced at Sarah and mouthed, "No flirting."

Sarah smothered a smile, then eavesdropped as her daughter peppered the young driver with questions about the tour.

"No, it's my dad's business," Mike was saying.

"I'm really proud of him. He built it from nothing. We keep it small—we run only two boats—but we're the best tour operator in Queensland. You'll have a great time today."

"I'm so excited," Lori replied. "This is going to be the highlight of our trip."

"That's our goal."

Sarah's attention was pulled away from Lori when the sunbather doctor's wife asked her where she was from. It came as no surprise that the obviously wealthy Minnesotans had been to Telluride, Vail, and Aspen but had never heard of Eternity Springs. "Next time you plan to visit Colorado, you should consider a stay at Angel's Rest, our new healing center and spa. It's a heavenly place. You'd love it."

"We'll keep that in mind," one of the doctors said.

"I adore spa vacations," his wife added.

"Is there golf?" the other doctor asked.

"No, I'm afraid not. But we do have some of the best trout fishing in the world nearby at the Taylor River."

"Taylor River Rainbows," he responded. "I've heard of them. We'll have to put your Angel's Rest on our to-do list."

Satisfied that she'd done her part as an Eternity Springs ambassador, Sarah smiled, sat back, and tuned into Lori's conversation once again.

". . . Next year. Dad really wants me to go to college, but I don't see it happening. School already interferes too much with my days on the boat."

"So what's your average day like?" Lori asked.

While the young man spoke of sun and surf and the deep blue sea, Sarah considered her daughter. Lori had never been a shy child, but she'd truly blossomed since leaving Colorado for college in Texas. She was a beautiful, intelligent, confident young woman, and her natural curiosity had been elevated to new heights. Lori never stopped asking questions, never stopped wanting to learn. *I'm so proud of her.*

For the second time that day, Sarah's thoughts returned to Lori's father. This time, however, the memories weren't bittersweet, only bitter. *You made a huge mistake twenty years ago when you turned your back on us, Cam. Lori is special. She would have made such a difference in your life. She could have brought such joy into your world.*

You blew it, Murphy. Our daughter could have been your redemption.

ETERNAL
ROMANCE

FIND YOUR HEART'S DESIRE...